HEATHER PINE

MOUNTAIN
getaway

A Lemon Grove Novel

CHAPTER ONE

$\mathcal{U}$sing the full weight of her body, Molly gave the trunk of her silver Toyota Camry one last shove, compacting the contents safely inside the vehicle. She was leaving for a two-week vacation and had stuffed her vehicle to the brim with every piece of camping equipment she found in her apartment. What didn't fit in the trunk, Molly placed on the backseat. She didn't want to find herself in the middle of nowhere without supplies and decided it was smart to pack everything.

Sure, the family campground near the mountains where she had booked her stay wasn't in the middle of nowhere, but campgrounds have limited supplies at their camp store and cost triple the price compared to the city's big box stores. She concluded it was wise to plan and bring what she needed from home than pay the price later. Her father always stressed the need to prepare. Whenever her younger self protested over carrying load after load of blankets, dry goods, and fire making supplies to her parents' minivan for their obligatory annual family vacations, he would remind her to always plan.

At twenty-four years old, the childhood lesson had sprung to mind as Molly began packing her vehicle for her first solo trip.

She had vacationed with her friends during a post-high school celebration, but this trip was different. This time it was just her. By herself. Alone.

"Are you sure you've got everything?" Leaning against the back bumper, Carla laughed as the trunk lock clicked. Her friend looked chic in her denim pants and knit T-shirt. Even the light breeze couldn't mess her styled blonde waves.

Molly dusted off her hands on her denim capris and tugged on the bottom of her sleeveless plaid shirt. She convinced herself it was the perfect outdoor look after seeing an online model wearing the same ensemble. That woman had looked confident and capable as she stood in the middle of an alpine meadow by her perfectly arranged campsite. It had spurred Molly to purchase the entire look, including the tent… and the lantern… and the wool blanket. She had drawn a line at the propane coffeemaker and solar-powered string of party lights that hung across the width of the campsite, although she worried about the quality of her instant coffee. She was hoping for a nearby coffee shop and to only use her supply of instant coffee as a backup. Working at a coffee shop meant she knew what a good cup of coffee tasted like, and instant grounds would be no match for the premium coffee she brewed daily.

Besides, she only needed caffeine to get through the work week and there would be no work when on vacation. Packing her car was the only work she had to do today, unlike Carla, who was supervising Molly and making herself late for work.

Molly smiled as she wiped a bead of sweat from her brow. "Thanks for helping, Carla. But you didn't need to take time off from work."

Carla smiled. "I wanted to make sure you got away okay." More like she wanted to make sure Molly didn't cancel her plans. Best friends know when someone is having second thoughts and Molly had them often.

Work at the coffee shop had been steady. They built a clientele of regular customers, and new customers were discovering them every day. Their shop had become a local hotspot known for excellent brew, tasty treats, and a comfortable atmosphere. For two years they built their business and loyal customers were the reward for their hard work. But being a small business meant few employees and Carla would mostly take on Molly's workload. Already, Molly regretted leaving her friend with the extra responsibility.

"Are you sure you can manage everything while I'm away?" Her thumb hovered over the trunk release on the key fob. All Carla had to do was say she couldn't manage without her, and Molly would start unpacking.

Carla gave her a knowing look and pulled the keys out of Molly's hand. "Remember who you're talking to. Everything will be fine. Besides, my cousin wanted to work a few extra hours this month to help pay her tuition. I've got help lined up if I need it." Carla wrapped her arm over Molly's shoulder and gave her a hug. "You need this, Molly. After the year you've had. You need some time away to get your mind off of—"

Molly lifted a hand to silence her friend. "Brad is the last person I want to think about right now. I wasted two years with him and I won't let him ruin this day when he's not even here." He should be here. After two years together, she had expected a proposal, not a breakup. There were no signs that something was wrong, and she had convinced herself his awkwardness was his anxiety over preparing to pop the question. It blindsided her when Brad announced he was moving away... with another woman. His coworker. How had she been so stupid? It had been two months since their breakup, but the wound was still fresh. Starting over was the last thing she expected.

Carla was right. She needed to get away from her routine and get her mind off him. Molly had lied every time she said she was fine, all while thoughts of Brad still gnawed away at her heart, leaving her with a tear-soaked pillow. She was supposed to have a fiancé and then be walking down the aisle by this time next year. Instead of planning a wedding, she was planning a two-week getaway to a family campground in Lemon Grove to heal a broken heart.

"Okay, okay. I won't say anything." Carla gave Molly a shove toward the driver's side door. "You will have a good time. Trust me." She reached into her purse and smiled as she handed Molly a small paper bag full of junk food. "For the drive."

"Thanks." She glanced up at her third-story apartment window and sighed. For two weeks she was leaving behind the comfort of her own bed and hot shower to sleep on an inflatable mattress. Molly laughed and shook her head. "What am I doing? There are better ways to clear my head."

Carla opened the car door and gestured for Molly to get in. "No. There's not. You know work will get in the way and keep you from getting the break you need. When you get back, we'll talk about expanding the business. Until then, you aren't allowed to think about it." She dangled the keys in front of Molly's nose. "Call me when you get there."

Molly started the engine and sighed. "You know, if I don't have a good time, it's all your fault."

"It's a risk I'm willing to take," Carla said with a smirk.

Molly closed the door and rolled down the window. "Thank you, Carla."

"You're welcome. Now get out of here before I drive you there myself."

Molly laughed and adjusted her seatbelt. With a wave, she set out in her overloaded car. With each mile she would drive closer to the mountains and further from her pathetic life.

For the first hour of the drive, she listened to music. The fast tunes fed her adrenaline as she navigated through the heavy traffic of the city's freeway until she exited onto calmer roads that led into the mountains. It was when the music transitioned to slower tunes and the adrenaline wore off that she reflected on her choice. There was no rule that someone must leave their home for a vacation. Taking a break from work might have been enough if she stayed at home.

Molly imagined the disappointed look on Carla's face and fought the urge to make a U-turn. She had promised her friend she would take a proper break, and Carla had sacrificed to make sure Molly had time off. Molly had to follow through. Not because she wanted to, but for her friend. She owed Carla that much.

A quick tap to the stereo switched the music to an audiobook, which took her mind off her indecisiveness long enough to drive another two hours. She had come too far to change her mind now. She was better off setting up her tent at the campsite and trying a night of camping than to turn around and go home in the dark. If she didn't enjoy the experience, she could pack up her equipment and go back home tomorrow... or to a pleasant hotel.

After grabbing a bite to eat at a small burger joint, she turned on the radio to catch the weather report as she sampled the bag of junk food from Carla.

"...And the heat wave continues for most of the region," the male host cheerfully announced. "It will be a scorcher for the rest of the week. You can expect milder temperatures as you move closer to the mountains, with occasional rainfall, but that system will pass by quickly, leaving behind pleasant temperatures for all those vacationers out there."

With that, any thoughts of returning to her apartment disappeared. The last thing Molly wanted was to sit in her apartment building with unreliable air-conditioning that the landlord refused to repair. Molly decided Carla was right. This was the perfect time to take a two-week vacation.

She had enjoyed watching the scenery change from tall

skyscrapers to farm fields, rolling hills, and forested communities at the outskirts of the mountains. The roads curved around lakes, where waterfalls streamed down beside roadways and dampened the asphalt. With each turn, she felt her stress melt away, along with any thoughts of... what was his name again?

Rolling down the windows, the cool air blew through her car and played with her hair, whipping strands against her face. Molly took a deep breath as the scent of damp pine and dirt filled the air. She glanced at moss hanging from tree trunks along the side of the road and the floral underbrush blanketing the ground. She would never see this in the city. Already she was finding the rest she was seeking.

Ahead, she spotted a simple black and white sign with a left-pointing arrow under "Lemon Grove Campground", followed by a green sign announcing the town of Lemon Grove at the next exit. Symbols showed lodging, recreation, and restaurants listed as amenities. If she found herself in need of groceries, or a good cup of coffee, she might not have to go far.

Off the highway, the paved road was rough. Her car rattled as it bounced over the potholes and uneven pavement, making her teeth chatter. Another white sign directed her to turn to the right, toward the campground. Loose stones struck the underside of her car before skipping off the road. The campground owner had designed a winding drive around trees rather than cutting a straighter path. It was a narrow road, with little room for recreational vehicles to squeeze past each other. Between the trees ahead, the white sides of camping trailers speckled the forest.

The road curved into an open gravel parking lot in front of a mobile home with "OFFICE" spelled out in large, red wooden letters nailed to a white painted board above the front door. Flower beds and hanging baskets adorned its front yard, along with a weathered, wooden wishing well and a metal bee with its wings spinning in the breeze.

Molly placed her car in park and stretched as she closed the door. Four hours was a long time for Molly to sit in a car, and any stops she made along the way hadn't been enough to prevent her muscles from tightening. She found the uneven stone steps between the garden beds and made her way to the open office door where a woman with short, wavy hair sat behind a cluttered desk. To one side, tourism pamphlets lined the shelves while assorted camping supplies and foods filled the remaining space. The campground staff had placed a small display stand of local stones and wooden carvings to the side of the desk, with a small orange paper stuck to the shelf noting the items at a twenty-five percent discount. It was an organized space, but tight.

"Can I help you?" the woman asked as she tapped a pen to a pad of paper.

Molly smiled and reached for her wallet inside her purse. "Hi. I am checking in."

"Do you have a reservation?" The woman's tone communicated her disinterest in any superficial chitchat.

"I do." Molly approached the desk with a smile. It seemed impossible for this place to receive multiple reservations. It wasn't as though Lemon Grove was a hotspot for tourists. Molly wouldn't have even considered it had she not stumbled across the advertisement in the tourism magazine and almost missed the plain text ad among the colorful print ads from much larger resorts surrounding it.

"What is your name?" the woman asked.

"Molly Banting."

"Ah, yes. Reservation for one."

Molly wondered if she felt irritable from driving, but she noticed the woman hang on the "n" a little longer than one would if they were speaking without judgment. Yes, it was a reservation for one and she was camping alone. She could have invited others to join her, but she wanted to be alone. Why would it be this woman's business that she was camping solo?

"Yes, that's right," Molly said, choosing to brush off her initial reaction. "I am looking forward to some quiet time." There. If the curious woman wondered why Molly was vacationing alone, she provided a perfectly acceptable answer.

"We don't see many young women traveling alone these days. No matter, no one should bother you, but if you have any problems, let me know." The woman filled out an information card, taking down Molly's details, including her license plate number and address.

The sound of heavy boots alerted Molly to someone coming up the steps. In the doorway stood a man in his late twenties or early thirties. His light brown jacket drew attention to his mousy-brown hair and dark eyes. Aside from the mud on his fitted jeans, he looked sharp, albeit a little sweaty. This was a man who liked the outdoors, and given how he filled out that outfit, Molly concluded photographers should feature him in advertisements for outdoor equipment. Speaking of advertisements, the campground never mentioned that attractive men lived in the area. Perhaps there would be more to see in Lemon Grove than just trees and mountains?

The woman glanced up from her paperwork and a wide smile spread across her lips. "Hi, Rick. He is at campsite twelve," she said, addressing the man that had their attention.

"Thank you, Glenda." Without another word, or an apology for his interruption, he turned and disappeared through the open door.

The woman reached for Molly's credit card and processed her payment before sliding a photocopy of the campground's map onto the desk. She grabbed a large marker and circled site number twenty-three.

"You are next to the creek and shower facilities. Because of the dry weather, there is a fire ban in effect, so no campfires."

"I understand," Molly said.

"Quiet time is at eleven P.M. sharp. Visitors are to leave by ten."

"I'm not expecting anyone."

The woman raised an eyebrow. No doubt Molly had confirmed any suspicions she might have had.

"Store your food in your vehicle at all times. We have bears roaming through the area. Garbage should go in our bear-proof cans by the showers. Do you have questions?"

Molly stared at the map. A large black arrow pointed to the south end of the map next to the words, "To Lemon Grove".

"How far is the town?"

The woman replaced the cap on the marker and tapped it beside the arrow. "This walking path will lead you to the residential area. Keep walking to the second street and turn left. The shops are about a fifteen-minute walk from your site."

Molly took the map and thanked the woman before returning to her car. Driving past campsite twelve, she tried to catch another glimpse of the man who visited the office minutes before but saw no sign of him. Instead, a family of four sat at their wooden picnic table, playing a game of cards.

She arrived at campsite twenty-three and exhaled. A thick forest of trees surrounded a small gravel pad across from a small brick building. A picnic table stood anchored to a block of cement at the far end of the site, still leaving plenty of room for a large tent or decent sized camping trailer.

Molly parked her car at the mouth of the site and stepped outside to walk to the edge of the gravel pad. Below the site, just visible behind the trees, was a flowing creek. She would have a perfect view from her picnic table and would fall asleep to the soothing sound of moving water. Stretching her back once more, she let out a long sigh.

"This will do," she said. Molly closed her eyes, listening to the sound of the creek and the breeze blowing the leaves on the trees. There were no sounds of construction or honking cars. No ringing phones at her work. Nothing but the sounds of nature to amuse her ears.

A drop of water hit her cheek. Molly opened her eyes and looked at dark gray clouds, which had covered over the once blue sky. She groaned. Of course a storm would hit on the first day of her vacation. Carla said she would have a good time, but like the meteorologists who gave the weather report, Carla could be wrong.

CHAPTER TWO

*A*ssembly of the tent might have only taken minutes with two people to do the work. The reviews on the online store stated building it was a simple task and claimed the user only needed to slide the tent poles into the slots, and the tent would pop into place. Molly laid the gray fabric over the gravel pad and oriented the door toward the picnic table for privacy, which also angled a side window toward the creek. Next, she snapped the poles together and slid them into the slots.

Raising the tent from the ground proved not as simple. Once one side lifted from the ground, the other fell, collapsing any progress she made. The raindrops increased in number, but they did not deter Molly. She glanced at the sky as darker clouds approached. The storm hadn't yet gathered momentum, giving her the time she needed to prepare her camp, or at least the basics.

Grabbing large stones from around the site, she raised a pole once again, lifting the tent roof from the ground. She stacked stones against the pole to prevent it from falling over or slipping out of its anchor. Molly knew the rocks wouldn't be enough to support the poles long-term, but it was enough to prevent the tent from collapsing before she rushed to the other side to secure the opposite end. With one pole end in place, she circled around the tent and secured the remaining poles. Minutes later, the tent was in place and upright. For the finishing touches, she slipped the fly covering in place and tied the remaining ropes to the pegs she hammered into the ground.

Taking a step back, Molly dusted pine needles from her hands and admired her work. She had erected the tent just in time as the rain and wind picked up speed. Molly ran to her car to grab her camping mat, sleeping bag, pillow and backpack full of clothes. She tossed the items onto the floor and climbed inside the tent, zipping up the flap to prevent the water from getting in.

Molly was pleased to have ordered the two-person tent instead of the single, as the interior offered more space than the single occupancy tent would provide. She wouldn't need a single tent forever, once she was no longer a single woman. Brad would one day see his error and come crawling back on his knees to apologize. Molly sighed. She had done it again. These thoughts were the reason Carla insisted Molly get away by herself. She needed time away to close that chapter in her life. Brad wasn't coming back, even if she wanted him to. Or did she?

"Two years wasted," she mumbled. She gritted her teeth as she spread out her mat and pounded a curled corner with her fist. Brad swept her off her feet the day he walked into the coffee shop. One of their first regular customers, he often sat in the shop for hours on his laptop and stealing frequent glances at Molly as she worked behind the counter. After a few months, he asked her out. She found herself unable to refuse the handsome guy with the charismatic smile and great sense of humor. He also left generous tips, which was a bonus. But later, his trips to the shop were less frequent, but Molly had attributed it to his busy schedule. She would not become one of those clingy girlfriends who demanded to be in contact with her boyfriend every minute of the day. Instead, she trusted him.

Molly groaned. "You're thinking about him again." She needed to chastise herself since Carla wasn't there to do it. This trip was an opportunity to get away from her previous life with Brad, but she still brought him along in her mind.

She laid her sleeping bag over the mat. Already, Molly noticed the lack of insulation and padding. Luckily, she bought that wool blanket from the online store, which she packed in the trunk of her car. She would need to get it before nightfall to stay warm. Her pillow at the head of the sleeping bag completed the space. It wasn't perfect like the images she saw online, but it would do.

Molly's stomach rumbled, alerting her to the time. Dinner was approaching, and it was several hours since she ate lunch. If she felt foolish enough to cook in the rain, she could unpack the camping stove from the car. From the sound of the storm outside, the rain would drench her if she attempted to raise the tarp she packed to hang over the cooking area and keep the rain off her tent.

She stuck her head outside the door and checked the clouds. The storm drifted by with no visible break in the clouds. Her stomach protested, but food would have to wait. Molly only brought a week's worth of clothing, and she wasn't about to soak her clothes on the first day. She planned a visit to the laundromat on the weekend, and getting wet or covered in mud would throw off her schedule.

Instead of catering to her stomach's demands, Molly pulled a book from her backpack and settled on her sleeping bag. This would be a quiet vacation in nature, away from people. With no obligations other than to read a book and listen to the rain, she got her wish, except her wish never included a rock pushing against her sleeping mat and into her back. Molly shuffled her bed to the side, away from the offending stone, and once again made herself comfortable on her sleeping bag. Before she even read a single word on the page, the tension in her back from the drive released. Just getting away from the city and her responsibilities was enough.

She sighed as she read the first line, once... twice... three times. Her mind wandered to her job and Carla dealing with an endless line of customers. Would it really be that difficult to relax and forget about her job? Molly brought the book to be a time waster and help her de-stress from the day-to-day when she couldn't be outside, but it wasn't distracting her from home. She wiggled against her sleeping bag and stretched out her arms. She even held her book above her head. Holding it in the air didn't help her focus on the words and only tired her arms, so she rolled onto her side where she found similar results.

Molly closed the book and tossed it to the side. She thought of what other activities she had brought with her to pass the time. There was her camera, but what memories would she capture inside her tent? She rolled up the window covering and looked through the screen that formed the window. Rain splashed against the netting, spraying her nose. If the weather cleared, she would walk beside the creek and explore the campground. The campground map highlighted more to see than the trees around the gravel pad, which Molly felt restricted to during the poor weather.

But wasn't rain part of camping? A little rain shouldn't frighten her into her tent. So what if she had to visit the laundromat? She should forget about schedules. There weren't any when she was a tourist in Lemon Grove.

Molly slipped on her shoes and pulled the hood of her coat over her head as she stepped outside into the rain. Rain had soaked the campsite and small puddles had formed between the gravel, while a stream of water poured over the edge of the picnic table. The sight made her happy.

Had Molly been camping with her parents, they would have ushered her inside, concerned about inconvenient trips to the laundromat or having rope strung across the site to form a clothesline. But her parents weren't here. If she wanted to be out in the rain on her camping trip and risk getting wet, it was her choice. She only needed to be mindful of how many sets of dry clothes remained in her bag, and an unsightly clothesline would fix that. Tomorrow, she would tie a rope to the trees and hang any damp clothes on the line to dry.

Molly walked over to her car and popped open the trunk. It was time to be a rebel, and rebels hung tarps in the rain. She unfolded the plastic and draped it over her tent. Tying the rope at each end, she hoisted the tarp into the trees, lifting it above her campsite, just over her head. She was thankful she didn't need to get it much higher. After standing on her toes, her arms reached around the tree as she fought against the thick, damp underbrush.

With the tarp in place, she removed her hood and ran her hand over her wet hair. The dampness always brought out her hair's natural waves, which she had worked to straighten before she left the city. On this trip, she would either need to embrace her waves or hide them under a baseball cap, which seemed to be every woman's go to when trying to hide a bad hair day on a camping trip.

Molly laughed to herself. How had she become so vain? She never used to care about her looks, but had become so as she tried to look the part of a professional businesswoman. Their coffee shop was in the city, and successful business executives often stopped by, so she had to look like she was at least trying. She had to try hard to look good, unlike Carla, who pulled together stylish outfits in her sleep.

The only part Molly was dressing for today was that of a camper who relaxes in nature and has access to a shower. It relieved her to be situated across from the facilities, although she didn't ask at the office if the showers were free or if there was a charge for their use. While she would like to have a hot shower in the morning, she wouldn't if the campground staff left the stalls covered in soap scum and random hairs from previous campers. Molly had brought sandals with her just in case, but she had her limits. She would rinse herself off in the creek before she'd wash in a gross and poorly maintained shower.

She checked her watch. It was almost six o'clock. Her picnic table was still wet from the rain and after setting up her campsite there was little energy left for cooking, even if the tarp covered the cooking space. Resigned to eating a meal in town, Molly hopped in her car to search for a restaurant. If the weather was better, she would have walked from the campground to Lemon Grove, but the rain prevented that from happening. No matter. This way she could investigate the town by car and see if the campground host was correct about the distance. And she was.

Molly had driven less than a minute before she rounded the corner and found the first row of houses. Two short blocks later, she reached a small community center covered in dark wood siding. The next street over had a general store with two gas pumps outside. It boasted live bait and hard ice cream on its signage.

Across the street was a café and its open sign, which featured an illuminated steaming coffee mug. From a distance, the café looked decent enough. It, too, had dark wood siding and a simple front door. Hanging baskets brightened the otherwise gloomy exterior, while a few picnic tables invited guests to eat outside. The tables were empty in the rainy weather, and the owner had secured a For Sale sign to the siding. Maybe business was poor in this small town?

Molly parked her car and rushed to the front door as the rain pelted her. Bells on the other side rattled, and she gasped as she came inches from colliding with a man exiting with a cup of coffee. He took a step back and smiled as he held his hand to open the door. It was the man from the campground, still dressed in the light brown jacket and the same mud-covered jeans and boots.

"Allow me to get out of your way," he said, gesturing to the interior of the shop, showing more manners than he had when he interrupted her conversation with the host at the campground office. Had this been the city, others would have cursed at her for rushing into the store with such carelessness. And no one would offer to step aside if they felt they had the right-of-way. Given how close he was to the door and that he carried a hot beverage, she should be the one waiting for him.

Molly turned sideways and slipped through the doorway. "I'm sorry. I didn't know someone was on the other side."

"Not a problem," he said, stepping through the door. Still not yet yelling or cursing, but appearing to chuckle. "Have a good day."

"Good luck, Rick," called the server from behind the counter before the door closed.

Molly stared at the space where the man once stood. This time she had gotten a better look at him, including the sharpness of his stubble-covered jaw and the dimple in his chin. His eyebrows framed his eyes in a way that highlighted their deep shade of brown. Not that she was really looking at them. Well, maybe she was looking, but only just a little. How could she not? His features stood out and he was practically in her face when she almost slammed into him in the doorway. She also couldn't help but notice he had an outdoorsy, woodsy scent to him that contrasted with the smells of the café. She would never have run into a man like him in the city.

Molly gave her head a shake and came to her senses, which meant noticing the familiar smell of coffee and fresh-baked goods. She turned toward the counter and glanced up at the menu.

The shop owner had decorated the chalkboard with a floral border and had drawn a loaf of bread in one corner below the list of soups and sandwiches. There was a good assortment. She would find something to eat here.

"I told my husband we should install a window on that door," the server said as she wiped her hands on her apron. She was older, which Molly guessed was around late-fifties, and had cut her gray hair into an elongated bob. The woman's eyes sparkled with a friendly warmth that drew Molly toward her. "A window would let in some light and keep people from running into each other."

"Does it happen often?" Molly asked, taking a moment to check out the dessert display in the glass cooler beside the register before standing in front of the counter.

"Almost daily. I expect the person who buys this place will put one in."

"I noticed the sign out front. You're selling?"

"I hope to sell one day," she said. "I would have sold it by now if I didn't care so much about who bought it." She leaned onto the counter and pointed to the menu above her. "What can I get for you?"

"I'm considering the roast beef sandwich and your vegetable soup."

"Considering or ordering?" The woman winked and tapped a pad of paper.

"Ordering," Molly said with a laugh. "That's one of the fastest decisions I've made after looking at a menu."

The woman joined her in laughing. She had a boisterous laugh. "I guess we're lucky the menu isn't any longer than it is. We could have been here all night."

"When do you close?"

The woman scribbled the order onto a piece of paper and slid it through an open window to the kitchen. "We stop taking orders around seven o'clock. We'll kick people out around eight if they are still in here, gabbing. They are welcome to sit at a table outside until they're done, so long as they toss their garbage in the bin and don't leave it out for the bears. Where are you from?"

"I'm from Millwood," Molly said. She handed her debit card to the server and took her receipt. "I am spending a couple of weeks here."

"So you're from the city. Are you camping with family?"

Molly braced herself for judgment. "No. By myself."

"Yourself?" The woman glanced over her shoulder and then leaned once more against the counter. "Aren't you a brave one? Most women I know wouldn't go camping alone. At least they don't choose to. They stay in a hotel where they can get their hair done at the salon or get a massage at the spa." Her laugh drowned out the refrigerated display beside her. "I guess some folks just need their alone time."

"That's me." Molly tried to laugh, although it was harder when she felt her private life being questioned by a stranger. "I needed to get away from things for a while."

"Would that include getting away from a man?" She leaned back and grabbed a cloth from under the counter, giving the surface a quick wipe. "You don't have to tell me, but I've seen it all before. Men are nothing but trouble, especially the one you almost ran over at the door. That one does nothing but frustrate the women around here."

Molly recalled his features and the woodsy smell. He was handsome: no doubt she wasn't the only one who noticed. She cleared her throat. "How does he frustrate them?"

"Did you get a look at him?" She gestured toward the door. "Rick is a nice-looking man, yet he's single. He says he likes the peace he finds by living on his own and bringing someone else into it would disturb all that. The nerve of him. Imagine a man like him refusing to marry. It is a travesty, if you ask me." Once again, she wiped the countertop and sighed.

"Where I come from, the girls have already scooped up all the nice guys. There are none left for the rest of us."

The server paused from her wiping and nodded. "They're taken or they are like Rick and are too hurt to date again. There isn't a woman in this town that doesn't want him, and he's refused every single one of 'em. Someone will catch him one of these days. I'd try to catch him myself if I was twenty years younger."

A bell rang from the kitchen, signaling that Molly's order was in the window. With her meal in her hands, she thanked the server and took a seat at a table by the window where she could stare out at what she could see of the quiet town. As she took a bite of her sandwich, she chuckled to herself and imagined a town full of women lining up to get a date with Lemon Grove's most eligible bachelor. To think, the most sought after man was one wearing mud-covered jeans.

CHAPTER THREE

*R*ick climbed into his pickup truck and dabbed wet coffee from his shirt with a napkin. He had hidden the coffee spill well enough with his arm when he held the door open. Had he not spotted the brunette beauty as she passed by the café window, he would have been less prepared for her to crash through the door, upsetting his coffee.

Patsy needed to install a window at the entrance to keep accidents from happening. She had talked about it enough but still hadn't taken action. This time, it was him who wore his coffee, leaving a poor cute girl embarrassed by their collision.

Rick swore he had seen her before but struggled to recall where. If she were a local, he would have recognized her. Rick knew everyone in Lemon Grove, so he brushed off the feelings of familiarity to either having bumped into her previously, or her resembling an acquaintance.

By hiding the damage, he hoped to ease whatever remorse she may have felt. It was just a shirt, and he was heading home anyway to take a shower and do a load of laundry.

He placed the coffee in a cup holder and backed his truck out of the parking lot. It wasn't his plan to get coffee this late in the day, but he had to make a quick stop at the general store for a carton of milk and needed a hot drink after working outside in the rain.

As he pulled away from the café, he noted the vehicles parked outside. He was familiar with all the owners, except for one: a silver Toyota Camry. The Camry must belong to the young woman in the shop. Rick chuckled as he imagined Patsy now talking non-stop to her new captive customer, peppering her with questions. At least he escaped the place with the excuse that he had to get home and change. From what he gathered, Patsy's fresh victim was newly arrived to town and about to learn first-hand what small town gossip was like.

He grabbed his coffee and took a sip. It was the right temper-ature. In all his years living in Lemon Grove, Patsy never got his order wrong. He would never get a cup of coffee like this in the city. The city lacked personalized service and seemed to consist only of popular chains with high prices and standard recipes. In a small town, café staff understood how to craft a coffee that catered to the customer, and they brewed his coffee how he liked it.

Rick drove past the campground and turned onto the high-way. It was quiet in Lemon Grove, and his choice to move away from the city five years ago, despite his family's protests, made him proud. They never understood his need for solitude when they craved the city nightlife. He argued that since it was possible to do his job remotely, he could work from anywhere, and trade in his view of concrete high-rises for trees and mountains.

They had come around to the idea when he agreed to allow them to use his property now and then as a summer vacation home. During their visits, the cabin was no longer his place of solitude, but sharing it with them brought peace to the family and it was peace he desired. The absence of their favorite urban amenities in Lemon Grove meant his family never stayed long. But it was the simpleness of Lemon Grove that Rick preferred.

Still, no matter how hard Rick tried to escape from the world of business, it had a way of finding him. Today was no different. As he pulled up in front of his home, he groaned. Most days, the sight of his dark blue, two-story home brought him joy. It was the sight of Robert Fletcher's black pickup truck parked by the pathway leading to his front door that made him wish he wasn't home.

Rick parked his old truck beside his unwanted guest's vehicle and glanced through the window. The truck was empty. He grumbled under his breath. Robert had no right to be wandering around his property uninvited, and it wasn't the first time he came here acting like he already owned the place. While he had bought up multiple houses on this stretch of road, Rick had no intention of letting Robert get his hands on the cabin. His long-term residence would never become part of some money-hungry resort owner's empire. If Robert wanted to expand Lemon Eagle Resort, he should do it in another direction.

Rick slammed his truck door and stomped around the back of his home. There were no signs of the man. At least Rick knew he had locked his home, and Robert wasn't interested in the cabin itself. Robert wanted the land and would knock down anything that didn't fit the resort aesthetic.

Had this been winter, Rick would have been able to track Robert's footprints in the snow, but in summer there were few signs of the direction he had headed. Rick looked at the bed of pine needles littered across the acres of land extending out from the back of his yard. There was talk of Robert Fletcher planning to develop a golf course near Lemon Grove. The only property standing in the way of his vision was Rick's. The thought of the trees protecting his home being ripped from the ground to make room for a fairway made his stomach churn.

"Are you sure you don't want to sell the place?" Robert Fletcher stepped out from behind a tree with his cell phone in hand. "I've told you, I will give you a good price."

Rick stood in place. "We've been over this, Robert. I'm not interested." He watched as the man approached him with his typical sales agent smile slapped across his face. It wasn't genuine. Robert was a man who smiled only to get what he wanted and treated everyone else around him like dirt when they had nothing to offer him.

Robert looked out of place standing among the trees dressed in a midnight black business suit. This was a backyard in Lemon Grove, not some executive conference room.

"With what I'm willing to offer, you would have the money to buy an even larger place in the next town over. Buy a penthouse in the city if you wanted."

Rick shook his head. This man didn't know him at all. "Why would I trade a place in Lemon Grove for the top floor of some cement block?"

Robert raised his hands. "Hey, it was only a suggestion. Do what you want with the money."

"I'm not accepting any offers."

"At least consider—"

"Robert, we've been through this enough. First the letters, then the phone calls…"

"You have to admit, I'm persistent." The laugh in his voice was still an attempt to charm Rick into a sale.

Coming from a business family, Rick saw through the sales tricks. He was not about to fall for some smooth talker pretending to be his friend. He took a step back toward his truck, hoping Robert would take the hint he was being escorted back to the driveway.

"Rick, I'd like to show you something." Robert headed back toward the trees, never once looking back to see if Rick was following him.

Rick glanced over his shoulder toward the front of his house and sighed. He would not get rid of Robert as quickly as he hoped. In order to get Robert to leave, Rick would have to hear him out.

He followed Robert deeper into the trees to where Rick had allowed the underbrush to grow in thick. There only so much property he maintained as a yard and the rest he allowed to grow wild. There was no need to interfere with nature. The animals did a good enough job keeping down the underbrush growth, and he enjoyed seeing the animals visit his yard.

Robert stopped and plucked a leaf from a bush before turning back to face Rick. "Can't even see your place that well from here, can you?"

Rick shrugged his shoulders. "That's the point."

"I thought you'd say that. A property of this size is difficult to maintain. You've only cleared the land up to here."

"It's how I like it."

Robert shook his head. "So, you like your cabin surrounded by a fire hazard?"

"It's called the forest, Robert."

"If you are going to live in the forest, you need to be responsible. You can't leave all this underbrush around. It will cause everything to go up in flames one day. Have you seen what is happening up north?"

Rick had seen the news reports. Wildfires, started by lightning strikes, were burning east of Lints and threatened at least twenty properties.

"And it has been burning out of control ever since," Robert said. "Imagine if those folks had taken care of their land..."

"Cutting everything down isn't the answer. We'd have no forests anywhere if that was the case." This conversation had gone on long enough. "I know what you're going to say, Robert, and I—"

"Hear me out." Robert raised his hand and turned back to face the unkempt forest. "I respect a man who wants to live out here.

My father was much like you, Rick. He bought his small piece of property to get away from the big city, and it was only after he and my mother missed having people around that they opened it up to visitors. They started with one or two tenting sites and built it up from there, adding space for trailers and then the cabins." Rick stared at the top of the trees. With Robert's back turned, he couldn't see Rick's complete disinterest in what he was saying. "People came and they continue to come even today. We are seeing the next generation bringing their families to experience Lemon Grove. Don't you want them to experience this place?"

Rick stifled a laugh. "You will tear this place down to expand the resort."

Robert turned in place. His smile remained plastered on his face but was a little more crooked than before. "No, no, no. I'm not sure where you got the impression that I was going to tear down the forest. We would have to do some pruning—"

"Is that what you call it when you rip roots from the ground?"

"Have you seen how many trees I plant on my property?"

"Those are decorative trees. They will never reach the same height, and you don't plant nearly as many trees as you remove."

Robert shifted his weight and discarded the leaf. "That's not true, Rick." He scrolled through his cell phone and held it up, turning the screen to Rick. "Look at this map." It was a rough drawing of the land between the resort and Lemon Grove. Robert had marked Rick's property with a red line outlining the place where they were standing to the southernmost part of his acreage and marked the area surrounding the cabin with a blue border. "What I am proposing is the purchase of your land from this point onward. You would keep your home and the land it sits on, along with a nice two acres to block out any views to your home. We would use this land as recreation for our guests."

"You mean to use it to develop your golf course."

"Not all of it." Robert cleared the screen and tucked his phone in his pocket. "A lot of it would remain as is, especially surrounding the course. Golf courses always need a rough."

"The rest of the land. What would you do with it?"

Sensing Rick might consider his offer, Robert's smile grew wider. "Good of you to ask. We are considering constructing a few cabins and short-term camping sites." Robert spotted the disapproval building on Rick's face and quickened his voice. "We're not talking about tall buildings here. They would be one, maybe two-stories high, and only four bedrooms. They would hardly be visible."

"And if you were to change your mind after you purchased the property?"

Robert shoved his hands in his pockets. "I'm an entrepreneur, Rick. Do you want to do business with me, or not?"

"My answer remains the same."

Robert shook his head and walked past Rick toward his truck, bumping his shoulder against Rick's arm as he passed. "You're making a mistake. This deal would give us both what we want."

"You're talking like I want to sell." He followed behind Robert, not to continue the conversation but to watch him leave. It was days like this that made Rick consider installing a gate at the entrance to his driveway. It would keep Robert and his business team from inviting themselves onto his property, which was becoming a monthly occurrence.

"You have to sell eventually, Rick. Why not sell when you can get a good price and afford another property to replace it with?"

Rick had invested his own time and money into this place without intention of ever selling. He planned to retire here one day and enjoy the simple life he had found in Lemon Grove. It was an excellent location, and he knew everyone in town. The thought of moving someplace new and starting over didn't excite him. And that wasn't even considering what might happen to the town if Robert Fletcher got his way.

"I don't think anywhere else could replace Lemon Grove."

Robert laughed as he opened the door to his truck. He pulled an envelope from the inside pocket of his jacket and handed it to Rick. It wasn't the first envelope Robert had given him, and Rick knew what he would find inside. Out of politeness, he took it and held it to his side.

"I'm ready to take your call whenever you change your mind," Robert said with a twinkle in his eye.

"I won't."

"You will." Robert winked. He turned his truck around and kicked up dirt as he drove toward the highway.

Rick sighed and slid his foot over the gravel, covering the tracks left behind from Robert's truck. Some would consider him a fool for turning down Robert's offer. Namely, his father. Robert had offered $1.2 million six months ago. That number rose to $1.5 million until reaching $2.0 million last month. After he had bought the place for four-hundred thousand three years ago, he stood to make an unimaginable profit.

He tapped the envelope against the side of his leg. There was no point in looking at the new offer. Since the resort was now looking to purchase less land, he expected the number to drop or remain the same. Not that he cared, although allowing Rick to keep his home was a new twist. He wouldn't have to move and could stay in the community, but would he be able to enjoy his home with resort guests milling about behind a revised property line? Already, the more adventurous types damaged his fence as they strayed from the trails and hiked through his property to reach Lemon Grove. It would only be worse with cabins nearby.

He grabbed his coffee and carton of milk from his truck and started toward the front door. It was time for dinner and he needed a shower. He would not give the offer another thought.

CHAPTER FOUR

*M*olly crawled out of her tent and let the crisp morning air fill her lungs. Dew dampened the ground and the inside of her tent, making her sleeping bag and clothes moist. Heavy fog settled over the campground, concealing her view of the mountains, but yesterday's storm had moved on, leaving the trees motionless.

With guests still tucked away in their beds, the campground was quiet. Had Molly not awakened this early, she, too, would be curled up inside her warm sleeping bag, but she needed to use the facilities. The early light of dawn lit the surrounding campground. She worried it would still be too dark to see, and with her flashlight in hand, she was ready to make the trip across the road, confident the flashlight was heavy enough to use for defense against human or animal attackers.

Seeing no signs of movement, she crossed the street. The campground remained silent, except for the sound of her feet on the gravel. Triggered by movement as she opened the door, the interior light of the restroom lit up and the ceiling vent roared, circulating the air in the small brick building. The campground staff had done a decent job of keeping the facilities clean. They painted the brick walls white, and the floor was still damp from the staff's early morning cleaning before campers emerged from their tents. A "wet floor" sign, placed in the center of the room near the sinks, warned guests of the slippery surface.

With no graffiti on the walls of the toilet stalls, either few vandals visited the campground, or fresh paint erased any messages. In her youth, Molly visited campgrounds with scalding or freezing water, so she grinned when the temperature of the tap water in Lemon Grove was neither hot nor cold. It was perfect.

Before leaving, she checked the showers and found no signs of scum or hair, but the showers were coin-operated.

"Fifty cents for three minutes?" Molly gasped. "Are they serious?" Outrageous prices, especially considering she paid thirty dollars a night to place her tent on a patch of gravel. At that price, they should have included hot showers. The owners were clearly making a profit from her and every other guest here.

Molly stepped outside and froze in place. Four brown paws were visible under her car. Her heart raced as she watched the paws pace back and forth along the edge of her tent. It was a light-colored animal and large, but from her position on the opposite side of the car, she couldn't make out its shape. Her fingers tightened around the handle of her flashlight, ready to defend herself from what was sniffing around her site. She kept the restroom door ajar, ready to rush back inside should the animal charge at her.

It didn't seem interested in the human across the road. Most likely hungry, the animal continued to sniff at the tent as it paced back and forth. Then, she saw its tail. A tall, pointy, wagging tail. Bears didn't have tails like that, especially a light-colored shaggy tail. That was a dog.

Molly tiptoed toward her site to get a better view. Not all dogs were friendly, and she was in no mood to become friends with a loose dog whose owners should have trained it to remain close.

Her foot tapped against the gravel. Her impatience caught up to her as the dog took its time searching each piece of stone around her site and every inch of fabric of her tent. She wanted to usher it along to allow her back into her own campsite. She had paid for the space, without ever intending to loan it to some stranger's dog.

"Go home!" Molly pointed toward the road.

The dog lifted its head.

She caught its attention.

The pup wagged its tail and looked in her direction before it headed down the road as she commanded. As Molly stomped toward her tent, the dog paused and turned to watch her cross the road.

"Silly dog," she mumbled. It was too early to deal with animals, especially out in the middle of the woods. Its owners should have been watching to make sure it stayed in their campsite and not allowed it to roam and pester campers. Had she been inside her tent and heard it sniffing the walls outside, it would have terrified her.

Molly lingered at the end of her campsite to observe the dog wandering down the road. It stopped to sniff the plants and lift its leg on the many stumps and campsite posts along the way. It seemed content enough, not at all concerned by its surroundings. She wanted to experience the same calmness as the dog. Instead, her temper flared. Molly wanted a break from the inconsiderate people she found in the city. She expected to hear a crying child in the campground, but never once thought she'd have to deal with a wandering dog. What if the dog had made a mess in her camping site? Would its owners expect her to pick up after it? She would have to do something if she didn't want to step in it. Imagine having to clean up after someone else's dog!

Satisfied the dog had headed back to its owner, she opened

the car door to grab a small carton of milk from her cooler, then moved to the trunk to grab a box of cereal, a bowl and a spoon. Dew covered the picnic table, so she opted to stand. She wanted to stretch her legs anyway after sleeping on the hard ground, and standing would also help her remain warm in the cool morning temperatures.

When choosing the campsite, Molly hadn't thought about how being so close to the mountains would cause chillier mornings. All she had wanted was a location where she would escape the heat wave in the city.

But this was cold. A bone-chilling cold. Her fleece hoodie would not be enough to keep her warm, and she determined she would need more layers.

Molly placed her bowl of cereal on the roof of her car and pulled a folding chair from the trunk. Setting up the dry chair by the tent, she grabbed an extra blanket and wrapped it around herself.

"Warmer already," she said, settling into the chair with her cereal.

Molly scooped another bite into her mouth and closed her eyes. This was going to be a good day. Despite it being her first night sleeping outside, she had a decent sleep and was excited to see what the day would bring. She may have resisted taking a break, but now she found herself looking forward to doing things at a slower pace without ever thinking about Brad.

She grimaced. Why did her mind have to remember she had someone she wanted to forget? Perhaps not saying his name would make it easier to redirect her thoughts to other things, like the bowl of cereal. She closed her eyes as she tried to distract herself.

A drop of milk hit her chin and her eyes fluttered open. Spotting the light-colored dog standing at the edge of the campsite sent her hand to her chest.

"You startled me," she said.

Its tail wagged as it held its position in the underbrush. The dog's dark-brown eyes stared at her, as if waiting for an invitation to visit.

"Didn't I tell you to go home?"

The dog beat its tail against the ground, happy that Molly acknowledged it once again.

"Are you wanting to play?"

Its ears lifted. She must have said a familiar word.

"I won't play with you."

Its ears lifted again. Molly thought of her earlier interaction with the pup. She hadn't shown kindness when she commanded it to go home. It was early, and she was hungry, not to mention only moments before she had feared for her safety after believing a bear was sniffing around her campsite.

"I am going to eat because I'm hungry," she said in a playful tone.

The dog smacked its lips and lowered its head. Whoever owned this dog had either neglected to give it breakfast or they were still asleep, as the dog was now begging from her. The worst scenario would be that someone lost their dog, but the odds were the dog belonged to a guest at the campground. As hungry as it was acting, all she needed to do was wait and it would run off to its owner.

She stared at its pleading eyes. "I can't feed you," she said. "I don't have any dog food."

The dog took one step forward.

"If I give you cereal, it could make you sick. Believe me, you don't want that."

The dog's tail wagged.

Molly leaned to the side and slapped the chair, beckoning the dog to approach. "Come on. I guess you want some company."

The dog scampered forward, kicking up gravel around its

feet. It nuzzled its face against Molly's hand, then sat at her feet, turning its head upward to gaze at her.

"You're friendly, aren't you?"

Its tail beat against the ground, clearing away the gravel until only a patch of dirt remained. The dog moved its head until Molly's hand slid to its ears, prompting her to scratch. She placed her cereal bowl onto her lap and gave the dog a two-handed scratch behind both ears.

"That feels good, doesn't it?"

The dog's mouth hung open as it panted and stretched its neck. With its nose pointed to the sky, the dog relished in the attention, allowing Molly to scratch under its collar, rattling its metal tags together.

"Let's see who you are." Molly held the tags in her hand, turning each over to inspect for a name. "These are only a license and vaccination tags. Do you have a name? I don't even know if you are a boy or a girl. Which are you? Huh?"

The dog laid down, and Molly leaned back, allowing her visitor to rest at her feet. "I guess getting scratched is exhausting."

Molly picked up her bowl and continued to eat her cereal. The dog groaned and sighed as it rested at her feet. It was awkward to eat in front of her furry guest, but she knew better than to feed a stray dog, and especially knew not to feed it unfamiliar food that would make it sick. The owner would feed the dog soon enough, and Molly was already being generous by giving the dog a good scratch. She should have sent it on its way again, giving the dog no attention at all, but she didn't and was glad she had invited it over. The dog at her feet brought warmth on a chilly morning.

In a campground this quiet and with wild animals in the surrounding forest, the dog had a calming effect on her. Her body relaxed as her companion protected her. She would be safe with it here, if it alerted her to signs of trouble.

The dog lifted its head and rose to its feet. She looked over her shoulder at the trees, but nothing had changed. Instead of barking or acting alarmed, the dog sauntered toward the entrance to her campsite.

"Where are you going?" she asked. "Bored with me already?"

The dog didn't look back and exited onto the road, turning into the campsite two spots away, wagging its tail as someone stepped out of their trailer onto their gravel pad.

Satisfied the dog had returned home, she continued eating her cereal, now aware that her once warm feet were cold. The dog had provided her with a little company, without being intrusive or talking back like people would do. It looked up at her, wanting affection, and perhaps a taste of her cereal. Receiving none, it remained at her feet, until its owners emerged from their trailer.

As much as it had bothered her to have a random dog wander into her campsite, she had enjoyed its brief visit. She didn't need to care for it and only needed to be a friend for a short time while it waited for its owners.

But… they should have at least had it on a leash or placed it in a crate, she grumbled. Even better, the dog could have slept inside the trailer with them rather than leaving it outdoors in the cold, where it might wander off in the night or roam where animals could attack it.

While her opinion of the dog had improved, her opinion of its owners had declined. Sure, some dogs enjoyed the outdoors, but when traveling in strange locations where someone could try to steal one's pet, the owners were irresponsible. That poor dog was lucky to have wandered into Molly's campsite, and it hadn't tried to steal an irritable camper's breakfast.

She filled a washbasin at a nearby tap and cleaned her dishes at the picnic table. Her fingers were numb as she rinsed soap from the spoon. Molly assumed the water from the tap must come from the creek, fed by the mountain glaciers, and decided tomorrow she would boil water on her camp stove to add to the ice-cold water and provide her hands with some warmth.

She dumped the dirty water into the drain by the shower facilities and returned her dishes to the trunk of the car. If her hands weren't so cold, she would drive into town to get a hot cup of coffee, but they were much too chilled to touch a steering wheel, which would not be warm. She tucked her hands under her arms and shivered before wrapping herself in her blanket.

From her chair, she looked up at the blue tarp hanging over her site. The problem with a tarp was how it blocked the view of the mountains and sky. It did, however, keep the covered portion of her site dry and she could always move her chair out from under the tarp to see the view, or go for a walk. She was glad she had braved the rain and hung the tarp when she did, and she would be thankful to have a dry place to sit after the next rainfall.

After her hands warmed, she unpacked a rope and strung it between the trees to form a laundry line. The washcloth needed drying.

"There," she said to herself. It was a decent clothesline that only sagged a little when she draped the cloth over the rope. She glanced down and saw the dog standing beside her, wagging its tail. "You're back. Did you enjoy your breakfast?"

The dog tilted its head. Molly scratched behind its ears and its tail beat the ground.

"Are you proud of my laundry line? It's saggy, but I shouldn't have to hang much."

The dog turned and looked across the road.

"Going somewhere?" Molly asked. The dog preferred not to stay in the same place for long. "You should stick close so they know where to find you." A rumble of an engine echoed through the campsite, along with the clang of metal. "It sounds like some people are packing up." But not Molly. She smiled to herself. Those poor folks may have reached the end of their vacation, but hers had only just begun. In fact, she had brought along an itinerary of activities in the area to consider exploring during her stay... if she wanted to. With clear skies, she might try to explore some of them today.

She checked her watch and quickly covered it with her sleeve. Time didn't matter here. This was the first vacation where she could sit and be lazy without being judged by her family or friends. The activities could be what she wanted without having to accommodate anyone else's interests. It was all about her, and she didn't feel guilty about liking it that way.

But what did she want to do? Trails surrounded the property, and most she would consider safe if she equipped herself with bear spray or stuck to the popular trails. That was her plan. But first, she needed to explore the campground.

"I'm going to go for a walk." The dog's ears lifted. "You should stay here. Alright?"

The light-colored dog sat on the ground and whined as it watched her walk toward the road. It had been well-trained. If only it would stay in its campsite near its owners.

She glanced over her shoulder to see the dog now lying on the ground with its head resting on its front legs. Its sad eyes begged her to invite it along with her, but coaxing it to follow her would lead the dog away from its owners.

Molly walked past the shower facilities to the first loop of campsites. Some sites were empty and ready for future guests. Another site sat occupied with campers already eating breakfast. Next door, a man worked to disassemble his tent. Engines started and the quiet morning Molly had enjoyed was ending. She hoped the noise was temporary. Once those who were checking out had left, all who would remain would be those staying at least another night.

Molly stuffed her hands in her coat pocket and kept moving. Already, her body warmed, just by keeping a good pace. A small dog on a leash barked by the steps of a travel trailer. The owner poked her head out the door to shush the pup with a wave of a finger. The dog grumbled and curled up on a woven mat at the base of the steps, giving a few stifled woofs for good measure. Molly's furry visitor was quiet. It was a silent guest and never said a word when it came by. This just proved what Molly had heard before about dogs. The small ones were yappy.

CHAPTER FIVE

*R*ick didn't know why he shoved Robert's unopened envelope into the back pocket of his jeans. He had glared at the envelope on the kitchen counter where he left it the day before, and yet he felt compelled to bring it with him until he decided what to do with Robert Fletcher's offer. His family raised him in a business-focused household where they gave each opportunity due consideration, even if they had already made up their minds. His father would have encouraged him to at least look at the offer and see for himself what he was rejecting. Opening the envelope shouldn't mean anything, yet to Rick, it did.

He wasn't interested in selling the cabin he saved to purchase on his own without the help of his family. His city friends encouraged him to continue to live rent-free in his father's condominium, but the city life wasn't for him and he wanted to live independently from his family.

His move from the city was the best decision he ever made. The transition to Lemon Grove brought a change in lifestyle and clarity. The distance to the city meant no daily visits to the office, which reduced the number of meetings the company invited him to attend. His family didn't expect him at every social gathering with their friends, most of which were also business contacts, and they often used the gatherings as another chance to close a deal.

Rick avoided playing the business game and chasing the dream of being rich, hoping money would one day make him happy. He already found what would make him happy.

It was summer, six years ago, when Rick had fallen in love with Lemon Grove, and he remembered the day he discovered the town with fondness. He had spent a long day completing a business deal after a senior sales associate botched the job. The deal shouldn't have gone sideways, but it did. His father asked Rick to fix the problem, which meant staying behind while the rest of the family left for their vacation without him.

He grumbled on the drive out of the city. All he needed to do was be the face of the family name and win over a customer. The sale would be easy since he could tell from previous interactions the woman was into him. Suggesting the meeting take place over dinner almost guaranteed the sale before anyone ordered their meal. Rick had influence over women, and his father knew it. He was lucky to inherit his looks from his mother's side of the family, and his father liked to exploit them for business at every opportunity.

"We give the customer what they want," his father would say with a wink. "Use those looks while you still can."

Rick hated the way his father paraded him around to flirt with the clients. It didn't matter if the women liked his attention, or even requested to work with him. He hated using his looks to make a deal. It was manipulative, and it ate away at his integrity. He didn't want a reputation as a playboy or as a sleazy business executive.

"It's part of the territory," his father argued against Rick's protests. "Embrace it, Rick. Many men would die to be in your shoes. Who wouldn't want to wine and dine beautiful women and close a business deal all in one night? You could have it all if you play your cards right."

Playing his cards right meant playing the way his father wanted him to. Six years ago, Rick realized his time as the handsome face of the family business had ended.

He didn't yet see his next move, but he was ready for a change. The further he drove out of the city, the more he thought about his need to break free. A little distance between him and the family business would create less stress for him and, he hoped, would improve his relationship with his parents. Boundaries were a healthy thing, at least that was what the television experts always said. But boundaries were something he didn't have when he worked for his parents and lived in their family-owned condominium. Something needed to change, and it needed to happen soon.

Perhaps his emotions had caught up and overwhelmed him and he needed a moment to regain his composure. Or maybe it was that he didn't want to join his parents at the, then, much-smaller Lemon Eagle Resort, but when he had spotted a sign for the town of Lemon Grove, he turned off the road to make a brief stop. The smell of nature captured his senses. The quiet as he sat in his car at the end of the road called to him and the rich green trees excited him. While he had been in nature before, he never stopped to appreciate it. The calming effect of the environment brought to the surface a sense of healing and happiness he hadn't experienced since he was a child. There were no pressures on him as he sat in the car while the wind blew through the open windows.

When he walked into Patsy's café and met the locals, their personalities and life sold him on Lemon Grove. Once he discovered the slower pace of the community, combined with the welcoming warmth of the people, he concluded quickly this was home. He never went to meet his parents at Lemon Eagle Resort, and they never forgave him for it.

Rick didn't care. He wanted to be in the town, and over the next year he put a plan into motion to move the rest of his life from the city to Lemon Grove. After living here for five years, it was still the best decision he ever made. He never regretted his choice. Not even once.

Nothing beat getting up in the morning to see the sunrise behind the trees and watch the deer graze in his backyard. He viewed a few homes before looking at the cabin, but this one stood out with its acres of trees, private yard, and a home he would one day grow into. This would be the place he would raise his family. Not the city. He would protect his future children from the constant pressure to work for the family business, and Rick swore he would never sacrifice family time for a company, like his father.

He looked forward to finding someone like-minded and starting a family. The children would enjoy running around the backyard while he sat on the back deck holding his wife's hand. Each time he visualized his future, he couldn't imagine selling his property to Robert Fletcher. That is why he never opened the envelope, yet he still carried it around in his back pocket out of habit. No amount of money could buy his dream. This place meant too much to him and selling it would mean selling a piece of himself.

The morning carried on as Rick walked around the northern end of his property to inspect the fence. No one bothered the low-horizontal fence by the road, and it fared well over the winter. A few boards needed replacement, and a fresh coat of white paint would sharpen its appearance and give it several more years of life. He made note of the repairs and continued along the fence when his phone rang.

"Hi, Mom."

"Good morning. I didn't know if you were already up." She knew. He had already responded to his work emails before going out into the yard, one of which he addressed to her. Rick noticed her cool tone. This was not a simple check in call, and there was something on her mind.

"Did you get my email about the changed deadlines?"

His mother gave a cheap laugh. She was never great at acting. "Oh, was that you?"

"That was me," Rick said as he gave one of the fence posts a shake.

"Yes, I see that now," she said. "Well, I understand Robert Fletcher came by the other day."

"He did."

"And?"

Rick pulled the envelope from his pocket and turned it over in his hand. "And what?"

Her exasperated sigh blew into the speaker. "How much was it?"

"I don't know."

"What do you mean, you don't know? Rick, when someone hands you an offer…"

Rick pulled the phone away from his ear and waited for his mother's deafening voice to quiet. "There's no point in looking at it when I'm not interested in selling."

"You should at least respect the man and look at his offer. It is what any decent human being would do."

Respect? For Robert Fletcher? He nearly snorted in his mother's ear. The man was proud and domineering and would stop at nothing to get what he wanted, which was why he reminded Rick of his father.

"I'm sure whatever Robert offered you was *more* than fair," she added in her most persuasive tone.

If Rick hadn't been holding the envelope, he would have pulled at his hair. This was how it always went with his family. Whenever they caught wind of something he did that they disagreed with, they would send in his mother to sway him in their direction. They wanted him back home in the city, and a deal with Robert Fletcher would fit with their vision for his life.

"Is this why you called me, Mom? To convince me to take Robert's deal?"

Her laugh became a nervous chuckle. Perhaps his voice had been louder than he had intended. "It would be nice to have you back home. Your father and I miss you." She had recovered well and the warmth of a mother's love oozed through the phone. However, Rick had already understood this wasn't about wanting the family back together. This was about their relationship with Robert Fletcher and not about their son's happiness. "Are you really going to pass up three million dollars?"

There it was. The confirmation Rick needed. "So, Robert told you."

"Of course, he told us. We all agree you're being stubborn about this, Rick. No one else would give you three million for that old cabin."

They didn't like the cabin because Rick hadn't torn down the building to build new. His family expected luxury, high-end... everything. Rick preferred the rustic touches the previous owner had put into the home. It had history and character, unlike the modern homes his family owned. He had made some changes since he moved in. The back deck was new, since years of weather had rotted the old one. He had updated the kitchen and bathrooms, and had new windows and doors installed. Besides a few other cosmetic changes, the cabin remained as it was, with its rustic plank floors, wood-trimmed ceiling, and even the ladder to the loft, which the previous owners had brought in from an even older barn. He had added his own personal touches to make it feel like home, and he liked it.

"That old cabin is my life, Mom." He glanced down at the envelope, now crumpled in his hand.

"I still don't understand what you like about that place. There is nothing there for you."

He faced his cabin. The front exterior was invisible from the fence-line, obscured by the trees and their branches. "You mean there is no *one* here. All you talk about is me getting married."

One more way they tried to control his life. The last time he listened to them on that point, it blew up in his face and blew his heart apart along with it. He wasn't going down that road again.

"Well, I imagine you all alone in that house and I worry about you being lonely." Again, with the motherly tone.

"I'm not lonely, Mother. I have plenty of friends."

"Friends are not enough. We may not agree on a lot of things, but you must realize I'm right about this. You are a good man, Rick, and there is a girl out there for you somewhere. I can guarantee you will not find her in the middle of some forgotten town like Lemon Grove. I want you to be happy."

"I am happy, Mother. How can I convince you of that?"

"I think I'm pretty easy to convince. Your father…"

Once again, Rick removed the phone from his ear. He didn't need to hear his father's expectations for his life, as he had heard them many times before. It was what drove him to Lemon Grove in the first place and why he was more convinced than ever, Lemon Grove was where he needed to stay.

"Mom," he said, interrupting her mid-sentence. "I'm sorry, but I need to go. There are a couple of things I need to wrap up before I get into my next work call."

"Of course," she said. Anything for business. "Maybe we can talk later after you have time to look over Robert's offer."

So, never. "Sounds good, Mom."

He breathed a sigh of relief when the call ended, and tucked his phone away. The wrinkled envelope remained in his hand as he carried it back to the house. It belonged in the trash bin with all the other offers Robert had given him, but three million dollars was a lot of money to throw away. His mother was right. No one else would make him the same offer, and he thought of what he could do with that kind of money, such as buy himself a newer place with a great-sized yard and even a pool if he wanted. With three million dollars, a custom-built home in the mountains with spectacular views wasn't out of reach… but it wouldn't be in Lemon Grove.

Rick tossed the envelope onto a small table beside the front door and headed into his office. The tall window offered its own spectacular view of the woods behind his house. Would he be willing to trade this in for something else? These woods have given him more than just a view. They had brought him focus, freedom from the city, and healed his broken heart.

Sure, the money would help him afford someplace new, but at what cost? Knowing what would happen to the forest he loved, he couldn't bear it.

He fired up his emails and saw a message of high importance waiting for him. It was from his father. Like Robert, Rick would make him wait for a response. There were several messages from clients waiting, and they should take priority over some conversation about a personal matter. He only wanted to push Rick to do his bidding and had no interest in what Rick wanted.

Rick checked his watch and noted the time. He still had a few hours before Glenda would call from the campground to tell him it was time to swing by. Another reason not to leave Lemon Grove. He had people looking out for him here, and he couldn't move when leaving would hurt a friend.

CHAPTER SIX

She had planned to only walk a quick circle around the loop, but Molly could not resist a detour on a short trail near the entrance to the campground. The carved wooden sign had shown the circuit as a thirty-minute loop, and Molly impulsively turned. Why not? The weather was beautiful with the sun fanning down through the leaves, creating a veil of light on the path. A light breeze turned the leaves into wind instruments as they beat together in a symphony. Best of all, there were no people. The entire trail was hers to enjoy.

A trail this close to the perimeter of the campsite meant she wouldn't be in danger. The sounds and smells of the guests would keep the animals away, so she was confident of being alone without a can of bear spray. Only a dog at her feet would make her feel safer. Even the dog from the campsite following her along the trail would do. But this was fine. She was close to the campground where someone would hear her if she called for help, and might even come to her rescue, especially since the sides of travel trailers were visible between the trees. It wasn't as if she had wandered too far into the woods.

The detour brought with it a change of scenery. A trickle of water from a small brook flowed under a mushroom-covered log before feeding into the larger creek. Pine needles littered the forest floor, giving it a reddish hue. Small shrubs were attempting to grow, no doubt struggling from the lack of direct sunlight and the limited rain penetrating through the canopy above.

A squirrel dug at the base of a tree to bury its treasure and Molly paused, mesmerized by the creature's stealthy behavior. No one in her family ever cared about squirrels and viewed them as a nuisance, always trying to steal food from their picnic table. Molly always liked them. She even bought a small toy squirrel at a gift shop to place on her childhood bed. The toy was long gone, but the memory remained of its plush tail and large, black plastic eyes. A static toy squirrel couldn't beat the real thing with their jittery movements, as if always startled and on edge.

The squirrel lifted its head and took off like a shot, scampering into the woods. Molly laughed at the thought of a silly squirrel spooking itself. There was nothing nearby to startle it, except for Molly, and she was motionless. Unless…

A quiet crack of a twig in the distance made the hairs on the back of Molly's neck stand upright. There was something else in the woods that she couldn't see, and Molly didn't want to wait to see what it was. Taking her cue from the squirrel, Molly moved at a jog, panting as she rushed to the end of the trail. She exited into the half-empty campground where she caught her breath and laughed. Nothing had chased her, and like the squirrel, she spooked herself.

With her nerves calmed, Molly took a fresh look at the campground. In this loop there were only three occupied sites, and the further she went, she discovered only twelve more occupied sites out of the forty-five capacity campground. There were fewer campers remaining than she thought. Given the nature of campgrounds, travelers would arrive later in the day and set up prior to their evening meal. She pondered if running a campground was profitable with so few guests?

Soon, she noticed the trailer near her camping pad had also vacated its site, and Molly experienced a wave of sadness. If the occupants of the trailer left the campground, the friendly pup would also be gone. The owners showed no signs of packing up their unit before she left for her walk, but they were efficient and pulled away before she returned. At this, she felt disappointed. From those few interactions she shared with the dog, she enjoyed having it around and as she stood by her tent, her campsite seemed empty.

She gathered her towel and a change of clothes and hummed an unidentifiable tune. After packing in the heat and setting up the tent the day before, she needed a shower, but after searching her wallet, Molly only found a single quarter. She emptied her dry groceries into the trunk and used the plastic bag to hold her clean clothes and towel, then walked to the office, hoping the attendant would provide change. The owners should, especially if they were emptying the coin collection in the showers every day.

The same woman who had checked her in sat behind the office desk. She had pivoted her office chair to face away from the door while working on a crossword puzzle.

"Good morning," Molly said in a cheerful tone.

"Morning." The woman sounded bored, as if she had already said the greeting many times this morning. "Let me know when you're ready." She hadn't even looked up to see who had entered the office.

Molly took a quick glance around the store. There was nothing inside she wanted, and as she had suspected, they inflated the prices. She approached the desk. "Can I get some coins for the shower, please?"

The woman tossed her crossword onto her lap and held out her hand to receive Molly's five-dollar bill. Molly attempted to maintain a neutral but pleasant expression as the woman reached into her cash register and counted out her change. There had been no mention of poor customer service in the campground's online reviews, but Molly might change that when her trip was over. While the place was clean, the woman at the front desk had yet to show any personality unless that man in the jacket had walked through the door. Now, she wouldn't even smile or look up at her visitor when Molly walked in and seemed annoyed by Molly's request.

At least she had the woman's attention, and Molly could learn more about the area and ways to spend her day.

"Which shops would be good to visit in town?" she asked, hoping to get some response out of the woman.

"Depends on what you're looking for."

Molly wanted to rephrase her question but didn't bother. She figured the response would be about the same.

"I guess you're right." She looked at the artisan display beside the desk. "What time do the shops close?"

"Hi, Rick." The woman's eyes lit up. Her face, only moments before wearing every expression of boredom, now wore an ear-to-ear smile.

Molly turned to see the man in the brown jacket standing once again in the doorway. Him again. He leaned relaxed against the doorframe, with one boot crossed in front of the other. It didn't matter that mud speckled the lower-half of his fitted jeans. His top-half was in a buttoned shirt and gave him a business-like look Molly hadn't seen him in before. What a difference a shirt made. Perhaps he was the reason this place had excellent reviews, as Molly was ready to give him a five out of five-star rating on appearance alone. Or four and a half stars because of the mud.

"Sorry to interrupt," Rick said. There were the manners Molly had been looking for yesterday.

"That's okay," the host said, as if it didn't matter that only moments ago Molly had asked her a question. "I see he's got you doing mornings again."

"Afraid so." Rick tapped the doorframe, and Molly wondered what his hand would feel like against hers. Would he have rough hands from working outdoors or soft skin like the men who worked in a city office? "Where can I find him?"

"Site thirty-eight, last I heard."

"Thank you." He smiled at Molly and her stomach fluttered. "Once again, I'm sorry for the interruption. As for shopping… sorry, I couldn't help but overhear. A lot of ladies like to shop at The Lemon Closet. And the shops close at six, but the corner store, restaurant and café are open later. Enjoy your stay." He uncrossed his ankles and stepped out the door before Molly could thank him for his recommendation.

Just as the server at the café had said, Rick attracted the women in the town, and Molly was falling under his spell. How could she not with looks and manners? It was the host who had addressed Rick first and avoided answering Molly's question. If she hadn't, he might have continued to stand in the doorway waiting for his turn to speak. But he took his time to tell Molly which store to visit, so she would at least check out The Lemon Closet. Maybe the next time she saw him, she would tell him what she thought of his recommendation.

The host handed Molly her coins and shoved the drawer to the register closed, rattling the desk.

"Is there anything else?" the woman asked, having snapped out of the man's spell.

"No, that is all, thanks," Molly said. She observed the woman taking one last lustful look at the doorway before resuming her crossword puzzle.

Molly walked back to the shower facilities and started the shower. She didn't enjoy using public showers with their misaligned stall doors and the flimsy shower curtains, but the owners had tried to make these as private as possible. They had proper doors between the sink area and the shower changing space. A glass door on the shower stall kept the water from splashing out onto the grated tile floor. Of course, this was the nicest of the three showers. The others needed updating.

Once a coin dropped through the slot, the water sprayed out at a good pressure and the temperature quickly rose to a pleasant warmth. Molly hopped inside and soon realized she had forgotten to pack shampoo or a bar of soap. A rinse would have to do, and she would need to add the items to her shopping list for her trip into town.

Cool air crept into the shower stall, chilling her exposed skin. She let the water pour over her scalp as she turned in place, trying to keep the warm water on her skin. And then the water stopped.

"Already?" Had she been washing her hair, it would have left her with a head covered with suds. The campground must really make a profit on the showers.

Her limbs shook as she quickly dried herself and attempted to balance on the grated floor on one foot while dressing into her clean clothes. At her campsite, she stuffed her dirty clothes into a garbage bag for a future trip to the laundromat and closed the trunk of her car.

Clean and dressed, Molly was ready to explore the town. She did not want to deal with the campground host or pay the outrageous prices, so she thought her best option would be to buy her soap at the general store. While there, she might also check out The Lemon Closet and maybe even get a good cup of coffee from the café.

Recalling the map, she walked to the lower end of the campground where a wooden bridge extended over the creek. She paused in the middle and gazed over the railing. The water was clear and sparkled in the daylight. Algae had formed over the smooth stones that lined the bottom and sides of the creek. Trees and underbrush stood along the banks, creating a picturesque setting as birds flew above. Now she wished she had brought along her camera to capture the scene. She would not forget it on her next walk.

After taking in the scene for several minutes, she carried on toward the town. As described by the host, the trail opened out into the residential area behind the campground. The road running along the edge of the forest was dry, except for the damp leaves that covered the shoulder. It was quiet on the road that ran east and west, with another road heading south into the neighborhood.

With her hands in the pockets of her hoodie, Molly ventured out onto the street. The route seemed straightforward enough, and after what she had seen of the town the night before, she knew it was small. If she became lost, it would be easy to find her way back to the campground. All she would have to do is go north, and if she reached the highway, she would have gone too far. To find the road that she took from the campground to Lemon Grove, she would walk east. For now, she followed the host's instructions and walked south to the first road, where she turned left.

A dog barked from a distant backyard in the second or third row of homes. It would seem there were only four streets extending to the east and west. Molly was at the westernmost point of the town, with only four houses remaining on the road to her right. The bulk of the residences were on the east side of the town, which she hadn't yet explored. The homes she could see looked like cabins, with their dark wooden siding and green rooftops. The owners had constructed fenced yards for gardens with chain-link used to support sunflowers and beans or peas. Nothing in nearby yards appeared expensive, which signaled the residents weren't rich and the town wasn't booming. It was a small resort community supporting a quaint, eclectic lifestyle, as confirmed by one home with an excessive number of pinwheels and garden gnomes as garden decor.

The town didn't seem to stir early; she still had yet to see a car pass by. Folks around town should still have to work, unless they were all employees of the town itself and were in no rush to get moving. Molly checked her watch. At ten thirty, the coffee shop and general store should be open. Lemon Grove's shopping hours shouldn't make it impossible for customers to buy anything. The town would never survive if that were the case.

As she reached the main road, Molly finally found the general store and the café. To her relief, both were open, and the bell rang as she entered the store, where a clerk sat on a stool behind the counter waiting with a smile.

"Welcome." The man in his seventies rose from his seat and moved closer to the counter. "What can I help you with today?"

This man understood customer service. Molly stepped around a shelf of candy. "I am looking for shampoo. Do you have any?"

"I do." He pointed toward a shelf near the back of the store. "Over there by the toilet paper. If you need anything else, please let me know and I'll be happy to help you."

"Thank you." Molly walked past the rows of cereal and bread to the shelf with toilet paper stacked on the top. Tissue paper, bug spray and hand soap also filled the hygiene section of the store. She grabbed a bar of soap along with the shampoo and cringed at the price. It was more here than in the city, but less expensive than the campground. Given how welcoming the store clerk had been when he greeted her, Molly would ignore the price if it meant not having to buy her supplies at the camp store or spend the time and money on gas to drive into the city to resupply.

The store bell rang, and Rick strolled in, waving to the shop owner. He seemed to be coming in Molly's direction so she urgently checked her appearance in the glass door of a freezer full of microwavable dinners. This was why girls brought hairdryers and make-up on camping trips. Only married women didn't care if they ran into the town hottie and were willing to let their appearance go. At least she was showered, but her hair was lifeless after being left to air dry, and her skin was pale without a little blush to brighten her cheeks.

Rick dipped into the aisle before hers and, noticing her, flashed a smile.

"It seems we keep bumping into each other," Rick said.

Her mouth went dry as she fought to find a response. "We do." She struggled with the informality and familiarity the tiny community offered. Here, people talked to each other, and he was standing across from her. In the city, it was normal not to make eye contact or to say anything more than a word or two — people stayed strangers because there were just too many of them. "I swear I'm not stalking you," she blurted. Molly noticed the heat rise in her cheeks. It would have been best not to say anything at all. Why did she bring up stalking? Of all the ridiculous things to have—

"That's what a stalker would say," Rick said with a wink. He didn't skip a beat, grabbing something from the shelf before turning back toward the counter. "I'd like to mail a package," he said to the clerk. He pulled a large envelope from inside his coat and handed it to the man.

"I think you are solely responsible for keeping our courier in business," the clerk said. He slid a paper and pen across to Rick.

"And I don't mind." Rick scribbled his shipping information on the paper as the clerk weighed the envelope, while Molly slinked along the hygiene aisle before moving to stand in line at the front of the store. She tried to not look obvious as she peered over his shoulder to see where he was sending the package, or if a woman was the addressee.

The clerk took the form and attached it to the package before tucking it under the counter. "You're all set, Rick."

"Thank you." He turned to Molly. "Have a good day." She smiled and caught her breath as the bells chimed on the door and he stepped outside.

"I didn't know you could mail packages here," she said.

"You sure can," the clerk said. "We're the post office and the bus depot."

"There is a bus in town?"

"It is more of a shuttle. It connects the small towns in the area to the city. Runs twice a day. Mornings and evenings."

"And you need a depot for a shuttle?"

The clerk handed Molly her change. "People need a place to catch the bus. Might as well come in here and buy something while they wait than stand outside at some sign." He winked and placed her items in a bag.

Molly thanked the clerk and walked out to the street but saw no signs of Rick. He had a way of appearing and disappearing, just like Brad, who had disappeared from her life. Right. She sighed. Brad. It had been several hours since she thought about him and that was a good thing. Molly had come to Lemon Grove to forget one man, and it seemed to work only because she was thinking about another.

CHAPTER SEVEN

*R*ick fired up his truck and let it idle. He had gone to the general store to send paperwork back to the office and complete the deal he was working on. Earlier that morning, he filed the electronic paperwork, but the company had yet to eliminate the last few paper forms. The option of electronic documentation and technology gave Rick the freedom to work from Lemon Grove, but he still needed the courier to make almost daily trips with the hard copies, and Rick paid a premium rate for the service.

With his office commitments completed, the rest of the day was his to spend as he liked. Rick had no additional obligations unless he booked them himself, and by now he would normally be eager to get back to his home to tinker in the garden. Today he wasn't as ready to return home, not after bumping into the cute girl from the campground for... how many times? The fourth time? He chuckled over her outfit. She was a city girl through and through, dressed in crisp, never before worn clothes. While he didn't consider himself a fashion expert with enough skill to identify old clothes from new, the "Size S" sticker stuck to her waist gave her secret away.

He had to admire how she embraced the adventure of being outdoors and at least tried to dress the part. She was among the first he'd seen to make the effort. The usual city girl arrived with perfect hair and nails done just so. They hid at the first sign of rain or bugs. Those high maintenance types would either arrive in a travel trailer or stay at the resort. Then there were the ones who tried to impress their boyfriends and claimed to enjoy camping until they arrived. Rick always heard their loud complaints from a distance and they never stayed long, leaving him wondering what happened to the relationship after they left.

This girl seemed different. Every time he saw her, she was alone. Was there no boyfriend to impress? She didn't fuss with her hair or make-up and let her messy, natural waves hang past her shoulders. The young woman looked like a genuine person and didn't hide behind some fake facade, except for the new outfit.

It was easy for him to see past clothes. When he moved to Lemon Grove, there were few outfits he owned which didn't belong in a boardroom. She might have had the same issue and needed to add more casual clothes to her wardrobe. The plaid shirts were stereotypical, and from what he had seen, she had purchased the same outfit in multiple colors. He liked the blue checkered plaid against her skin more so than the red. Sadly, he didn't notice if the blue color matched her eyes. In their previous interactions, he never looked at her eyes, having found himself too overwhelmed by everything else about her, like the way she wore an annoyed expression whenever he walked into the campground office. It was what prompted him to apologize for interrupting her conversation with Glenda for a second time, and only after he stood outside the door listening to their conversation. Her voice was sweet and intoxicating.

She was already up the front steps by the time he arrived at the campground. A girl like her was hard to miss in Lemon Grove. Anyone who didn't live here stuck out, and she was right out in the open. For a third time, she was alone, which was odd. If she were traveling with family or friends, he would have seen her out with someone.

Now he had seen her a fourth time at the general store, and she was just as cute as the first time he saw her. He questioned talking to her in the toiletries aisle. The last thing he wanted was to make it awkward, but he had to say something. He got a smile out of her and he wanted to see her beautiful smile again.

Rick sipped on his coffee and watched her flit across the road, with her plastic bag from the general store dangling at her side, and into the café. Who was she? If he was going to keep running into her, he had to learn her name.

He looked down at his paper cup full of coffee and sighed. If he hadn't made a trip to the café before mailing the package, he could have used buying a coffee as an excuse to bump into her for a fifth time. She disappeared through the café door and he took another sip before tucking the cup into the truck's cup holder.

There was no rule stating he couldn't get a second cup of coffee if he wanted. Besides, only Patsy was aware he visited the café only minutes earlier. With the girl, he could play off them being in the same place at the same time as mere coincidence. Rick glanced in the rearview mirror and ran his fingers through his hair. His appearance would have to do. She did just see him in the general store, so it was too late to make any major improvements to his appearance. He turned off the ignition and unbuckled his seatbelt. "Who's the stalker now?" he whispered to himself.

Taking a quick breath, Rick set out across the road before doubt sank in. He came to a halt five feet from his truck, re-thinking his plan.

This was a bad idea. What if she thought he was following her? If she were worried, Patsy would vouch for him and say he was a nice guy. After six years of filling his order, he had come to know the owner of the café well. He had even attended her husband's funeral two years ago. It saddened him to learn Patsy wanted to sell the business she had worked with her husband to build. Rick had promised her he would be a loyal customer until the day she closed the doors.

On the other hand, Patsy had a way of calming people, and if her customer seemed nervous about Rick, Patsy would be sure to set her straight. Besides, he would say the young woman was the one trying to find him and had timed her trip to the café to align with his visit. Of course, she would deny it.

A car honked at Rick, snapping him out of his reverie. He waved to the annoyed tourist who had stopped for him while he stood in the middle of the road. He dashed across to the café door and paused. He could change his mind now and not walk inside, but she had captured his attention, and he had to figure out why.

Patsy wore a puzzled expression when Rick re-entered the café. He tried to appear neutral, then surprised when he spotted the young woman by the counter. He had to sell both women he wasn't expecting to run into the visitor for a fifth time. It was time to put those old high school drama classes to good use.

"You're back," Patsy said. The young woman turned at the counter and her mouth hung open. "Was there something wrong with your coffee?"

"No." Rick strolled forward and leaned against the wall beside the cooler. "I came back for another."

"Another?" Patsy wiped her hands on a towel. "Since when do you drink two in one day?"

He shrugged and shoved his hands in his pockets. "What can I say? You make excellent coffee." The girl looked at him and smiled. "We meet again."

"It appears so." He couldn't read her expression. There was a slight smile mixed with a look of embarrassment as she glanced down at the floor.

Rick bent down to peer into the cooler and hold her gaze. "If we keep meeting like this, we should tell each other our names."

Patsy raised an eyebrow and smirked before turning around to face the pass-through window into the kitchen.

"Well, I understand your name is Rick."

His muscles weakened as she said his name. That had never happened before. "How do you know that?"

"Because everyone in town calls you by your name."

"Right." As he stood upright, he saw Patsy with her back toward them, shaking her head. "Since you already know my name, it is only fair for me to know yours."

She passed her plastic grocery bag to her opposite hand. "My name is Molly."

"It is nice to officially meet you, Molly."

"Same."

Patsy laughed and stepped up to the counter with Molly's order. "I could write her name on her cup if that would help."

"I don't think everyone needs to know my name." Molly chuckled and took her cup of coffee. "Thank you."

"Enjoy shopping at The Lemon Closet," Patsy said. "Make sure you check out those shoes I was telling you about."

Rick rushed ahead of Molly and held open the door, allowing her to step outside unobstructed. He lingered in the door as she turned onto the sidewalk.

"Did you really come here for a second coffee?" Patsy called. She leaned over the counter, observing Rick take one long stare. "I'll keep your secret."

"What secret?" He strolled back to the counter.

"That you only came in here to talk to Molly."

"I did not." He pointed to the chalkboard menu. "I'll have an Americano."

Patsy lowered her chin and held her pen to her paper.

"I'm serious," Rick said. "Stop looking at me like that."

She scribbled his order onto the paper and passed it through to the kitchen. "This has to be the first time you've ever ordered a—"

"Second coffee in one day? It has been a long day."

"It is going to last even longer if the caffeine keeps you up all night."

Patsy was onto him, but he shouldn't leave without a coffee in his hands if he was to run into Molly again. It is one thing for Patsy to figure out he had only come to the café to talk to her, but another for Molly to see through his plan. He didn't want to scare her off before he had the chance to talk to her again.

"If it keeps me awake, I'll remember your warning." Or he'd think about Molly and come up with fresh ways to talk to her. They won't always run into each other at the campground office. Since she is only visiting, he would need to move quick to stand a chance at seeing if she was someone who—

His phone rang, and his father's name displayed on the screen. Rick rolled his eyes and Patsy stepped back from the counter. People knew his name in town, and they also knew about his father.

"Where are the papers?" his father demanded.

"Hello to you, too."

"Don't get snarky with me. I have important business to attend to and I need confirmation you sent them."

Rick took his second coffee from the counter and nodded to Patsy. "I sent them to you today. The courier will have them to you by the end of the day."

His father groaned. "If you didn't insist on living in that backwards town, we wouldn't have to wait on things like paperwork. The papers would be right here in my office."

"The deal is complete." Rick squeezed the phone between his ear and shoulder, freeing his hand to open the door. "I only have to send in the papers as a formality."

"It is the formality that makes it legal."

"We have a verbal agreement and I had everything electronically signed."

"Until those papers show up on my desk, I consider nothing final. Things can happen in business—"

"Dad, trust me. The paperwork is on its way, as always."

"Yes, yes. I'm sure it is." Rick's father had dropped the conversation too soon, and Rick leaned against the side of his truck to brace himself for the real reason his father had called. "Have you thought about Robert's offer?"

Rick kicked his heel against the front tire. "I've thought about it."

"Your mother and I have been talking and we feel you shouldn't turn him down."

"Mom already called and talked to me about it."

"And you didn't listen to her, did you?" Listening meant Rick doing what he was told. It wasn't good enough to allow his mother to talk and share an opinion. Her opinion was the only one that mattered and the opinion they expected Rick to follow.

Rick took a sip of coffee. "I listened."

"And?"

"And what? I don't want to sell, especially not to him."

"So you'd sell if it was to someone other than Robert Fletcher. That's not good business."

"I'm not saying that."

"You aren't talking sense. Robert Fletcher has offered you a large sum of money. It is more than what your property is worth and you are telling me you are turning him down?"

Rick laughed and took another sip of coffee. His father's calls weren't humorous, they were frustrating, and laughter was the only thing keeping him from hanging up or saying something he might regret.

"Your mother and I have been patient with you while you lived out this little adventure of yours, but it is time you looked at the practicalities of this arrangement."

"There is nothing wrong with working remotely. Many companies are doing it these days."

"Companies only permit their staff to work remotely if it doesn't have a negative effect on the business and productivity. This arrangement has been nothing but a frustration to me."

"A personal or professional frustration?" Rick realized his words after they had flown from his mouth. He turned and mimicked banging his head against the frame of his truck.

"You are lucky you are my son or I would have you fired for your disrespect."

"You're right. I'm sorry." His frustration had taken hold of him. An apology wouldn't be enough. "I understand me being here has been difficult for you—"

"Difficult? Is that what you want to call it? We're here running the day-to-day of the business, managing staff, keeping the lights on, and what are you doing? You're out in the woods pretending to be a mountain man."

"Dad, I—"

His father's desk rattled in the background. His fist had struck the surface. "I don't want to hear another word about how city life isn't for you. This is where the money is. Until you can understand that, perhaps working for me isn't the best option for you."

Rick held his breath. This wasn't the first time his father held Rick's employment over his head. It had become tiresome and Rick had considered looking for work elsewhere. With nothing lined up, he couldn't afford to lose his job. Not yet. He'd have to find something with the same flexibility in working arrangements and location, or it would force him to move back to the city. If his father fired him, he couldn't afford his mortgage, which would lead to needing to consider Robert's offer. He needed time to search.

"I apologize for my choice of words," Rick said with a level voice. "I am doing my best to make this work. My performance hasn't dropped since I moved here. I'm making more deals than ever, which means the company is making money. Why don't you and Mom come out here for a few days and see my set up? It might help to understand how I do my work. Maybe we can talk through your concerns face to face?"

His father couldn't argue with the facts. Rick was the top associate even when he was the head of the advertising department and not in sales. He had proven to his father he didn't need to be in the city, or flirt with the ladies, to make a sale.

"Fine. I will speak with your mother, but in the meantime, I expect you to speak to Robert and give it some real thought. Don't disregard it because you dream of a life in the woods. It is time to look at things like an adult."

Rick took another sip of coffee. It was better than biting his tongue. With their call ended, he slinked into the front seat of his truck and slipped his second coffee next to his first. He had made a mistake. Not in speaking to his father, but in getting a second coffee. Patsy was right. The caffeine would keep him awake.

CHAPTER EIGHT

*M*olly woke to the sound of breathing near her head. She froze as her heart pounded and her chest tightened. She dared not move, worried it would alert whatever was outside to her presence. Molly convinced herself it would leave if she remained still. She calmed her breathing and listened to the surrounding movement.

From the glow of the light outside her tent and the songs of birds, it was morning, but she wouldn't know the exact time until she moved to check her watch. Her legs shook in the sleeping bag while the heaviness of fear held her in place.

A pebble skipped across the camping site. It was to her right, closest to her laundry line. Perhaps she hadn't cleaned the rag well enough after doing her evening dishes and the scent had attracted a —

Molly held her breath. It had better not be a bear. Her bear spray wasn't inside her tent, and if it tore through the fabric, she had nothing with her to use as a weapon. The bear would find her an easy target, wrapped in her sleeping bag like a burrito.

As her tiredness lifted, her mind now understood the breathing to be sniffing, and it traced along the edge of her tent to the door. The sniffing only paused when it sneezed. Metal clanged together, followed by a flapping and slapping noise. There was a whine and a long sigh as the metal touched the gravel.

Molly exhaled. A bear wouldn't wear metal tags. She inched to the window and peered between the flap that covered the opening and the side of the tent. A shaggy light-brown tail rested on the ground.

"What are you doing here?" The tail beat against the dirt in response.

She smiled, happy to see the dog again. Then, she frowned. Why *was* it here? She had guessed it left with the previous guests at the nearby site, as once the spot was empty, she no longer saw the dog. Did they leave it behind? Was the dog lost? Sadness came over her as she imagined a lonely dog wandering in the woods, searching for a kind stranger to feed it scraps from their picnic table. She would be a kind stranger and help it.

Molly checked her watch. It was eight thirty. "I slept in," she said in an animated voice through the fabric to the dog. She rubbed her eyes and stretched. The cool morning air greeted her as she climbed out of her sleeping bag. Molly stuffed her arms into a clean shirt, pulled on the same pair of pants she had worn the day before, and zipped up her hoodie tight around her neck before she climbed out of her tent.

The dog sprang to its feet, tail wagging.

"Good morning, good morning." She scratched the dog's head, and it panted, vocalizing with quiet groans. "How long have you been awake for?" She plucked fragments of twigs and leaves from its fur as it enjoyed her attention.

Molly looked across at the site left empty the day before. Her stomach twisted with concern as she continued to scratch the dog's head. "How could someone leave you behind like that? They're horrible people." The dog stared up at her with its brown eyes and open mouth, enjoying each stroke. "Did they at least feed you before they left?"

In the distance, someone dropped a metal object on the ground, capturing the dog's attention. Another camper was packing up their site. With the campground once again silent, the dog tilted its head upward to bring Molly back into view. "Stick with me," she said. "I'll see what I can do for you, okay?" The dog's tail beat at the ground as it wiggled in place. "People like that don't deserve a dog like you."

Knowing someone might be so cruel as to abandon a sweet dog like the one staring up at her made Molly's emotions swing from anger to sadness. A pet was something a person committed to. An owner should not throw away their dog once they grew tired of caring for it. Her throat tightened and tears welled up as her strokes of the dog's head became even more gentle and the dog closed its eyes. She vowed to protect the dog until she could pass it along to someone local who would take care of it. If that meant a nearby shelter, that would have to do. As much as she would love to take it home, a city apartment was no place for a dog as large as this.

But a city apartment was no place for Molly, either. The constant crowds and traffic left her feeling claustrophobic, making her long to escape the noise. She often imagined leaving the city for the suburbs or moving even further out. Her apartment was conveniently located close to the coffee shop. With their business thriving, they needed her at the store. Living outside of the city would limit her availability. Even though owning her own business had been her dream, being trapped in the city was not part of the plan. If it weren't for the coffee shop she owned with Carla, she would have left the city and lived somewhere else. A place with a yard big enough for a large dog like this one.

If only there was some way she could make it work to live away from the city and still support the business. Since the coffee shop was doing well, they had talked about expanding to a second location. Could she convince Carla to pick a place outside of the city?

Molly walked to her car with the dog at her heels and opened the trunk to pour a bowl of cereal, sprinkling the flakes with a dash of milk from the cooler in the backseat. The dog followed her to the chair and sat at her feet as she ate, twisting its head back to gaze at her. She patted the dog on its side.

"You don't look skinny. You seem well fed." The dog tossed its head back and shuffled itself onto its hind legs. "You really wanted me to get up this morning, didn't you? I do like spending time with you, but I don't believe I can take you home with me. You really wouldn't enjoy living in my apartment. Even I don't like it."

The dog remained at her feet until she finished her breakfast, and jumped to its feet to follow her to the basin where she washed her dishes, and again over to the shower facilities to dump the dirty water. It followed her from task to task, remaining at her side while looking up expectantly.

"Is that your dog?" a camper called from another site down the road. "It came by our site this morning."

"It's not mine," Molly called back. "I thought it belonged to the people who had been in the site over there, but they left yesterday."

"Did they leave it behind?" The woman stood with her hands on her hips, shaking her head.

Molly sighed and stroked the dog's head. "It looks that way."

"We're going to head out," the woman said. The dog's ears lifted, listening to their conversation. "We can stop by the campground office and let them know. Maybe they can call someone."

"That would be wonderful. Thank you." At least there were still kind people in this world. The dog was lucky to have found Molly and this woman. Together they would help the dog out of its sad situation and help it find a better life.

"It's such a shame," the woman continued to shake her head, "it is a sweet dog."

Molly smiled at the happy furry face that stared back at her. "Sure is."

The camper walked back toward her trailer and Molly strolled back to her site to place her empty basin in the trunk of her car. She grabbed a book from the tent and wrapped herself in her blanket. With the knowledge that the woman would notify the office, she could relax for a bit and keep the dog occupied while they waited. With the dog at her feet, she read. It was another pleasant morning and Molly would go to Lemon Grove for coffee from the café once they took care of the dog. For now, she would take a break from her morning chores to relax and read.

The sound of a car engine made the dog perk up its ears. The woman and her husband backed their SUV out of their site and waved before driving toward the office. Molly scratched the dog's back as its head rested on its paws. "We're working on getting you somewhere safe. You're such a good girl."

The dog looked up at her.

"You are a girl, right? I think you are a girl. And you're very sweet."

Molly noticed the dog rest its head on her foot, and she turned the page in her book. Soon, she found herself immersed in the story, forgetting about time and what she had come to the campsite to escape. Now and then she would feel the dog flip over against her legs, or twitch as it ran in its sleep. They no longer needed to keep each other warm as the sun shone onto her campsite. Molly smiled. It felt good to have a morning with no commitments, other than to help a dog that needed a home.

A blue pickup truck rolled up the road, making its way around the loop. Molly and the dog lifted their heads and watched the truck approach before it stopped at the end of her site. The driver rolled down the driver's side window and flashed a gorgeous smile, making Molly's stomach flutter. It was Rick.

Molly turned her head away and adjusted her hair, tucking a few strands behind her ears and smoothing down the hair at the top of her head.

"Hello there," he called out.

Molly hoped she didn't look too much the part of a disheveled camper.

"Have you seen a large brown dog? I heard he was last seen at your site."

"This one?" Molly pointed to her feet and pulled the blanket back to give him an unobstructed view of the pup.

"There you are!" Rick put his truck in park and stepped out onto the road. "Hudson. Come on, boy." The dog lifted its head and lowered it back to the ground, letting out another long sigh. "It's time to go."

The dog rolled onto its side, refusing to acknowledge him.

"You know her?" she asked.

"Him, actually," he said, rounding the front of the truck. He still wore the same jacket, but paired it with a clean pair of jeans and a V-neck shirt. "He's mine."

"Yours?"

"He's my buddy. Just a couple of old bachelors keeping each other company. Ain't that right?" Neither looked that old to her. It is too bad for Rick that wisdom didn't come with his looks. No one was perfect, and after running into him multiple times, and liking what she saw, she had found a fatal flaw. "I'm sorry," Rick said, strolling into the site. "He's always coming here to beg from the campers."

Molly looked at the disobedient dog lying at her feet. "His name is Hudson?"

"Yes. He is twelve years old and does this every day. Glenda calls me from the campground office to let me know when he gets here, although it is getting tiresome to come here in the morning. I much prefer the afternoon."

Molly shifted in her chair. To think he would allow his dog to wander like that. It was irresponsible. "You mean he visits the campground every day?"

"He sure does. I can't even get mad at him anymore. It's just what he does." He shook his head and gave the dog a scratch on his belly. "Have you been pestering the campers again, Hudson? Come on. We need to go home now. Your adventure is over."

"Adventure?" Molly rose from her chair and the dog stood on his feet. "Don't you care that he could have gotten lost?"

Rick laughed and placed his hands on his hips. "Hudson has lived here his entire life. I'd be more worried about me getting lost before I'd worry about him."

The dog slapped his tail against the ground.

"Do you think this is funny?" Rick said to the dog. "I've got better things to do than drive you around town. Let's go." He patted the side of his leg to encourage the dog. "Come on, Hudson."

Hudson flopped himself on the ground and groaned.

"Don't you give me that attitude. You're lucky I don't make you walk home."

Molly stepped forward and narrowed the gap between her and Rick. "He's tired." The dog could stay if he wanted, especially a twelve-year-old dog. That would make it a senior, and Rick didn't need to be threatening him, even if he was joking.

Rick smiled and shook his head. "He isn't tired. He's just trying to see what we will give him to get him to go to the truck. Lazy dog. You want a treat, don't you?"

The dog's ears pointed straight and his tail wagged. No longer sitting, the dog stood at attention, waiting for his reward. Rick was right about the dog, but it didn't mean his actions were.

"You should take better care of him," Molly blurted out. She bent down and stroked the dog's head, facing Rick as if to prevent him from calling the dog away.

"Excuse me?" Rick stood straight.

Molly rose and placed both hands on her hips. "You should make sure he doesn't get out of your yard. He would be content to stay if you took him for a walk every day. Bored dogs get into trouble."

Rick shifted his weight to one side and ran his hand through his hair. "Have you ever owned a dog?"

"No. But I sure know how someone should treat one." Caring for an animal was common sense. Molly didn't need to have owned a dog to know if you cared for someone or something you provided for it. While most might believe food and shelter was all a dog needed, it also required them to give it proper exercise and to keep it safe.

Rick laughed and turned on the spot. "Typical."

"What do you mean by that?" This man already made her blood boil, and she didn't even know him. He was the one who was typical. A typical irresponsible pet owner.

"It is always the ones who have never owned a dog who are the experts on how to care for one."

What did he know? Molly had read books, watched television programs about animals, and had he forgotten about the internet? She understood enough to see where he was lacking as a pet owner.

"My grandparents owned a dog." As soon as the words left her lips, she realized it was a ridiculous statement, but if he was going to question her knowledge—

"So, it's in the genes." Rick laughed and shook his head. "I find your ignorance over my dog amusing. He likes to walk and was a wanderer before I got him. His previous owner allowed Hudson to wander all his life. When he died, I took over caring for Hudson. He is always on the move and at twelve years old, I'm not about to change what he's been doing his entire life."

"At twelve, he is a senior and is more prone to injury. What if he forgets where he lives?"

"He has a good sniffer. Hudson will be fine."

"You think an animal this old should be able to wander free and risk an injury? How is that right?" There was no getting through to this man. This was a dog that should enjoy a quiet life by a warm fireplace and not one where it wandered through cold creeks and thick forests in search of food from strangers at a campground.

It seemed to Molly that Rick would not be convinced. He led Hudson by the collar toward his truck. "Is it more humane to tie him up, or let him walk? He hates being stuck in the yard. I know this because I tried to keep him contained when I first got him, but he dug holes under my fence. When I fixed those, he pushed boards free. When I fixed the boards, he figured out the latch on the gate. This dog hasn't known a life in a fenced yard. The community knows him and they tell me when he's here and I don't mind getting him when he's done. He knows how to take care of himself. You do not understand—"

"I have enough of an idea." She followed Rick to his truck and tapped her foot on the gravel, her arms crossed. Maybe no one at the campground told him the truth about what they thought about a dog roaming around their campsite. Who wants to look after someone else's dog because the owner is incompetent? "If you cared enough about your dog, you would keep him in a safe place."

"He's a dog," Rick said, patting the seat of his truck. Hudson hopped inside and wagged his tail as he took his place in the passenger's seat. "He's doing what dogs do."

"He will get in trouble if you let him do whatever he wants. You are his owner and set the rules. Just like you would do with children."

"Are you an expert with children, too?" Molly's mouth hung open at his comment. "He's twelve years old, and he hasn't died yet. I think I'm doing a pretty good job of taking care of him. Isn't that right, Hudson?" The dog beat his tail against the seat, excited by their raised voices. "See? He agrees."

Rick closed the door to the truck and walked toward the driver's side.

Molly followed. "That's right. Ask the dog. You wouldn't let a child wander in the forest alone, so why let a dog?"

He laughed. "You've once again proved that you have no clue what you're talking about. Hudson doesn't wander in the forest. He takes a trail from my cabin into town. He then walks past all the houses, stopping to visit his dog friends along the way. Everyone knows him."

"You have everyone else looking after your dog because you aren't doing it yourself? That's splendid."

"I don't think we are going to see eye-to-eye on this one. Hudson and I will go now. Thank you for giving him attention this morning. I expect he will be back tomorrow."

Molly sighed as he climbed into his truck and slammed the door. The dog stared out the windshield expectantly, only turning away to kiss Rick on the cheek with his tongue.

"How odd," Molly grumbled to herself as she watched them pull away. "Back tomorrow. Some people shouldn't own dogs."

She tidied up her site, then grabbed her wallet and keys. There was no point in sitting around her campsite getting frustrated over Rick and his stubbornness. She had better things to do, like walk to town where she could enjoy a good cup of coffee. She needed one after the morning she had, but first, she needed to stop by the office and let the woman at the front desk know what she thought. No one should be permitted to let their dog roam through the campground. Having a spat with a pet owner was not how she had pictured spending her vacation. Same with worrying about a dog wandering alone through the woods.

Rick was lucky his dog finds his way. One of these days, he

might not make it to his destination. Her heart sank at the thought.

She stepped into the office where the host sat at her desk laughing on her phone. It was the most animated Molly had ever seen her, until the woman spotted her. The laughter disappeared.

"I will have to call you back," she said in a monotone voice before hanging up her phone. "Can I help you?"

"Good morning," Molly said. She cleared her throat and tried to settle her emotions. "I have a question," she said. "There has been a dog wandering around the campground—"

"Yes, yes. That would be Hudson." She slid her crossword puzzle off the desk and onto her lap. "Rick will be by to pick him up any time now."

"Don't you think that's odd?"

"What? That he comes to get his dog?" The woman shook her head and raised her crossword puzzle into view.

"No. That he allows it to wander free."

The woman held a pencil to the paper and shifted her gaze away from Molly and onto the puzzle. "It doesn't bother me any. Hudson is nice enough and is good with kids. As long as he doesn't cause any trouble, he's welcome here. The guests cause more trouble than he does." She waved her hand to dismiss Molly.

A dog wandering free and visiting her campsite is less of a nuisance than the people who pay to stay? This town had a unique approach to caring for animals and a different view of customer service.

She backed out of the office, sensing an even greater need to get away from the campsite and distract herself with a good cup of coffee. If she were the only one concerned about the dog, she would have to let it go. Besides calling Animal Control, there was nothing more she could do. In her frustration, she was making good time stomping along the path into town. It also helped her remain warm. Molly could understand not wanting to change a dog's routine, and the old boy didn't look to be suffering. She just wanted to know he was safe, loved, and protected. Anything could happen in the big world outside one's backyard. Molly would know. She wasn't in her own backyard anymore. She was in a small town where people let their dogs run free, and the coffee shop…

…was closed on Sundays.

Molly stood at the locked doors of the café. Now what was she going to do?

CHAPTER NINE

*T*he resort guests did more damage to his fence this year than in years past, and Rick had grown tired of the repairs. It was ridiculous and costly to erect a fence in the middle of the woods, but it deterred people from entering his property with their rented off-road vehicles. In the summer, they rode dirt bikes and ATVs. In the winter, they drove snowmobiles. Signs identifying his land as private property didn't deter them, and even if the resort marked trails for them to follow, the more adventurous guests wanted to make their own path, bringing them into Rick's backyard.

Even with the fence in place, it didn't matter. Guests took down the boards to make room for their vehicles to pass through. While they may have assumed they were being sneaky, it was impossible for them to hide the noise from their motors as they cut through the woods on their way to town and back.

Rick's complaints to Robert got him nowhere. Every time, Robert gave him empty promises to mark the trails and request guests sign a waiver declaring the vehicles would remain on the path. The guests still came and from what he had observed, Robert created no additional paths on resort property. It had only grown worse, as if Robert didn't care or encouraged it, hoping if the resort guests annoyed Rick enough, and disrupted his life, maybe Rick would be more willing to sell? Not going to happen. He would keep making repairs and, if needed, he would continue improving the fence into something indestructible.

He should have taken a break already. His hands and back ached, but Rick remained determined to fix the fence, or at least continue to distract himself from that insufferable woman at the campground, Molly. Who did she think she was, telling him how to care for Hudson? She accused him of not caring when that was far from the truth.

Rick glanced over his shoulder at the dog lying on his side next to a tree in the shade. Having already explored for the day, Hudson followed Rick into the woods to watch him work. Watching soon turned into taking a nap, and he woofed and batted his paws in the air in his sleep. She had called Rick irresponsible and said he shouldn't make others look after Hudson. Molly did not understand. Everyone loved Hudson and would feed him treats when he visited. If she had paid any attention in the campground office, she would find a little box by the office door full of dog treats for campers to give him.

As an urbanite like his family, she had her opinions she wanted to push onto him and anyone else she met. Women like her had led him to swear off relationships for the time being. He wouldn't have another person try to control his life like his parents, and was determined to find someone who appreciated his lifestyle. There was no place for preachy city folk in Lemon Grove.

He grumbled and slammed a nail into the fence board. There he was, thinking about her again. While the fence needed repairs, he worked for longer than intended to erase any memories of their encounter. Swinging a hammer felt good on the first twenty boards, but it grew tiresome and soon failed to achieve the effect he was hoping for. Even in the middle of the woods, hammer in hand, fence boards being mended, he still couldn't get her beautiful petite features out of his mind.

As she was giving him a piece of her mind, he found the fire in her eyes to be even more captivating than the shy sparkle he saw the days before. He flustered her and he knew it. While angering a woman was not the way to win one over, he found some amusement in how they sparred over the care of Hudson… at least, it amused him for a short while. He even liked how her feistiness brought out a little crease above her right eyebrow.

An argument was not something to build a relationship on. She viewed him as an incompetent pet owner, but he wasn't about to change how he cared for Hudson. He would decide how to care for him and not some visitor from the city, no matter how cute she was. All city folks were the same: loud, opinionated, and selfish. He recognized now that she was not as quiet as she appeared and, through her volume alone, shared her opinions on his pet ownership with the entire campground. The jury was still out on if she was also selfish.

He checked his watch and discovered it was almost time for lunch. The morning went by fast, as he had spent more time thinking about her than about the work being done. It was a blessing and a curse.

Rick drilled the last screws into the new railing, securing it to the freshly dug post, and took a step back. He had come a long way from the white-collar lifestyle he had been born into. His father never got his hands dirty and had never mentored Rick in the ways of home repair. Rick learned by watching the repairmen his family hired, being the annoying child peppering them with his constant line of questions. Over the years, Rick had discovered personal satisfaction in physical labor, especially when it involved swinging a hammer. Were he born into any other family, someone would have nurtured his skills and interests. Luckily, the community of Lemon Grove assisted him with any knowledge gaps he had.

The cabin needed work when he bought it, but that never bothered Rick. At the time, his father understood Rick was flipping the house to resell it and didn't raise too much of a fuss. When Rick announced he intended to move in long-term, his father could no longer hold on to the belief that Rick had been fixing up the cabin for profit. Spinning the conversation to invite the family to stay there as a vacation home softened the blow, but it took time for them to comprehend he would not be coming back to the city.

They tried everything to bring him back home, and their plans almost worked… until they didn't. Setting him up had almost worked, but his parents would never forgive him for calling off his engagement to Valerie. If he had married her, he would have committed himself to a doomed marriage and a city life. For a time, Valerie feigned interest in his outdoorsy lifestyle by participating in the occasional adventure. She even posted the odd picture to social media of her experience… although he assumed the role of photographer and followed her direction to frame the photo to her liking. At first, he laughed at her poses, which looked unnatural in an outdoor setting, and how she deleted anything she didn't like. He never understood the need for the multiple filters she applied, adding a whimsical, otherworldly twist to the mountain backdrop. Soon, he found the role of social media photojournalist tiresome.

After a year and a few months, Rick realized they both were trying too hard to make the relationship work and staying together would have made them both miserable. His family viewed their breakup as a mistake. Their marriage would have created a business empire, as her parents ran an equally successful company, and if the two families worked together, they might have merged the two companies. His parents saw dollar signs, but Rick saw potential family drama.

The longer the relationship dragged on, the more he sought refuge at his home in the woods and avoided commutes back.

Wanting to limit his travel became the deal breaker for Valerie. She all but demanded he change his mind and return full-time to the city. His parents' plan of encouraging his relationship with Valerie as a tool to convince him to return home failed, and the experience left him wondering if the next girl he met knew his parents or not. If steering clear of relationships helped him avoid drama, Rick would make the sacrifice… at least until he knew for sure.

Rick sighed and gave the post a shake. After the work he did to secure it, the post wouldn't be going anywhere unless someone tampered with it. A laugh erupted from within. How foolish had he been to think running to a small town would help him avoid drama? It followed him here. Robert Fletcher with his plot to purchase his cabin, and his parents' constant badgering to convince him to move home. Now, Molly the opinionated girl from the city with the cute but predictable outfit. There was no escaping the drama with the latest caused by his dog.

He turned and slapped the side of his leg. Hudson stretched and rose to his feet.

"Hey, buddy." Holding out his hand, Rick knelt and waited for Hudson to wander over for attention. "Are you hungry?"

Hudson lifted his ears and opened his mouth, panting as Rick scratched the top of the dog's head.

"Let's go inside and look for something to eat."

Hudson's front paws lifted in a hop before trotting alongside Rick in the cabin's direction. Rick could trust Hudson. This dog was loyal and would never try to push Rick toward a relationship for his own gain, unless that someone had treats.

The instant coffee wasn't at all the same level of quality as what she might have enjoyed if she bought a freshly brewed cup at the coffee shop, but it hit the spot. If only the coffee did more to soothe the lingering burn of anger she experienced from that morning. Molly would be lucky to get her mind off of the arrogance Rick had shown when he argued with her over the obvious. How could he believe he was doing right by the dog, by letting it roam through the woods unattended? Where she came from, pet owners faced fines from Animal Control for far less, yet in Lemon Grove no one seemed to care. Even the campground host was unconcerned when Molly attempted to talk to her about the issue. The host was clearly among those women blinded by Rick's handsome looks. Looks would only get Rick so far, especially with such an obviously flawed character.

Molly took another sip of coffee and spat it back into her cup. Instant granules had settled into the bottom of the cup, giving her a mouthful of ground bean powder. "Ugh. Gross."

Nothing about this day was going well. While the trip had started out promising, it was falling apart like she knew it would. First, it was the rain that dampened her site, then Rick who wouldn't even consider her concerns, and now she couldn't even enjoy a cup of coffee. What would be next? A hole in her tent? Stepping on a beehive? Molly intended this to be a relaxing trip with opportunities for her to clear her head, but it was turning into nothing like the vacation Carla had painted in her mind when she insisted Molly get away for a few days. This vacation was full of stressful situations, and while they might have taken her mind off her previous concerns, the situations were not bringing her peace or relaxation.

It was Carla's fault Molly shivered in a campsite with an inadequate cup of coffee. Carla would be at the coffee shop breathing in the smell of fresh beans, thinking Molly was having a great time away when it was far from the truth. She needed an update.

Molly pulled her phone from her pocket and dialed. Carla had to know what was happening, so it wouldn't surprise her when Molly walked into work several days earlier than planned.

"How is paradise?" Carla chirped exactly as expected.

Molly laughed and swirled the coffee grounds in a circle at the bottom of her cup. "I need to get my money back due to false advertising."

The background noise of the busy coffee shop subsided as Carla moved to the back of the store. "What's wrong? You're not enjoying yourself? I heard the weather was good out that way."

"There was some rain, but it cleared up."

"Then why are you being so gloomy?"

"It's the people here. They're… different."

Carla let out a loud laugh. "You're different."

"Shut up." Carla knew how to break her out of her negative mood. A little gentle teasing always made her laugh.

"So, what's the deal? Where are you at?"

"I'm at Lemon Grove Campground, which is nice when I don't have to pay a fortune for the showers. The host has no personality unless Rick comes by."

"Who is Rick?"

Molly glanced over her shoulder at the half-empty campground. Given the number of times she had bumped into him, the odds were good he'd be standing behind her as she gave Carla her report. "He's this guy who lives in the area that all the women love."

"Oh?" Carla's tone communicated her curiosity and flirtatious spirit. A man the women loved must have sounded to her like an opportunity.

"You wouldn't like him. I don't."

"Why not?"

"Because he is a jerk." Molly paused and shook her head. "Maybe that's too harsh. He's not a jerk, but he doesn't take care of his dog."

"How do you know he doesn't take care of it?"

The campground was still empty, with no sign of the dog. Where the dog was, Rick would soon be.

"His dog is old, and he lets it wander from his house all the way to the campground every day, and then he comes by to pick it up. He claims everyone in town is fine with it and doesn't see the problem with allowing an old dog to walk alone through the woods where it could get injured or lost. I thought he was a nice guy until he showed me how stubborn he was."

"Have you seen him more than once?"

It had been comical the number of times she had bumped into him around town, and now she wanted to avoid him. Had this been the city, she would only see someone this often if they were a frequent customer at the coffee shop or if they took the same bus. So far, she had seen him in three different locations: the campground, coffee shop, and the general store. Hopefully that would be the end of their encounters.

"We keep running into each other. The town isn't that big, so you always see the same people."

"But he was nice?"

"Yes. He was polite whenever I saw him, until this morning."

"What happened this morning?"

Molly stared down at her feet and the bare patch of gravel where the dog had earlier settled to rest. She could see where the dog's body had pushed away stones, forming an outline of the dog's back and legs.

"His dog came to my campsite like it had done a couple of times before. I thought it was lost and was getting concerned that someone had abandoned it. Then Rick showed up asking if I had seen his dog, so when he told me it was his and how old the poor thing was..." Molly paused as she felt her breathing increase, along with her volume.

"What did you do?" Carla asked. Her question wasn't backed by curiosity. Carla and Molly had locked heads before over the direction of their business, and Carla had witnessed Molly's stubbornness firsthand. It was why Molly felt defensive the moment she heard her friend ask what happened next.

"I didn't do anything," Molly shot back. "All I did was point out how his dog was old and he shouldn't allow it to walk through the woods alone."

"I take it he didn't take your advice so well."

Molly laughed, remembering Rick attempting to lure his dog away from her and into his truck. "He couldn't wait to get out of here."

"I hope the next time you see him things will be better."

Molly gasped. "Next time? I don't want there to be a next time."

"Why? You said yourself he seemed like a nice guy and it is a small town. You're going to run into him again. Try being nice to him next time."

"Whose side are you on?"

"I'm on whatever side ends with you enjoying the rest of your vacation."

CHAPTER TEN

The following morning, Molly woke again to the sound of the dog sniffing around her tent. She fought against the urge to talk to him, which would encourage the dog to stay. She knew if Hudson stayed, Rick would follow to pick him up. She guessed if the dog lost interest in her, it would move on to another site before Rick arrived. But maybe there was still time to give Hudson some attention.

She dressed and climbed out of the tent to give him a short greeting, which turned into a longer greeting as she scratched Hudson behind the ears and the dog nudged her hand for more. Instead of sitting in the chair to allow the dog to lie beside her, she remained on her feet while eating her bowl of cereal. Next, she cleaned her dishes and started down the road, leaving Hudson at the end of her campsite.

Molly wanted to call the fluffy, old pooch to her and encourage him to follow. If Rick listened to her, she wouldn't be as hesitant to interact with him again, but she met his type before. Men like him were arrogant and best kept at a distance unless she wanted to risk getting hurt again. The warning signs were all there with Brad, but she had ignored them. Brad only wanted to do the things he found interesting and always came up with excuses to turn down Molly's invites to activities that interested her. Whenever Brad bought something new, he needed to show it off to anyone who would give him five minutes of their time. It became clear to Molly, he cared more about himself than about her. Brad didn't even care about animals, often shouting at a barking dog or complaining about the odd strand of fur on his clothes.

Rick seemed different in that regard. Distracted by the mud on his jeans, Molly didn't notice right away the dog fur on his clothes that hinted at an engaged, caring owner.

She scolded herself for thinking about him again and gave her head a shake. Wait… were her thoughts about Brad or Rick? Did it matter? They both gave her plenty of reasons to get her mind off them. She had found some success forgetting about Brad. Getting away from the city seemed to work and now she only had to work on forgetting about Rick, which was difficult to do at the campground while his dog stood at the end of her site to watch her walk down the road.

Completing her circuit around the campground, she added a quick stroll through the trail near the entrance and came back to her loop. Ahead, she spotted Rick's truck parked a few sites from hers.

Molly's stomach muscles tightened as she slowed her pace. She thought she caught herself speeding up when she spotted Rick's truck, which was ridiculous. She wasn't excited to see him. She wanted to avoid him, which was the whole reason she had taken the walk.

Rick walked around the back of the truck to the driver's side, and Molly inhaled. Even though she wasn't interested in him, he still looked appealing. He was missing the brown jacket and wore a gray T-shirt that left his arms exposed and Molly longing for a closer look. The brake lights lit up and Molly stood in place watching the truck pull away.

While she successfully avoided Rick picking up the dog, it gave her no happiness. The whole situation of avoiding Rick in his hometown was ridiculous. What should it matter to her what that man did? He lived in Lemon Grove, and she was a tourist.

It occurred to her that sitting around a campground in a small town she didn't know, while attempting to avoid a man, wasn't any fun, so she decided visiting another town where he didn't live might be a solution. According to the map she had noticed when she was booking her stay at the campground, there was a town another twenty or thirty minutes away. She should hop in her car and explore. Tourists explored, and she was the tourist.

Molly climbed into her car and exited the campground onto the highway. As she pulled away from Lemon Grove, the first drops of rain splattered against her windshield. She missed noticing the clouds earlier. Maybe it had been clear, and it was just how fast the weather changed in the mountains, but she was thankful the rain hadn't started while on her walk.

In less than a minute, the rain was pouring down, forcing her to put on the windshield wipers. She wouldn't be able to do much exploring without getting wet. All she could do now was note points of interest and plan to return to visit it another day.

Molly's car slowed as the engine sputtered and stalled. She glanced down at her fuel gauge and saw the meter below the final red line, then slammed her hand on the steering wheel and let out a yell. Why didn't she check how much gas was in the tank before she left? She always checked it before she left to go anywhere, but not today. She pulled her car onto the shoulder as it rolled to a stop and Molly fought back tears. Nothing about this vacation was going right. This was not the adventure she had signed up for.

∾

Rick paid for his supplies and slid his wallet into his pocket. The hardware store owner came around the counter and handed Hudson a treat, who wagged his tail in anticipation. People in small towns went the extra mile, and little things like a dog treat made Rick a returning customer. They would never permit him to bring his dog into a store in the city. They welcomed Hudson at Lakewood Hardware whenever Rick needed to grab a few things for the cabin and never once told Hudson he wasn't welcome. In fact, it became part of their routine after collecting Hudson from his wanderings to make the twenty-minute drive to Lakewood every Monday to gather supplies for the week.

He exited the store and patted the truck's passenger seat, signaling for Hudson to jump inside. Hudson pulled himself up onto the bench, then stared out the windshield and waited for Rick to enter on the opposite side. Rick had learned from Hudson's previous owner how much the dog enjoyed car rides, and whenever Hudson saw Rick getting ready to leave, he would beg Rick not to leave him behind. Hudson's expressive personality was what Rick liked about the dog when he met him, which made it an easy decision to take the old pup in when his owner became too ill to care for him.

Hudson was well trained and behaved better than most dogs in town. He already had a reputation for being an obedient, mellow dog. Hudson had been making his wandering circuit every day for twelve years, alone or accompanied. The only problem Rick discovered was training the dog to return to Rick's cabin and not to the vacant home of his deceased owner. It had taken a year for Hudson to learn to return to Rick's cabin, and it wasn't because Hudson couldn't find his way home. Hudson missed the old man and was waiting for him to return.

It had been two years since Hudson began returning to Rick's home, but over the past five months he became too tired to make the return trip from town. Hudson started napping at the campground, finding empty camping chairs to climb onto or doormats at the base of trailer doors. That was when Rick arranged with Glenda to call him when Hudson arrived. Calling Rick would give the dog the chance to continue to have the freedom he enjoyed, even if it cut into Rick's day. He didn't mind the interruption, but apparently some people did. People like Molly. Rick tried to see it from her perspective. Hudson was getting old, it was true, but Rick wasn't ready to take away the one thing his dog enjoyed. He would know when it was time to stop the independent walks, but not yet.

Pulling away from the hardware store, he turned onto the highway toward Lemon Grove and replayed his encounter with Molly. She hadn't been complaining about Hudson being at her campsite like others had done before, but rather Hudson's well-being concerned her. She was thinking out of an urban context, and she misunderstood Hudson's inclination to roam, but her heart appeared to be in the right place.

Part of him wanted to go to the campsite and apologize to Molly for their conversation the day before. Had he kept his cool, he might have been able to better explain Hudson's history. He loved this dog as if he had raised it from a pup and would never allow Hudson to be where he might get hurt. If she understood that, then maybe she would recognize Rick was doing a good job caring for Hudson, and Molly wouldn't judge so harshly.

But why did it bother him that she judged him? That's what people from the city always do, so it was no surprise when she passionately shared her views on pet care. Like her, he came from the city, and Rick didn't think he was all that bad. Not everyone was like his family, and if he was around Molly long enough, she might show him that she was different. For one thing, Hudson seemed to like her, and for a dog, he was always an excellent judge of character. Rick should have listened to Hudson's groans whenever Valerie used to come around, and he had promised himself he would trust the dog next time. Hudson seemed to have gained some wisdom over his many years.

Ahead, Rick spotted amber hazard lights from a car stopped along the side of the highway and he slowed his truck. Anyone stopped along this stretch would have a long walk ahead of them to reach Lakewood, and cell-phone reception was spotty if calling for help. Their best chance would be for someone like Rick to help them out.

As his truck approached, he got a good look at the driver and snickered to himself. Of all the people to run into again. He liked the way the corner of Molly's upper lip curled as she attempted to mask her disappointment when she saw the identity of her rescuer.

"Well, Hudson," Rick said. He applied his brakes. "Should we help her out?"

The dog turned his head and lifted his ears. Hudson didn't understand, but was happy Rick spoke to him.

Rick steered the truck to the shoulder and made a U-turn back to where Molly sat waiting in her car. He brought his truck to a stop behind her car and Hudson wiggled in his seat.

"You stay here." Hudson took a step toward the open driver's side door. "Stay."

Hudson whined as he watched Rick approach the car. Since the rain had stopped, Hudson would have a clear view.

Molly rolled down her window and smiled. She replaced her expression of disappointment with a relaxed, pleasant curl. Perhaps he misread her expression earlier?

"You look like you need some help," he said, leaning into her window.

"Thanks for stopping." Her voice filled with more relief than he had assumed would be there. "I ran out of gas."

"Out of gas?" He wanted to laugh. Someone who expressed concern over the care of animals couldn't even care for herself. Who wouldn't think to check the fuel gauge? "The next gas station is in Lakewood up the road. I can take you there, if you'd like."

Molly took her time to respond. If she was weighing her options, she didn't have many. She could accept his offer, or wait for a tow truck, which wouldn't come unless someone called from cell-phone range. The only tow truck was owned by Ed Halton. He only took his truck out when someone called for help, and no one called for an empty gas tank when most locals were willing to help a stranded driver.

She nodded. "If it isn't any trouble."

"No trouble at all." Rick had told the truth. He had only planned to take Hudson home to play in the yard like any responsible dog owner would do. Play comprised of throwing a ball a short distance as Hudson couldn't run like he used to, and he already had his morning walk. "Hudson won't mind the trip back to Lakewood. He enjoys the company."

Molly looked over her shoulder to the truck, and her smile widened. She must like his dog. "Thank you. I'll just grab my things."

Rick took a step back as she grabbed her purse from the empty seat beside her and rolled up the window. She locked her doors and followed him back to his truck. "I appreciate you stopping. I was considering walking up the road until I found some cell reception."

"You would have walked right up to the edge of town." Rick opened the passenger door and encouraged Hudson to jump into the backseat. "Into the back, Hudson. You'll get to go back in the front in a bit," he said. "We have a guest."

Hudson groaned and moved to the back. It had been some time since Rick had someone sitting in the passenger seat and Hudson became accustomed to having the seat to himself.

"Hi, Hudson." She climbed into the seat and stretched out her hand to the dog, who nuzzled and licked her palm. "Thank you for rescuing me. You're a good boy."

"You're welcome," Rick said, before closing the passenger door. He enjoyed watching her through the windshield as her cheeks reddened. He couldn't help but tease, although he rarely teased strangers. Not everyone had the same sense of humor he did. "I'm surprised you're not at the campsite searching for stray animals."

"I don't have to search. Strays find me." She reached back to Hudson and gave his head another scratch.

Rick laughed and pulled the truck onto the road back toward Lakewood. "I guess you're right. Although this one is not a stray."

"It's hard to tell when a dog is wandering around alone in a campsite."

"About that," Rick cleared his throat, "I wanted to apologize for coming off so defensive yesterday. You had his best interest at heart."

"I was worried about him." Hudson stretched his neck forward and licked Molly on the cheek. "I'm sorry for trying to tell you what to do with him. He seems happy." She rubbed her forehead. "Oh, gosh. I'm so embarrassed."

"Don't be," Rick said. They both had acted poorly yesterday. "When you come from out of town, you wouldn't be familiar with dogs like—"

"I don't mean over that." Molly sighed. "I've never run out of gas. I feel so stupid for not checking how much gas I had before I left Lemon Grove."

"Not to worry," he said. "It happens." But not to him.

"I've been sitting in my car wondering what I was going to do. Not many drivers passed by, and none of them stopped."

"They weren't locals. Folks who live out here would have stopped." Rick could have said the drivers who passed without stopping came from the city, but decided to check this chip on his shoulder for her benefit.

Rick struggled to keep his eyes on the road. The pretty girl in the seat beside him had the loveliest, gentle features. Molly seemed too delicate to be camping alone in the woods, but her personality made up for her petite frame. She had some spunk to her, and he admired it.

She rested a finger against her upper lip with her elbow against the truck door. Her forehead creased with worry while she stared out the window, and Rick wished there was something he could do to take away her concerns. Driving her to the gas station had to help, which it did, as her back straightened at the sight of the station sign.

"There it is," she said. Molly ran a hand over her cheek and smiled. Had she wiped away a tear? Rick couldn't tell.

Molly fussed with her purse and Rick put the truck into park, jumping out before she pulled out her wallet. "I've got this." As he closed the door, he saw her mouth open to protest, but he left before she could say a word.

Rick pulled his empty jerry can from the bed of his truck and stood beside the pump, watching the numbers rise. After yesterday's conversation, he hadn't pictured paying for her fuel, but here he was filling the jerry can to the max.

As he climbed back into the truck, Molly was counting her cash. He placed his hand over hers, covering the bills and coins. He never expected the rush of feelings he experienced when he felt her hand under his. Rick also hadn't expected his own fingers to wrap around the side of her cool hand to feel her warmer palm.

"You don't have to give me anything," he said, softly.

"But, I—" Her eyes met his, and he saw the worry had left her face. There was a sparkle as she held him in her gaze. He didn't want to turn away, or move his hand, but he had to. Even in that moment, he couldn't help but remember that she wasn't from Lemon Grove and would leave once her vacation was over. Visitors were an easy ticket to getting hurt.

"Consider it a thank you for looking out for Hudson."

Rick turned the ignition, and they drove in silence to her car, still parked where she left it. She thanked him many times as he emptied the can into her car's fuel tank, and he remained at the side of the road until she pulled away. He knew it was the right thing, stopping to help her. Now he needed to do the right thing and keep his distance before he was the one in need of help.

CHAPTER ELEVEN

*M*olly's eyes shifted from her hands on the steering wheel to the road ahead. She had felt a tingling on the back of her hand since Rick covered hers with his, and she experienced nothing like it before. The sensation could have been from nerves. Only moments earlier she had been counting cash from her wallet, hoping to have enough to pay him back for the fuel. Watching the meter climb on the pump, she wanted to ask him to stop filling the container just in case the gas station didn't have an ATM available.

Then, as she counted, he stopped her. His tender touch had caught her off guard. She hadn't expected the feelings that surfaced as she noticed the warmth of his skin. While her body froze in place, she caught herself holding her breath and she almost reached for his hand before he pulled away. That never happened with Brad. There were no butterflies in the stomach or wishing he would stay a little longer. She had always assumed people only experienced those feelings in fairy tales.

Today, she felt it, and its lingering effects. How ridiculous that she became swept up in emotion so soon after meeting someone. Even Carla wouldn't approve. Or would she? Carla knew better than anyone how little Molly felt for Brad, or she thought she felt a little until he left. Carla said the feelings were mourning being in a relationship, and given how unhappy Molly had been throughout the relationship, yet refused to end things, Carla pigeonholed Molly as afraid of being alone. Had she really been so desperate not to be alone that she missed out on feelings like this?

Molly glanced again at the back of her hand as she passed the Lakewood gas station. She had gas in her tank because of Rick, and it was by fuel pump number five she was grateful to have run into him again. Sure, being rescued from the side of the road was nice and so was having someone help pay for gas in the car, but the spark in his eyes as he told her she didn't need to pay had her attention. She needed to look at those dark eyes again.

But why should she get caught up in physical reactions over a man she would leave behind in a few days? He wasn't the only man in the world. There must be others who could catch her off guard with a gentle touch. She shouldn't have to head off into the wilds to find a man, right?

Another few blocks into Lakewood, she found a row of shops and parked. She had arrived a little later than she expected, but there was still plenty of time to explore. The reason she had traveled there in the first place was no longer valid. The whole point was to avoid Rick, who she ran into anyway while waiting along the side of the road. Maybe this was one of those meant-to-be things?

Without looking at the sign, she stepped into the first shop. Kayaks hung from the ceiling, and shoes and hats lined the walls, along with an assortment of backpacks and ropes. Clothing hung from racks near the front of the store with camping supplies placed in the back half. Since she was camping, it was a good store to wander into.

"Let me know if you need anything." The clerk was a man in his mid-thirties who dressed like he should live closer to the ocean in his baggy tank-top, long shorts, and flip-flops. While he had greeted her, Molly could sense the clerk didn't expect to make a sale.

She browsed the clothing racks, looking at the many shirts resembling the ensemble she already wore. She needed something different. Something cute and not plaid. While not a shirt, she found a jacket with ties to cinch the waist. She also found a couple of T-shirts from the discount rack, which were much better suited to her figure.

Not wanting to buy more than she should, Molly walked to the counter to pay. The clerk rose from his chair and smiled.

"You found something?" He should have tried to hide his surprise.

"I did." She stared at a large map covering the wall behind the counter. It was an enlarged map of the area surrounding Lakewood with a large star marking the Lakewood town site.

"Why was the town called Lakewood?" Molly asked. "I don't see any lakes on the map."

"There used to be a lake. About a hundred years ago, a rockslide blocked off the river that flowed into it. Now all that's left is the dry lake bed and the debris it left behind. Folks love to visit it and take pictures."

"The place sounds fascinating. I should make a point of seeing it."

"It is a sight, that's for sure. But you'll never make it in your little car." He gestured to her car parked outside and slid her items into a plastic bag. "You'll need a truck. The road is sketchy sometimes and a little car wouldn't make it through some of the rough patches."

"Oh." Molly lowered her head. For a moment, she had something else to look forward to. A trip to an old, dry lake would have been a great opportunity.

"If you don't have a vehicle to get you up there, you have a couple of options," the clerk added. "There are tours out of

Lemon Eagle Resort, but they are rather pricey. There is another gentleman who books tours out of Lemon Grove Campground."

"That's where I'm staying."

"He's your best bet then." He pulled a brochure from a rack on the counter and slipped it into her bag. "I'd ask at the campground if anyone else has already booked a tour. You might luck out and join one that's already happening."

"I will ask."

After browsing through a few more shops, Molly hopped into her car to head back to Lemon Grove, stopping at the office to check if someone had already booked a tour. She was in luck, the tour guide had scheduled an older couple to go to the lake bed the following day, and the host added her name to the tour list. Molly skipped back to her car and waited out the afternoon. Tomorrow, she would explore a new area and she would bring along her camera.

Rick pulled up to the office and checked the list of guests. Three people had signed up to see the old Lakewood Lake site. When he first started offering the tours, he only received one booking per month, but lately it had grown to twice per week. It was word of mouth that was bringing in the business. That, and offering a cheaper rate than Lemon Eagle Resort. Perhaps one day his side hustle would bring in enough money to allow him to quit working for his father and do something he enjoyed.

He looked at Hudson with his head sticking out of the passenger window, smiling and panting. Knowing they were going to be visiting the lake, Rick had kept Hudson from his morning adventure, afraid he'd be too tired to do both. At first, the change in routine seemed difficult on the pup, but Hudson came to understand a missed stroll through the forest alone meant a fresh adventure was coming.

Sometimes Hudson seemed too tired, and Rick would leave him behind. Today, Hudson needed to be there, especially after the host gave him the name of the third guest. He didn't always add another person to a tour after someone else already booked, but he recognized the name. This gave him the chance to see her again.

He had to catch his breath when he spotted her walking toward the office. She wore a fitted green jacket and jeans, but this time he noticed her brown hiking boots with just enough mud on the edges to tell she had worn them outdoors at least once.

"Good morning." He tried not to sound too eager.

"Good morning," she replied with a warm smile. Hudson stuck his head out of the passenger window and Molly's eyes lit up. "Hudson." She greeted him with a scratch to the head. "I was wondering where you were."

"I kept him home today." Rick walked down the stone steps and stood beside Molly to give Hudson a scratch under the chin. Hudson closed his eyes, taking in attention from them both. "So, you're going on the lake tour?"

Molly paused her scratching of Hudson's head mid-stroke. "How did you—"

"Meet your guide," Rick said, taking a bow.

"No. Really?" Hudson surprised her with a quick kiss to the cheek. Rick never wanted to be a dog more than right then.

Interrupting the moment, the other couple approached. They were in their sixties, dressed in shorts and light spring jackets. Between them walked a little white terrier.

"Are you the one doing the tour?" the man asked.

"I am. I see you brought a dog along." Rick stared at the little frizzy haired pup that sniffed at his feet.

"We hoped it wouldn't be a problem, since you had a picture of your dog on the brochure."

"You're on the brochure?" Molly asked.

Rick laughed. "Yes, Hudson and I are on the brochure. You must have seen it if you called for a tour." At least, he hoped it was the case.

Molly shook her head and laughed. "If I had known, I… The clerk at the store in Lakewood recommended you and said I should ask the host at the campground about a tour. I never even looked at the brochure. It's still inside the bag."

"How long is the tour?" the woman asked.

"Let's see, it is ten thirty now. It will be forty-five minutes to get up there and another forty-five to get back. We'll have lunch and it depends on how far we walk. There is an easy loop trail we can take, if you're interested."

"I'm not sure if my knees will take a hike," the woman confessed.

"There are a few small hills, but most of it is flat. We can always turn around if it is too much. We'll do whatever you are most comfortable with and I'll let you stay for as long as you want." Rick reached through the open passenger window and grabbed a clipboard from the dashboard. "Before we get going, I will need you to fill out a waiver. I promise I'll take good care of you while we're up there, but I still need you to sign."

"Not a problem," the man said.

He didn't enjoy requesting his guests sign a waiver, but it was for his protection. Even though he didn't like it, he had grown to appreciate the waiver and the warnings it provided. He had, at one point, concluded that some relationships should come with waivers. A relationship waiver would warn the couple of potential issues and either could decide if the risk was too great to proceed.

"Do you need me to sign?" Molly asked.

Rick blinked and took the clipboard from the couple and stared at Molly.

"Sign what?" he asked.

"The waiver." Molly held out her hand.

"Oh. Yes, please."

He watched her complete the form, which included her contact information. Now he had her number... unless she had given him a fake one.

Rick opened the back door to the truck cab and stood to the side as the couple stepped forward.

"I don't know if I can climb in there," the woman said, placing one foot on the truck's running board. "It's too high."

Rick lifted a step stool out of the bed of the truck and placed it in front of the woman. "Let's see if this helps."

He held out his hand as the woman gripped the panic handle and climbed into the rear seat. Likewise, he helped the man up the steps into the cab and lifted their little terrier into their waiting laps.

Molly slid into the front passenger seat next to Hudson, who glanced back at the wiggling terrier.

"Are we ready to go?" he asked from the driver's seat.

"We are," said the couple.

Hudson whined and stuck his nose in Molly's ear as she pulled on her seatbelt.

"Yes, I'm going with you."

He had never seen Hudson react like this toward anyone before. While the dog was always on the lookout for a sucker to give him a treat, it was unlike him to show interest in someone, even after repeated exposure to them. He had his favorite people and kept his list limited. Hudson had become attached to Molly, and it warmed Rick's heart, especially when it seemed that affection was being returned in the form of attention.

"Come on, Hudson," Rick said. "Give her some space."

"You have a beautiful dog," the man said. "How old is he?"

"Twelve. And he thinks he is still a puppy."

"We're all young at heart," his wife said with a smile.

Rick pulled out onto the highway and looked up at the sky. "It looks like the weather is going to be decent for us. We're in the mountains so things can change. If we're lucky, it will hold off any rain until we're done."

"That would be good," Molly said. "I'm looking forward to this."

Rick's lips split into a smile as he tried to maintain his composure. It didn't matter if she was referring to the tour. She was looking forward to three hours with him... or longer, if he could drag it out with a few other scenic stops along the way. Molly was expecting a tour of the lake and she would get all the time with him she needed and he wanted.

CHAPTER TWELVE

*M*olly enjoyed the drive up the mountain with its winding roads and steep drops. The couple in the backseat cried out many times and broke into laughter after Rick navigated the truck around stumps and positioned it precariously along the shoulder while reassuring everyone along the way.

As the truck bounced over a rock, Molly reached out and grabbed Hudson's collar, hopeful Rick would once again cover her hand with his. If he was shy about it, all he needed to do was take one hand off the steering wheel and offer comfort to Hudson, then find her hand already there. Molly left her hand on Hudson's collar, disappointed the moment she had envisioned did not materialize quickly. She allowed her hand to drift from Hudson's neck to a space on the cloth seat beside her. Rick should have seen her hand on Hudson and seized the opportunity, but he might be cautious about getting involved with a tourist. Maybe the kind gesture at the gas station was nothing more than him offering to pay for the fuel to make up for their earlier argument? And perhaps she read more signals into something than were really there.

And now Molly felt like a fool after dangling her hand, bait to a disinterested fish. To make matters worse, she was sitting close to him in a truck with a happy couple in the backseat, but longed for the happiness they appeared to share.

She stared out the window at the trees and steep embankment below. Her previous relationships mimicked this back-country road. She had always navigated close to the edge of disaster and encountered many obstacles and rough patches along the way. While Molly enjoyed the adventure of relationships, she didn't like the danger. She needed to find something less risky with someone who she would be with long-term. It was time to stop settling for the dangerous roads and choose a safe, paved high-way… or residential street. Whatever that equivalent would be for safe relationships.

"We're here," Rick said.

Hudson whined as Rick parked the truck beside a clearing surrounded by tall, thin coniferous trees.

"Where is the lake?" the man asked, pulling his camera out of a bag.

"Behind the row of trees. The clouds are moving in, so we will need to keep an eye out. Should we eat first?"

They agreed to eat their lunches before they set out on their loop around the lake. Rick had purchased sandwiches, potato chips and cans of soft drinks from the café, which were as delicious as Molly expected they would be when she heard Patsy made them.

With the lunch cooler locked inside the cab of the truck, they set out toward the old lake. A narrow unmarked trail led them from the clearing to where trees were further spaced apart, giving them a view of the large dirt field where the lake once existed. The void extended to a line of trees in the distant north, east, and around a bend to the west. Logs and tree stumps lay scattered along the ground, while grass and saplings had begun the long process of reclaiming the land.

"My goodness," the wife said, holding her terrier's leash.

The husband fiddled with his camera, taking his time to get the right shot.

Molly took a step forward from behind the couple to take in the view. She was glad she had seen the map and asked the clerk about Lakewood's history. She might have missed out on this otherwise. While it was terrible to think that in an instant a rock-slide had taken away the lake's water source, so much beauty emerged from the destruction. Molly raised her camera and snapped a photo.

Rick stood back. From his vantage point, he had the perfect view of Molly standing next to Hudson as she looked out at the dry lake bed. She was something else in her green jacket. The belt ties showed off her waist, which would be perfect to wrap his arm around. She had tied her hair back and loose strands hung beside her ears.

His heartbeat accelerated, watching her reach down to scratch the top of Hudson's head. He liked her... and maybe Hudson did, too. Spending more time with her, it appeared her interest in the outdoors was genuine. Molly may have arrived in crisp and new clothing, but it meant she had limited opportunity to be outdoors. All it would take was for her to spend a few more days camping and her clothes would be broken in and it would look like she belonged out here. As she stooped to feel the texture of some freshly sprouted herbs, he noticed she didn't mind getting her hands dirty, which was refreshing. Most girls visiting from the city concerned themselves with the possibility of ruining their manicured nails, but Molly seemed to understand dirt under one's fingernails was part of the adventure.

Rick had seen her rest her hand on the back of Hudson's neck throughout their drive, and during his many glances he saw no sign of a ring on her finger. A missing ring didn't mean there wasn't someone already in the picture. No ring possibly meant someone hadn't asked her yet, or she didn't want to get a diamond covered in mud and left it tucked away at home. He made a mental note to inquire on the subject.

The husband put his camera away and Rick called Hudson to his side so they could continue as a group down the narrow dirt trail. Letting the couple set the pace, it was a slow walk. It suited Rick just fine as he walked next to Molly with their hands nearly brushing against each other. He lifted his pinky finger, bridging the gap between them. Then, he felt it. Not just the touch of her skin, but the electrifying sensation he felt when he covered her hands in the truck the day before. The urge to grab her hand returned, and he stepped away, calling Hudson over to walk between them.

"He was enjoying smelling the plants," Molly said.

If only he could explain he hadn't called the dog because he didn't want him near the plants. Walking beside her made him want to pull her close. It was too soon, not only because they had recently met, but he wasn't ready to try again. Relationships took sacrifice, and he had sacrificed too much with Valerie. The next woman he let into his life needed to be different. Someone he could trust.

"Tell me about Hudson." Molly looked up at him. Her eyes filled with curiosity.

Hudson turned in acknowledgment of his name and returned to sniffing the ground between them, following the couple's scent ahead.

"I got him trained from his previous owner. They did a lot of outdoor activities together, so Hudson loves being outside. Being kept inside is like a punishment to him. I think the old man tried to wear him out by keeping him busy, but there is no stopping Hudson. He needs his time outdoors."

"He has quite the personality."

"He does." Enough about Hudson. If he was going to find out more about Molly, now was his chance. "How about yourself? What do you do in the city?"

Molly chuckled and glanced out at the old lake. "I work with my best friend. We own a coffee shop together."

Her best friend? A best friend who was just a friend or a best friend who she had a history with? He needed to learn more. "A coffee shop. It would make sense why I ran into you at Patsy's."

"I guess so. I can't get away from coffee even when I'm on vacation."

"How long have you been co-owner of a coffee shop?"

"Two years. It has been doing well and I am a bit of a workaholic, so Carla said she'd take care of things while I got away to get my mind off of…"

Off of… what? "Lemon Grove is a good place to be when you want to take your mind off things."

"I've found that to be true." She smiled at him and his knees almost buckled beneath him. He searched his mind for more things to say or do to make her smile again.

"Do you want to see a view of the town?" he asked.

"From here?"

"Yes, just ahead is an extra loop we can take to a viewpoint. Ten minutes, tops."

"That would be lovely." The smile had returned even wider now.

Rick called ahead to the couple and guided them to the path toward the view. Molly's stride lengthened and Rick heard her boots crunch against the trail. Even the couple picked up their pace. His suggestion of stopping at the viewpoint brought a new level of excitement to the group.

He caught himself sneaking quick glances in Molly's direction and she appeared to be keeping her eye on the trail, watching for the upcoming view with little thought to the man at her side. Why would she want to look at him? Molly was a city girl and was most likely attracted to success. It was his connections to his father and his father's money that made him a catch to the ladies in the city. In Lemon Grove, he was only a guy with a dog. Even his truck wasn't impressive. Sure, he didn't look all that bad (if he did say so himself), but what else did he have going for him? From what Molly had seen, not much. No wonder she hadn't seemed to react when he touched her hand at the gas station. He concluded that anything he had experienced came from his own head and was one-sided. There was no sign to lead him to believe she might be looking at him the same way.

But what did he feel? Curiosity. Attraction. It had to be an interest in someone unfamiliar. She was new to town, and he needed to talk to someone outside of his usual small social circle in Lemon Grove. He needed to keep his thoughts in check and recognize them for what they were. Time with Molly had become a break from the mundane and nothing more.

"I see the town," the wife called excitedly from the front of the line.

They gathered together at the unmarked viewpoint where no trees grew on a large rock overlooking the valley below. Nestled in the trees were the rooftops of Lemon Grove.

"The trees to the left of town are the campground."

"And those large buildings over to the right?" asked the wife.

Rick sighed. There was no missing the five-story building and the other outbuildings sticking out among the trees. "That is Lemon Eagle Resort."

She grimaced. "I'm sorry, but it's kind of ugly."

"I can't argue with you there," Rick said. The way Robert Fletcher changed the landscape with his eyesore made Rick hot with anger. The town should never have granted the resort the permits to develop the area as they did. It made Rick wonder who Robert paid to make sure they built the resort according to his plans, no matter how much of an impact it made on the area.

Molly took a step toward the edge, and Rick grabbed her elbow, pulling her back.

"Sorry," he said. "It's instinct. Don't get too close." The last few words were for him as he left his hand on her arm a little longer.

"Where do you live?" Molly asked. She fixed her eyes on the buildings below. Her elbow still in Rick's grasp.

He moved closer. "You can't see it from here. My home is to the left of the resort. Between the house with the red roof and the last resort building."

It was impossible to make out the red roof or the last resort building from where they stood. Those unfamiliar with the area would probably struggle to pick out his home among the thick trees, but Rick knew where his house was.

Molly turned to him and held out her camera. "Would you take my picture?"

"Of course." Molly tucked her hands inside her jacket pockets and smiled for the camera. He checked the picture on the screen. She was beautiful in a photograph, too. "Got it," he said.

"How about the two of you together?" The husband took the camera from Rick and gestured for him to stand beside Molly.

Rick mimicked her pose, slipping his hands in his pockets, and stood by her side.

"Come on." The husband waved his hand in the air. "Put your arm around her."

Rick smiled and watched Molly's face for her approval. She gave a nod and as he slipped his arm around her waist, he thought his heart would burst.

"There." The husband returned the camera to Rick and laughed. "You two make an adorable couple."

"Oh," Molly's cheeks reddened, "Rick and I—"

"Thank you," Rick said. His face smiled back at him in the photo on the LCD display. "This is a great picture of us."

The husband held his wife's hand as he walked proudly down the trail with their terrier leading the way.

"I want a copy of that," he said to Molly. "Can you send it to me?"

"Don't you have a picture of yourself with the town already?"

He shrugged. "I think I like this one more." Leaning close, he showed her the image of the two of them smiling side-by-side.

"It is a wonderful picture," she said softly.

It was a keeper. And from Rick's perspective, so was Molly.

Molly had never looked as happy in photographs as she did standing beside Rick. Even in pictures with Brad, there was still a hint of sadness behind her eyes. But here was evidence it was possible for her to be happy with someone. Even someone she was still getting comfortable with.

She turned off the camera and tucked it away. Relationships had a way of going sour once she got to know someone better, as they were never the same as they first appeared. On the surface, Rick might appear like a small town guy who loves his dog, but there had to be more to him than that. He didn't like people questioning his care of Hudson, however, he knew how to apologize. It was a trait Brad lacked.

"Be careful around the roots. Don't trip." Rick had his eye on everything from the trail, the couple, the dog... even Molly.

She found comfort in being with someone who wasn't only looking out for himself. Rick had put thought into this trip to create an enjoyable experience for his guests. From reassuring the couple and offering them options to packing lunches, he now called out hazards on the trail, and it seemed to come naturally to him, which put Molly at ease. She would be happy with someone like Rick. Someone who would put other's needs before himself. Someone who might put her first.

Molly didn't mean to trip on the root, but the toe of her shoe caught the edge and sent her tumbling forward. There wasn't even time to gasp before her arms waved in the air as she searched for something to keep herself from landing on the ground. And her arms found Rick. He grabbed her hand and pulled her toward him to stop her fall. His grip tightened into a light squeeze and then his hand relaxed, leaving her hand in his.

"I'll make sure you get over this rough patch," he whispered. It was the same reassuring voice he had used at the gas station. The soothing voice. Now, instead of covering her hand, he held it entwined with his.

Her heart beat fast with every step their hands remained locked in their hold. Neither released the other as they continued down the trail hand-in-hand and Hudson walked beneath their outstretched arms.

While Molly had cautioned herself not to get caught up in a relationship with someone she would soon leave behind, she saw no reason she couldn't hold hands with him. As long as she recognized this as a perk that came with the Lakewood Lake tour package, she could let it slide. If it continued after today, she might need to set a few more boundaries for herself. She assured herself it wouldn't happen again. Rick was being helpful, and the lingering of his grasp was a pleasant and harmless surprise.

The walk continued on with the couple taking additional pictures of the empty lake. With its little legs exhausted from the walk, they carried their small terrier in their arms. Despite Hudson's age, he trotted along just fine, keeping up with his human companions.

Molly was thankful for the slow pace. She didn't know how much time had passed, but knew she had held hands with Rick for half the length of the loop and she estimated they would soon be back at the truck.

A raindrop hit her cheek. Another soon followed. And another. Then the clouds unleashed their worst, sending down sheets of rain.

"Get under some branches," Rick called to the couple.

They tucked themselves under the shelter of a pine tree, which caught much of the rain in the branches above. Rick pulled Molly to a tree off to the side of the trail. Once hidden under the branches, Rick wrapped his coat and arms around her, further shielding Molly from the rain. Her mind swirled as she breathed in his outdoorsy scent. Holding hands was one thing, but her head resting against his chest was another. The longer she remained in his arms, the more she begged the rain not to stop.

A drop broke through the branches, striking the side of her face. As she lifted her arm to wipe it away, Rick leaned back and ran his thumb across her cheek. Molly rolled onto her toes, inching herself closer. His hand remained on her cheek for a moment, his eyes staring back into hers before he pulled her back against his chest.

"This shouldn't last long," he whispered, or the rain drowned out his voice. Molly couldn't tell which.

"It shouldn't?" Her voice trembled from excitement, or it could have been the chill of the rain. Her heart knew the difference.

He wistfully replied, "Nothing like this lasts forever."

CHAPTER THIRTEEN

*S*tepping through the front door to his cabin, Rick whistled a cheerful tune. This day took a turn he could never have predicted. Only twenty-four hours before, he had been planning a tour for a retired couple, and it caught him off guard when Molly joined them. The tour had started innocently enough, but when she fell into his arms, he didn't want to let go.

He took a risk when he held her hand. Molly could have pulled away and refused to talk to him for the rest of the hike. Through the corner of his eye, he had seen her tumble forward and in an instant he grabbed her. Then as they walked, any awkwardness of taking her hand for the first time had drifted away. His heart soared when she left her hand, small and cool, in his. He was sure he felt her slide her fingers between his... or maybe he had done it? It happened in a second.

The weather was out of his control. He wanted to take credit for the rain that forced them to seek shelter under the tree. Normally, he complained about his clothing being drenched, the raindrops streaming down his spine, but he would stand in the rainstorm for hours if it meant she would still be in his arms. Sadly, there were others he needed to think about on the tour.

At the first break in the weather, he directed the couple to lead the way back to the truck. Even with the poor weather, there was laughter and smiles from everyone, including Molly. He hoped she enjoyed herself and didn't find it awkward to spend the day with him. It seemed she had when Molly agreed to meet him for coffee tomorrow.

"It's a date," he had said, leaving her with a stunned expression. She didn't disagree when he dropped her off at the campground. And so, he whistled his merry tune on his drive home and continued whistling as he walked into his bedroom, where he peeled off his damp jacket and T-shirt and found a set of clean, dry clothes from his dresser. His phone rang in his jacket pocket. Was it her?

Checking the call display, Rick saw his father's name and his positive mood drained away with every chime of the ring-tone.

"Where have you been all day?" his father demanded.

"I was giving some folks a tour of Lakewood Lake."

"I'm not paying you to give people tours."

Rick trapped his phone between his ear and his shoulder as he wrestled himself into a dry pair of jeans. "That would be why I booked the day off. One second." He dropped the phone onto his bed and pulled a dry T-shirt over his head. "What can I do for you, Dad?"

"While you were off sightseeing with friends, I was working on a business deal."

"Sounds promising." Rick knew there was more to his father's phone call than just another round of criticism. He needed something and expected Rick to deliver.

"I need you here tomorrow to finish it off."

His father always had a way of ruining his plans. "I'm pretty busy here."

"Anything you can do there, you can do here."

Rick couldn't have his coffee date with Molly in the city, and his father would never accept a date as an excuse. "I have another meeting."

"With who?" Not getting an immediate response from Rick, his father continued. "Any other meeting isn't as important as this one. Cancel whatever you have scheduled and meet me in my office at nine."

Rick ran his hand through his hair. "Do you realize how short notice this is? You can't ask me to drop everything because you—"

"Listen, Rick. Your mother and I can't be the only ones sacrificing for this company. How many times in the past year have I asked you to come back for a meeting?"

There were other requests. Paperwork. Equipment reviews. Staff parties. His father had plenty of non-meeting demands for Rick to comply with.

"I'm asking for more notice than to call me in for a meeting the evening before."

His father exhaled into the phone and made the hair on the back of Rick's neck stand upright. He had been on the wrong end of his father's temper many times before. "Don't you tell me how things are going to be. If you won't respect me as your father, you will at least respect me as your employer, and I am telling you I expect you in the office tomorrow."

"Fine."

It was a crushing end to what had been a spectacular day. If not for this meeting, his good momentum with Molly would have carried over into tomorrow. Instead, his family was unknowingly stopping the momentum in its tracks. Without even being here, his father messed things up for him and brought the drama into his life.

He flopped backward onto his bed, thinking of how he would need to break the news to Molly. At least he had a reason to call her and hear her voice one more time before the day was over. Luckily, he had her number written on the waiver.

Molly knew the date was too good to be true. Rick hadn't even waited twenty-four hours to change his mind. She never even had time to call Carla to tell her about Lakewood Lake, the hike, and the rainstorm before he called to cancel. He should at least have been honest with her about not being interested than pretend he wanted to reschedule. Now she understood why he was single. He couldn't commit and would come up with lies to get out of a date. *Sure,* he needed to go to the city. She dodged a bullet there.

"I didn't know they were going to ask me to come in."

Mm-hmm.

"I tried to get out of it."

Sure.

"Let me make it up to you."

She heard it all before, but from someone with another name. Somehow, in her effort to forget about him, Molly ended up in Lemon Grove, where she had apparently found his small town twin. Why was it she always attracted the same men? What vibe was she giving off to draw them all to her? For once, she should be entitled to meet a nice guy who would treat her like she was his priority. At some point, her bad luck had to run out.

For now, there would be no morning coffee date. Rick *might* be back in time for a dinner date, but no guarantees, and Molly saw through it. He had no intention of making a second attempt at a date. It was time to move on. Was it fun while it lasted? Perhaps. If only she could erase the memory of Rick holding her as they stood under that tree. She wouldn't soon forget the way he stared back at her as if he was reading her thoughts. If only she could have read his.

Rick was right, nothing like that moment would last forever.

As the early morning light spilled between the buildings, Rick pulled into the asphalt parking lot, and took a breath. He was a stranger in the land of concrete and asphalt. This was not his world anymore, yet his family still dragged him back. The staff parking lot was full, leaving only a handful of visitor stalls to choose from. As the son of the owner, any empty parking stall was available to him and he could force an employee to park on the street. He chose visitor parking. He would not be staying long and had no desire to displace any of the employees for the sake of his convenience.

Pulling his phone from his pocket, he checked for messages. There were none, although he wished for an important phone call to whisk him away from the anguish he was about to endure. He would take any call at this point. A call to say the pipes had burst at his cabin would do. If only he had thought ahead and asked a friend to call during the meeting to save him.

There was only one more thing to do before he went inside. He needed to switch his mind away from the negativity he had been thinking about work, and focus on something positive. Rick knew what to do.

He scrolled through his phone contacts and found Molly's number. She would be awake as Hudson stopped by for his morning visit.

The phone rang, and she answered.

"Hi, Molly. It's Rick."

"Hey. Aren't you in the city?"

"I just got here," he said, unbuckling his seatbelt. Hearing her voice, he became energized, forgetting all about his troubles. The sooner he got through this meeting and finished the deal for his father, the sooner he could get back home and take this woman out to dinner. "If Hudson isn't there yet, he will be there soon."

There was a delay in her response. "He's here. I'm surprised you didn't keep him home if you weren't going to be here to pick him up."

"That's why I'm calling. I usually ask someone in town to look after him while I'm gone. Would you be willing to let him spend the day with you?"

"But I have nothing to—"

"Glenda has a leash for him at the campground office. I've also left a small bag of food and treats there in case he needs them. There is another stash at Patsy's café if Glenda isn't around."

The tags of Hudson's collar clanged together in the background. She must have been petting him.

"I guess I can." Her voice didn't have the same energy Rick had grown accustomed to. It was monotone and slow. Perhaps he had called her too early?

"You're sure it won't be a bother?"

"No. I was hoping to check out a trail today, but he might be too tired for that."

Rick laughed and switched his phone to his other ear before grabbing a briefcase from the passenger seat. "If it is a short trail, he'd love to go with you. Try the waterfall or the river loop trails. They are beautiful locations and wouldn't be too long for him."

Silence lingered. He didn't want to hang up, but he was at the door to the building and would soon bump into familiar faces.

"Thank you, Molly. I will pick up Hudson and take you out to dinner."

"That sounds fine." She had little reaction to his comment, but she was no doubt distracted by Hudson's need for her attention. Still, their brief conversation was all he needed before he ended the call and flung open the door to the marble-floored lobby. His father strode across the room from a bank of polished elevators and checked his watch.

Rick slowed his pace. The man had a commanding presence. With his shoulders, his arms barely swayed at his side as he stepped. His hair had grayed over the years and rather than color it, like Rick's mother had, his father embraced the gray saying people respected a man who didn't hide who he had become. In his father's case, it was a sixty-year-old version of his twenty-year-old ambitious self. Never slowing down, his father knew who he had become and was determined to make something out of Rick.

"Where have you been?" he asked through his teeth. His father always slapped on a smile whenever he dressed Rick down in public. Appearances were everything. He grabbed Rick by the arm and pulled him toward an open elevator. "They've already been here for twenty minutes." His father pushed the button, directing the elevator to the tenth floor.

The lift was quiet and sparkled from every chrome surface. The gentle movement of the elevator left the occupants to focus on their business conversations and not on the stability of the cables that prevented them from descending into the basement.

Rick answered, "But the meeting isn't until nine o'clock."

"Well, they wanted to socialize beforehand. You could have shaved before you came."

His father's first rule of business was to always have a clean face. No one wanted to do business with someone who tried to hide himself behind facial hair. Not even five minutes into his arrival, Rick had already arrived later than the clients and he didn't look the part of a business executive or his father's son.

"Who are we meeting with?"

"You'll see." His father adjusted his tie and tugged on his suit jacket before running a single hand over his hair.

Rick's tongue stuck to his mouth as he tried to swallow. He ran his hand over the stubble on his jaw and stared down at the floor. Maybe he could have shaved before he left home, but his father still wouldn't have liked the length Rick would have left it. While the look might not be satisfactory to his father, it made Rick happy.

The elevator doors opened onto the tenth-floor lobby and seated on a leather-upholstered couch, Valerie's red-lined smile greeted him.

"Rick," she purred. Valerie strutted toward him, placing a hand on his shoulder with a slinky smile. "My, you're looking rather rugged."

His father stood between him and the elevator. There would be no escape from coming face-to-face with his ex. Valerie wore her blonde hair in a bun and her favorite tight black skirt and fitted floral blouse. It was an outfit that showed off her figure and her family's money. If she was trying to show Rick what he was missing, it wasn't going to work on him. Not anymore. Finally, he noticed the two other men standing nearby who now attempted to look busy as they stared down at their phones.

"It's good to see you." He stepped past her, loosening her grip on his shoulder. His father cleared his throat. Clearly, he expected Rick to give Valerie more attention. "Are you here for the meeting?"

"I am." She grabbed the back of his arm. "Sit with me." Unable to politely detach himself from her grasp under the watchful eye of his father, Rick allowed Valerie to guide him toward a meeting room at the end of the hall. Now he understood why his father summoned him back.

Valerie's father rose from his chair. "Rick. So good to see you."

"Mr. Turner." He greeted Rick with a firm handshake, as if he still was in the running to become his son-in-law.

"When we started talking with your father about the deal, I told him we wanted him to put his best man on the job."

"He has plenty of those to choose from."

Valerie's father laughed and moved his chair closer to the table. "Nonsense. Ever since I met you, I saw your potential. I still don't understand why you continue to work with your father instead of coming to work for me. We could use a man like you at our company."

"Should we get started?" Rick's father glared at his son from across the table. Leaving his company to work for someone else would be the ultimate betrayal, even if it suited Rick to do so.

It was a three-hour meeting with Rick leading the negotiations. Occasionally, Valerie would rub his arm in encouragement whenever she sided with him. They weren't together, yet she put on a show as if they were. Much like their former relationship, the meeting ended without a commitment.

"I think," Valerie said as she leaned in closer to clasp his arm, "we should continue this conversation over lunch."

Rick rose from his chair while Valerie still clung to him. "As much as I'd like to, I need to head back."

"Come on, Rick." His father also rose from his chair. There was a smile on his face, which to anyone other than his son would read as a pleasant expression. To Rick, his father was sending him an obvious message to not turn down Valerie's offer. "Stay for lunch before you hit the road."

Rick cast his gaze toward the meeting room's newly installed and fresh Berber carpet. If he wanted to keep his job, he needed to prove his worth and get the deal done. He nodded.

His father clapped his hands. "Ah, very good. I will get my assistant to make reservations… unless the two of you want to go someplace without us old men tagging along."

Both men laughed while Rick stood in awkward silence beside a blushing Valerie and her intense eyes.

"Is it a business lunch?" Rick asked.

Mr. Turner smiled and placed his hand on Rick's shoulder. "Lunch will be whatever we make of it, isn't that right, Charles?"

"You are correct." His father opened the meeting room door and stood to one side.

Mr. Turner led the way toward the elevator and smiled. "Any chance you might move back to the city?"

"I haven't—"

"Robert Fletcher has made Rick a rather significant offer on his property," his father interrupted. "Isn't that right, Rick?"

Once again, he nodded. "Yup."

"Oh, Rick." Valerie tightened her grip on his arm. "That's wonderful. I've been waiting for the day when you'd move back."

"I haven't decided, yet."

His father laughed. "He doesn't want to jinx it."

"He is a businessman, like his father." Mr. Turner slapped Rick's back. "You're wise not to make plans before the ink is dry. You never know when things fall through and you end up with an unexpected surprise."

Rick laughed as his jaw tightened and the minutes dragged on. He had already spent more time in the city than he had agreed to. Now, it would be hours before he could escape back to Lemon Grove.

CHAPTER FOURTEEN

She couldn't say no. Not to Hudson. When Rick called, those little brown eyes stared up at her as he lay at her feet and she couldn't refuse Rick's request. Of course she would take care of Hudson while Rick was in the city. It wasn't because she remained hopeful for a date, but because the poor old dog needed someone to look out for him. For a moment, she had considered suggesting someone from in town, but Molly changed her mind when Hudson let out a long sigh. If the dog appeared relaxed about the entire ordeal, she would be, too.

She refused to allow Rick's comments of promising to do his best to be back in time to have the effect he had been hoping for. She wouldn't sit around pining for him. Until he showed up at her campsite, she would consider his promise to be a line he fed her to soften the blow. He needed someone to watch Hudson and nothing more. A meal would be payment for her babysitting services and not some romantic gesture.

Molly considered herself among the lucky ones. At least she had seen through his act before getting sucked too far into his game. A few days later, she might have ended up like the other women who waited on him as he gallivanted around meeting who knows who in the city. Maybe he thought it easy to call upon visitors to Lemon Grove. He could flirt with whoever he wanted, knowing they would leave in a week or so. There was no commitment needed when relationships came with a pre-determined time limit. It was another bad relationship avoided, and it was a close call.

"At least you're a good boy."

Hudson beat his tail against the ground as she stroked his head and waited for his walk. As Rick had said, Glenda had an extra leash at the campground office and spare food, which Hudson gobbled up. Glenda questioned Molly as she encouraged Hudson to eat faster. She asked why Rick had chosen Molly to look after Hudson and not someone local, like herself. Molly gave her no answer, instead telling Glenda to ask Rick when she saw him. If he wanted to string multiple women along, he should be the one to sort out his mess. Molly was only babysitting Hudson for the day and wasn't his mediator. Whether Rick paid her with a meal or not, it didn't matter to her. She wanted company on the trail, and she had a furry companion to accompany her.

Hudson leapt into the passenger's seat of her car and whined as she exited the campground. He was excited to spend time with her, even if Rick had found other things to do, or people to be with. They would still have a nice day together.

Finding the parking lot at the waterfall's trailhead was easy on the single-lane gravel road that reached a dead end at the river's edge. There was nowhere else to go but turn into the hard-packed gravel circle that would have been tight to turn around in on a busy day. But did Lemon Grove ever get busy? Today, the parking lot was empty and Molly chose a spot in the shade nearest to a laminated map attached to a bulletin board and two pegs stuck in the ground to mark the start of the trail.

Hudson pawed at the window and wiggled in his seat before Molly opened the door for him to exit.

"Are you ready to go for a walk?"

His tail brushed away the dirt from the polished stones embedded in the sand.

"Alright. Alright."

Molly leaned back, attempting to keep Hudson from pulling her off her feet.

"You're strong when you want to go somewhere." Hudson ignored her, stretching the leash as far as it would go to reach the post, where he lifted his leg. "Of course," she giggled. "You mustn't walk down a trail with a full bladder."

Molly scanned the map, noting the route from the parking lot to the waterfall, and saw it would be a good two hours to complete the round trip. She glanced down at the pup as it continued to sniff the ground near her feet.

"Do you think your old legs can make the trip?"

Hudson continued to sniff. He let out a large sneeze and shook his head.

"Hopefully, that is a yes."

She led him to the trail and down a gentle slope into the trees. The temperature was perfect for a walk. It was warm, but with a cool breeze preventing the exercise from making her overheated. The breeze also helped to keep the bugs away, and insects were the one downside to being outdoors. Birds sang from nearby branches while the forest was otherwise silent. She and Hudson had the trail to themselves. Molly exhaled and stomped out her frustrations. Without the bugs, Molly imagined herself spending more time in the forest.

If only life was this simple. All she needed was a dog and a trail. Everything else, such as work and men, just added frustration to her life. Life was so full of demands, she had missed out on the quiet moments like this. She needed time to be alone with her thoughts and let her mind wander to what might be.

What would it be like to live in a place like Lemon Grove? The smells of the forest had a much more pleasant scent than car exhaust, and the singing birds were preferable to trucks and their air brakes or car horns. If she had to work nine-to-five every day, she needed to be someplace where she could recharge, and living in an apartment overlooking a city street didn't make her heart sing. The trees did.

She would consider moving to an apartment near to the park, but that would come at a cost and the rent was already at the top end of her budget. And then there was the location. While she would enjoy the view of a park, she would be further away from the coffee shop, which would mean added commute time.

Again, life wasn't simple like the trail. All she needed to do was walk from point A to point B. She didn't even need to meet a timeline. This was at her own pace and she could take all the time she needed… as long as Hudson didn't get too tired.

He seemed to do well for the first ten minutes and the next fifteen. At forty minutes into the hike, he slowed to a crawl. Lowering his body close to the ground, Hudson inched forward. He paused and looked up at Molly.

"Are you getting tired?" she asked.

She heard the rushing water in the distance. When they reached the bend, she might catch a glimpse of the falls.

"Just a little further and we can go back."

Molly took another step and Hudson dug in his paws. She gave his leash a tug, trying to encourage him to follow.

"Come on, Hudson. We haven't reached the falls yet."

He lowered his head, and his collar slid up to his ears.

"I don't want to be stuck here while you're too tired to go up or down the trail."

Molly attempted to walk forward, hoping Hudson would reconsider. As the leash reached its full length, Hudson growled and sprung to his feet, rushing ahead to block her path.

"Will you go a few more feet?"

She lifted her foot and leaned forward. Hudson bared his teeth.

"Okay. Okay." She took a few steps back, away from the direction of the falls, and his face relaxed. With his head lowered, Hudson followed her, stopping only to glance behind him. "I guess we won't be seeing the falls today. You might have at least warned me you were getting too tired."

Hudson continued to walk behind her on their return to the car. Molly reached back and gave his head a scratch.

"It's okay. I guess it was too much."

She shouldn't have listened to Rick. He had said Hudson would manage the walk to the waterfall after his morning adventure, but was it a lie to keep her from turning down his request? What if Hudson had been too tired and collapsed on the trail? It would be impossible for her to carry him back on her own. Would Rick have expected her to abandon Hudson on the trail? She would rather sit in the dark with a tired dog sleeping at her feet until he was ready to walk again than leave him behind.

At least he hadn't reached that point. He communicated they had gone far enough and was escorting her back to the car. It could have ended poorly had his old legs given out. Perhaps Rick knew Hudson would tell her when he reached his limit, but he should have warned her how he'd react. She didn't like him showing her his teeth as he had. Hudson never showed signs of aggression before, and she hadn't expected him to intimidate her into turning around.

Now that they started on their way back to the car, his demeanor had improved and his pleasant personality reemerged. It took thirty minutes before his body appeared less tense, which Molly took to mean he smelled the end of the trail ahead.

"You can have a good rest at the campground when we get back. How does that sound?"

Molly's phone vibrated in her pocket, and she checked her messages. It was Rick.

I'm delayed in the city and won't make it back in time for dinner. Are you okay to keep watching Hudson? I'm sorry about this. Can we try again tomorrow?

She tucked her phone in her pocket without punching in a reply. It would be easy to use the excuse with Rick of being on the trail and not having a signal or not feeling the phone vibrate in her pocket.

Why was she not surprised he canceled dinner? Probably because she saw it coming. What she didn't see coming was him asking her to continue to watch Hudson without giving a time when he would return. Was she supposed to keep Hudson overnight? Was that what he meant by "tomorrow"? That would take his ask too far. One doesn't allow a dog to wander around town and then not come back in time to take it home at night.

A moist tongue licked the side of Molly's hand.

"What was that for?"

Hudson wagged his tail and trotted at her side. Ahead, Molly saw the trail posts at the parking lot and Hudson took the lead, pulling her toward them.

"You're ready to get back, are you?"

She opened the door to the car, allowing the warm air to escape and the outside air to cool the interior. Hudson jumped into the seat and sat waiting for her to join him.

Her phone vibrated again.

I'm trying to get back as soon as I can. Please let me know if tomorrow will work.

She sighed and checked her watch. It was five o'clock. Rick should have sent a message earlier if he was going to skip out on dinner. Waiting so long showed he wasn't considerate when changing plans. He was about to find out she wasn't the type to accommodate his lack of manners.

That's unfortunate. I already made plans for tomorrow, she typed. *Don't take too long. Hudson is tired.*

And she'd had enough of his games. She tucked her phone back into her pocket and climbed into the car, where Hudson gave her a kiss on the cheek. "You don't need to apologize for Rick." His ears lifted. "You're a good boy."

Hudson panted, and Molly started the engine to cool the car with the air conditioning. If only it cooled her temper. She shouldn't have let her guard down with that man. Her instincts had been right when they first fought at the end of her campsite. He was irresponsible not only in how he cared for his dog, but he couldn't even follow through with his own plans.

Molly exhaled and focused on calming her emotions. The day had not played out the way she had expected. No coffee date. No dinner date. She couldn't even see the waterfall. The day was a bust by most standards, but she still was away from the rush of work… and that other dead-end relationship. Thank goodness that was over.

This trip had made her smarter. Now she saw them coming and could protect her heart from being hurt again. The vacation had given her the space to reflect, figure out what she needed, and identify what she wanted to avoid. In Lemon Grove, what she wanted to avoid came in the form of Rick. If only he didn't look so good.

Pulling into the campground, she stopped by the office to pick up more food for Hudson and headed to her campsite to warm a can of stew. A meal from a restaurant would have been better than the cubes of potato and unidentifiable meat she stirred at the bottom of her bowl, but it was cheap.

Hudson would have cleaned her dish had she allowed him to; however, a responsible pet owner didn't feed a dog from the table or let it lick a dirty dish. She settled into her chair with her book, and Hudson sat at her feet as she immersed herself in the story. Her day hadn't gone well and the character in the book was having an even worse day, making hers seem like a breeze. At least Molly didn't have some crazy murderer stalking her. She rolled her eyes. Carla had recommended the book, and while it was not at all her type of story, it passed the time. As the hero arrived to save the day, the daylight faded around her and the headlights from Rick's pickup truck lit the road leading to her campsite.

Hudson rose to his feet and walked toward the road.

"Wait," Molly said. She wasn't about to let him get hit by the truck. Hudson stood in place as Rick parked the truck and turned off the engine.

"Did you miss me?" he called to Hudson as he closed the door and knelt beside his furry friend. "I'm sorry that took so long. You know that hardly ever happens. I hope you had a good time."

"I don't know if Hudson enjoyed himself today." Molly stood a few feet away, folding her arms across her chest.

"What do you mean?" Rick asked, giving Hudson a good scratch on the head.

"I don't know what it was, but just before we reached the waterfall, Hudson started acting strange. He could have just been tired."

"What was he doing?" Rick looked down at Hudson, who wagged his tail and nudged his head against Rick's hand.

"He lowered himself to the ground. He wouldn't move anymore, and when I tried to get him to go, he started growling at me and blocked the path. After we turned around and went back, he lightened up again. Like I said, he might have been tired or—"

"Good boy." Rick ruffled the top of Hudson's head and smiled.

"Good boy? Why are you praising him for growling at me?"

"Because he protected you. He sensed trouble up ahead and kept you from walking into danger. Isn't that right, Hudson?"

"I saw nothing. Are you sure?"

Rick nodded and scratched Hudson's belly. "I'm confident. It wouldn't surprise me if there were a bear up ahead. He has steered me away from many bears in the past."

Molly knelt on the opposite side of Hudson and rubbed his back. "Did you protect me from a big, scary bear?"

"I knew he'd take care of you." Rick held her in his gaze. "I'm sorry about today. My father insisted I come in for this business deal, and the clients wanted to complete the deal over dinner. If I bailed on that…" He sighed and lowered his head. "Believe me, it was not where I wanted to be tonight."

Molly rose and took a step back. "It was unfortunate."

Rick moved close. "I'm not a guy who cancels out at the last minute. Please, don't let today change your opinion of me. I still want to take you out for coffee, if you'll let me."

"I do like coffee." That was the truth. It still didn't fix the fact that he had canceled twice in the same day. "But you'd have to promise not to cancel next time."

He took her hand and held it against his chest. "I promise. I wouldn't let anything get in the way of our coffee date." He took a breath. "Are you still busy tomorrow?"

"I might have an opening for coffee."

"Around eight o'clock? When I come by to pick up Hudson?"

Molly nodded. She looked at how his fingers wrapped around her hand and felt the beating of his heart. Glancing up, she saw his eyes staring back at hers and she lost her fight against the urge to forgive him. One more chance. If he blew it this time, he'd have to find someone else to watch Hudson in the morning.

His smile grew, and he continued to hold her hand until he climbed into his truck to drive home. Molly stood at the edge of her campsite and watched the taillights disappear behind the trees. Tomorrow she would know if he was telling the truth or playing another game. At eight o'clock tomorrow morning, she would decide if he was worth her time or if she had already wasted enough on Rick.

CHAPTER FIFTEEN

*I*f she wasn't so wide awake, the sweet melody of her cell phone's ring-tone would have put Molly to sleep. When Molly answered, Carla's chirping voice on the other end jolted her awake.

"You're not asleep yet?" Carla asked. "I thought all that fresh air would have worn you out."

Molly chuckled and rolled onto her side. "I'm afraid not. I've had a lot to think about out here."

"Are you talking about Rick?"

"Yes. Why can't things ever be easy?"

"Relationships are never easy, but the good ones are worth the effort." Carla took a sip of a drink on the other end of the phone. Her evening cup of tea. "Tell me what's going on."

Molly sighed. She hated the thought of dumping her complaints on her friend late at night, but this was not the first time they shared personal conflicts over hot tea. "Rick asked me to give him another chance after canceling breakfast and dinner today. Before he arrived to pick up Hudson, I had prepared what I was going to say if he asked, but…"

"But what?"

"Then I saw the look in his eyes and he looked really sincere when he apologized."

"And so you decided to give him another chance?"

"I did." Molly sat up and pulled her knees to her chest. "We're going to have breakfast together tomorrow. Am I making the wrong decision? How many times does he have to blow me off before I stop giving him chances?"

"Stop freaking out. Here's what you're going to do." Carla took a deep breath. "You are going to get up early tomorrow morning and make yourself look gorgeous. Make him feel guilty about canceling today. If he's interested, he'll make sure he never makes the same mistake again."

Molly chuckled and rolled her eyes. Carla always knew how to scheme. "So you think I should go ahead with the date tomorrow?"

"I do. Cut the guy some slack... but only a little."

"What does someone wear to a coffee date?" Rick stood in front of his closet, sliding hangers across the rack. He held a dress shirt against his chest and shook his head. "I'm not going to a business meeting."

The clock ticked. At seven thirty, he needed to decide what to wear and finish getting ready to be punctual. After canceling on her twice, he was not going to be late. It would be even better if he arrived early. At least Hudson would be there to keep her distracted until he arrived, but he couldn't count on that dog to do everything. It's not like Hudson could take Molly out for coffee.

Three shirts later, he settled on a red plaid, short-sleeved, button shirt. The buttons would give her the impression that he tried to dress up, even though he was taking her to the café in Lemon Grove, and not some fancy restaurant in the city. Staying at a campsite, Molly probably packed nothing dressy, so this outfit struck the right balance.

Dressed, hair styled, and teeth brushed, he looked somewhat ready. His palms were sweating and his stomach twisted in knots as he watched the clock. He hadn't been this nervous about getting coffee since… well, ever.

He never had to ask out Valerie. Their families orchestrated their first date and scheduled lunch for them, with his father overseeing what he wore. After a while, he went along with the setup and a relationship developed, but it lacked a spark. It was convenient and bland.

This was his choice, and he liked this girl. Things seemed to go well after the tour of Lakewood Lake, and he could have kept things going if not for being called into the city. Now, Rick hoped she would forgive him, not just for canceling coffee but also dinner.

She could have turned him down and refused to have coffee with him this morning, and she could have also pulled her hand away when he held it the night before. Instead, she listened and agreed to give him another shot.

He ran his hand over his hair and gave himself one last look in the mirror.

"That will have to do," he said before laughing to himself.

All this fuss over a woman he only met a week ago. Some people fall for their partners the first time they laid eyes on them. In Rick's case, she caught his eye that day in the campground office, but the moment she berated him for how he cared for Hudson… in that moment, he noticed the spark.

He always wanted a spark. The only thing close to it was the urge to move to Lemon Grove, and the more he tried to push away the idea, the more it consumed him. He experienced the same draw with Molly. She would eventually have to go back to the city, but that was only a drive away. He imagined he would make the trip if it meant giving the spark another chance to burn and grow into a genuine relationship.

If she was willing to forgive him for yesterday, then perhaps she feels the same? Why else would she put up with a guy who cancels last minute? He'd seen friends dumped for less than that. Molly didn't seem high maintenance like some other girls he'd met, but he knew he needed to make her feel respected. Coming across as an ignorant loser who puts work ahead of a woman would not do him any favors.

Today was his chance to prove to her he is a gentleman who was serious when he first asked her out. He swiped his keys from the dresser and threw on his shoes. To pick her up on time, he needed to leave now.

Like the day before, Molly spent money on the campground shower. She would not smell terrible on a coffee date. She checked her phone for messages and found no message to say he canceled. Satisfied enough that Rick was still coming, she took extra time to fix her hair, twisting it around her finger as it dried to encourage its natural waves.

She probably wouldn't have fussed as much if not for Carla's encouragement the night before. As she returned to her campsite from the showers, Hudson arrived and licked her hand in greeting. "Good morning, Hudson. You're here on time. Is Rick coming?"

Hudson followed her to her car where she prepared her breakfast. She used the last of her milk and unwrapped the last yogurt and cereal bar.

Molly stretched and yawned before lowering herself into her camping chair. "I hope he comes soon," she said. "I need my coffee."

She checked her watch. Seven fifty-five. Five minutes left before he was—

Molly heard the roar of his truck as Rick drove up the road. Hudson didn't rise and remained at Molly's feet, moving only to lift his head in acknowledgment. Molly remained seated in her chair and waved to Rick as he pulled into the campsite to park.

"Good morning," he said with a wide smile.

He looked good in his button-down shirt and denim pants. The man understood how to dress, and she had no complaints with no mud on his clothes.

"You made it." She hadn't meant it as a comment on the day before, but her stomach twisted as she worried Rick might interpret her words the wrong way.

Rick laughed and knelt down to pet Hudson. "A few minutes early."

"Really?" Molly pretended to glance at her watch. He didn't need to know she watched the clock. "I never noticed. Hudson distracted me."

"That's why I sent him. Should we get going?" Rick rose and slapped his leg. Hudson groaned.

"Come on, Hudson. We're going to go for a walk," Molly said. Hudson lifted his head and lowered it back to the ground. "Do you think he's too tired?"

Rick shook his head and held Molly's hand, leading her toward the road. "He thinks I'm trying to make him go home."

"We aren't going to leave him behind."

"Just wait." They took a couple of steps onto the road where Rick whistled over his shoulder. Hudson sprung to his feet and ran to their side, wagging his tail in excitement. "See? He needed to make sure we weren't going to the truck."

Molly laughed at a dog being so stubborn. She hadn't been around dogs enough to observe one behave like Hudson, or at least the dogs she had been with displayed little personality. Hudson had a mind of his own and wasn't afraid to make humans do what he wanted. He seemed to have learned a few tricks, but who did he learn them from? Perhaps the one holding her hand? Every time she seemed to guess Rick was up to something, he ended up innocent. His trip to the city could have been innocent enough, and she became more inclined to forgive him since he showed up this morning, surprisingly on time. He also seemed to dress up for the occasion.

She breathed in, taking in the scent of the trees and some woodsy soap. He made an excellent choice, and she leaned in to take it in even more.

"Tired?" Rick asked.

"Hmm?" Molly's cheeks flushed. She hadn't realized how far over she had leaned. It was too early to be leaning against his arm, but her cheek had brushed against his sleeve. "No, I was trying to look between the trees over there." Her heart raced with the fear of being caught smelling him. What would he think if he realized what she did? He'd most likely laugh at her, and then what?

Rick slowed their pace and bent his knees to see from Molly's level. "There's not much to see over there."

"I just like looking at the different trees and the bark. There aren't many to look at in the city."

"True."

His thumb glided down the side of hers and back toward her wrist. Molly would have almost frozen in place if she hadn't reminded herself to be cautious. She was still learning about Rick. Why get caught up over a small, gentle touch? A touch that made her fight the urge to return the gesture. Shouldn't she show her interest? Even a little? If she gave him nothing at all, maybe he'd think she didn't like him and he'd move on? He could have a list of ladies to move on to if she rejected him.

Then again, the fear of other women shouldn't be what spurred her toward flirtation. In fact, it should push her in the opposite direction. To be in a relationship with someone, she needed to be confident no one else was in the picture. Another already dumped her for someone else, and she needed to spot warning signs early to prevent it from happening again. But had Rick triggered any serious red flags?

She stole a glance at his eyes, not wanting him to see she was looking at him. A person could learn a lot about someone by looking in their eyes, such as if they were hiding something, or if they were relaxed, or happy. Rick had happy eyes, at least by Molly's definition. They differed from Brad's and it wasn't only in their color. It was how the corners and the bridge of his nose creased when he smiled. There was animation in his face, which she never saw with Brad. It didn't appear that Rick was trying to control his emotions, which naturally displayed on his face, unless he was an excellent actor.

Given that everyone she had met in town seemed to like Rick, it inclined her to believe this wasn't an act. How tiring it would be to act one's way through life in every interaction. This had to be the real him she was seeing, which was reassuring. He had proven to her he wasn't perfect, but who was? If she were looking for a perfect man, she'd never find one. What she needed was to find the perfect man for her. Someone who cared about her and wanted to spend time with her. Rick was spending time with her… until she had to leave in a week.

Rick led them over the bridge, but instead of walking into the residential area, he veered left onto a narrow path.

"Where are we going?" Molly asked.

"It is a nicer walk along the creek."

It was. The path was barely the width of their feet and traced the edge of the creek bed. Rick walked in front of her, holding her hand behind him. He held back branches and waited for her to pass by or blocked them before he let them go and they sprang back into place.

Through the trees, Molly heard dogs barking in town, which made Hudson's ears perk up, most likely excited to hear his furry friends. Dew coated the leaves of the plants, giving them a sheen. If only they didn't dampen her clothes as they passed by. The birds had sung their morning tunes, and the cool morning air enhanced the scents of the surrounding forest. She smiled to herself. This was a pleasant walk, and she found comfort in being close to town in the company of Rick and Hudson.

She looked ahead at Rick as he walked in front of her and noticed how his hair had been trimmed at the back of his neck. She observed his stride as he moved along the path. He was strong and was used to hiking in the outdoors. His clothes fit him well… a little too well, and Molly shifted her gaze away. For years, she had prided herself on noticing others' accomplishments rather than their physical assets, but she had never met a man like Rick before. This was a man of the woods. Those men didn't exist in the city, and if they did, Molly had never met one.

Rick was the type of man Molly now realized she found attractive. She didn't know she had a type until now, and she never would have known if she hadn't taken a vacation to Lemon Grove. To think she was going to settle for the likes of Brad without ever knowing genuine attraction.

At the side of the coffee shop, Rick tied Hudson to a picnic table where a small metal bowl, already filled with water, rested on the grass.

"Patsy leaves the bowl out for Hudson to drink from whenever he comes by."

"That's kind of her."

Uninterested in having a drink, Hudson flopped down beside the bowl and closed his eyes as Rick walked Molly to the front of the café and held the door.

"Good morning. I'll be with you in a minute," Patsy said. With her back turned, she prepared an order behind the counter and turned around. Her mouth dropped open at the sight of Rick holding Molly's hand. "I wasn't expecting to see the two of you. Well, I did… but not now… together… I mean, I didn't think I'd see you until later… separately… I, uh, I'm going to get this to my customers and I'll be right with you." Patsy grabbed a tray and rushed to the corner of the room to deliver two breakfast bagels to two men seated at the far wall.

Molly smiled as Rick tightened his grip on her hand. She hadn't expected walking into the coffee shop would fluster poor Patsy, but it seemed it had. Hopefully, it wasn't because Patsy had wanted to be the one on the end of Rick's arm. Molly hadn't meant to make anyone jealous and was here for a morning coffee, which happened to be part of a date with Rick. Molly had enjoyed getting to know Patsy these past few days and had no desire to upset her.

"Did you want to get something to eat?" Rick asked.

"I had breakfast, although those bagels look good." Eggs and bacon stacked between a sliced bagel looked delicious and was something to consider adding to their menu back at the coffee shop. She would need to mention it to Carla.

"You should try one then."

"I don't know. Maybe tomorrow."

"Go ahead. I'm buying."

Molly shook her head. "We're only here for coffee."

"And if you want a bagel, I won't keep you from it."

"I only said they looked good."

"What if I split one with you? I haven't eaten breakfast myself."

Molly encountered a wave of guilt. She hadn't even considered if Rick was hungry and had only thought of herself. Rick shouldn't be forced to skip breakfast because of her.

"Splitting it is fine, unless you want the whole thing."

Rick smiled and gave her hand a squeeze. "I want you to try the bagel. We'll split it."

"Sounds good," she said.

Patsy hurried around the counter and wiped her hands on the

cloth. "So, what can I get you two?" Her cheeks were red as she avoided eye contact.

"A breakfast bagel," Rick said. "Two coffees. Molly, what kind of coffee would you like?"

"Oh, a mocha would be lovely this morning."

"Of course," Patsy said. She turned to Rick, seeming to have regained her composure, looked at him and smiled. "The usual for you?"

"That would be great. We'll be outside with Hudson."

"Hudson is here?" Patsy's shoulders bounced as she laughed. "Then I will bring him out his treat. I'll have your things out to you right away."

Rick paid for the breakfast as Patsy winked at Molly, who wondered if it wasn't a common occurrence for Rick to pay for someone's coffee at the coffee shop, or to be holding someone's hand. What she knew was word traveled fast in small towns, and townsfolk liked to visit coffee shops. By the end of the day, everyone in Lemon Grove would know Patsy saw her at the coffee shop with Rick, and Molly would find out soon enough if it was good or bad being the talk of the town.

CHAPTER SIXTEEN

*R*ick was under her spell. Not once did he turn away from the stunning woman sitting across from him at the picnic table. He might have snuck a peek at Hudson to check up on the pup as he slept at their feet, but Molly had his full attention. He couldn't take his eyes off of her and her lips. He loved the way they curled into a smile and how they moved when she spoke. She was enchanting, and he wanted to keep her sitting in front of him for as long as possible, or at least spend as many hours with her as she would allow him.

After his trip to the city, Rick figured his father owed him the time it took for him to travel to the meeting. If he were late getting to work today, he would argue it was better than asking for money. He'd accept time with Molly over any cash bonus.

His heart soared with the beautiful company in front of him. Her laugh made his heart sing. She couldn't be more perfect… except for that minor issue of her living in the city. This distance was a problem, but one they could figure out. For now, he was content to be here at the café and stare into her beautiful, sparkling eyes.

"What do you think?" she asked, snapping him out of his trance.

"I think… that… uh…"

"You weren't listening, were you?" The look of disappointment on her face was unmistakable.

He shook his head. "I'm sorry. I was—"

Molly sighed and shuffled in her seat. "It doesn't matter."

"No. It does. Please, repeat what you were saying."

"From the beginning?"

Rick took a breath and smiled. "From when you said your friend Carla wanted to talk about the next steps for your coffee shop."

"So, from the beginning."

"Y-yes?"

Of course, he had to get caught up in her pretty smile rather than stop his mind from wandering. She had this way about her that, for the first time, rendered him helpless. In business, he always entered the room in control of the conversation. He had a plan in place that would move the discussion toward sealing a deal to benefit the company. With Valerie, well, she was the one in control and he had to stay on his toes.

With Molly, he had no agenda. The conversation unfolded as they talked and rather than listen to her words as if he was hoping to steer the conversation toward an end goal, he allowed himself to imagine other opportunities, such as what it would be like to hold her hand again, to smell her hair, kiss her lips… It was those thoughts that were getting him into trouble, and they would do so again if he didn't pay attention to what she was saying.

"I don't want to open another one downtown, but Carla is certain it is the best place to make a profit. She wants to have a second store at the other end of the city so half of our clients don't have to travel as far."

"But by doing so, you're cutting half of your profits at your current store."

"That's my argument, I think we should open one in a unique area that would build a new client base."

"That's a good approach. In a new area, you reach people who don't know you yet. If they like you enough, they will keep coming back and you will gain more clients with word of mouth. Either approach you settle on will be good. No matter what, you can't have growth without risk."

Molly nodded and turned to the side of the café. "How long has Patsy had this place for sale?"

He stared at the weathered for sale sign on the side of the building. "For a good year or more, but I don't think she's in a rush to sell." He made a connect in his head that started his heart racing. "Why? Are you considering buying it?"

"Could you imagine?" Molly laughed and shook her head. "Carla would never agree to it. This is so far away from the city, she'd think I was crazy if I suggested it."

"It has an established customer base with everyone in town coming through. You get those that always hit it up on their way through to the city, plus tourists."

"How many people stop in Lemon Grove?"

"Many people stop here just for Patsy's café. She has some very loyal customers."

Molly sat in silence and ran her finger along the surface of the table. Now Rick had a new expression to appreciate. A dimple emerged on her chin when Molly was deep in thought, and her right eyebrow rose a fraction as her jaw shifted to one side. He would have mistaken it for a smirk if it weren't for the blank stare that threatened to bore through the tabletop.

"Are you considering it?"

Her gaze shifted to his. "I can't. As much as it would be nice to live in a small town like this, away from the craziness of the city, I wouldn't be able to get the support of Carla to get the money I'd need to buy it. This place would be great though."

"What makes this place so great?" He leaned forward and propped his chin on his fist with his elbow planted on the table.

Molly giggled. "Oh gosh. It's a cute place and, like you said, it has loyal customers. I like Lemon Grove."

"And?"

"And what?"

"Well, I kind of hoped if you bought the place I'd be your favorite customer. I might even move my office from my cabin to a café table."

"You wouldn't." She looked down at the ground as her cheeks reddened. Rick watched her lift her fingers to her lips before she pressed both against the side of her face, no doubt attempting to hide her expression.

"We'd be by every day. Wouldn't we, Hudson?" Hudson lifted his head before lowering it back to the ground and letting out a long sigh. "There'd be no place he'd rather be."

"Well," she said. "That would be very sweet of you, but I don't see that happening. Maybe the two of you could come out to the city to visit me at the shop there?"

Rick leaned away from the table and faked a smile. Given how infrequently he visited the city, he wouldn't make it to her coffee shop often, and Hudson no longer enjoyed long rides in the truck. The short trip here and there was manageable for the old dog, but anything longer than an hour and he was ready for bed or his truck needed a cleaning. Keeping trips short and close to home was best.

"I guess we will see what happens." Rick wasn't about to rule anything out. It was possible to figure out a way to double up on a trip to the city. His father would like to see him come to the company office now and then, so his father might approve of a young lady with the power to persuade Rick to come to the city. It was getting harder to get his father to like anything he did or anyone he met from Lemon Grove. Molly wasn't from here, and that would make his father happy.

But would Rick be happy? He hated the drive to the city and found it difficult to picture being back there permanently. Then again, being with Molly made him happy, and this was the happiest he had been in some time. Molly made him smile and laugh. She made him want to think about the future, beyond quiet moments at the cabin. He had a renewed outlook on life whenever she was around, and that wasn't something that could be dismissed easily.

Rick's phone rang in his pocket and he checked the display before placing it on the table beside him.

"Aren't you going to answer that?" Molly asked, gesturing to the phone.

The last thing he wanted was to answer a call from Robert Fletcher. "He can leave a message."

"It's okay," she said. "I don't mind." Molly leaned over and stroked the top of Hudson's head.

The phone continued to vibrate and chime on the tabletop before coming to an abrupt stop.

"See?" Rick pushed the phone to the side. "Not important."

Once again, the phone chimed and buzzed. Robert was calling again.

"Maybe it is important."

Rick sighed as he held the phone, hovering his finger over the phone icon. He took a breath and answered the call.

"Robert."

"Rick, my boy. How are you?" Robert's voice seemed more energetic than usual.

Rick looked across at Molly and rolled his eyes, trying to communicate his displeasure over the caller on the other end. "I'm good, Robert. Just out having breakfast."

"Are you at the café? I could swing by and—"

"No, thank you. I'm with a friend. What can I do for you?"

Robert cleared his throat and laughed. "Well, Rick, I heard from Valerie's father, Charles Turner, that you were ready to look at my offer."

"You heard wrong." His firm voice caught Molly's attention, who sat straight in her seat.

"Oh, he assured me you were serious. He mentioned something about you and Valerie getting back together."

Rick's eyes widened, and he struck his knees on the underside of the table as he rose. "I don't know where he got that from."

"It's not true, then?"

He turned away from the look of concern on Molly's face, while trying to hide his own. Too many people in Rick's life were connected to Robert. Charles Turner, his parents, Valerie... Anything he said on this call would get back to them and he wasn't ready to deal with the consequences that would follow if Robert spun the conversation to put Rick in a tight spot.

"Alright, I might have said something to them about you bringing by another offer."

"And?"

Rick ran his hand through his hair and took another breath. All he needed was time to figure out what to do next. It is one thing to turn down Robert Fletcher, but a whole different issue for Charles Turner to think he was getting back together with Valerie. That meant his parents thought the same, and even Valerie. All because he had to go back to the city for that stupid meeting.

"You asked me to think about it, so I am. I won't let you rush me, Robert."

"Oh, of course not. Take your time. I'm happy we're talking. Let me know if you have questions. I'd be willing to meet with you any time."

He felt sick as he placed the phone back on the table and slid back into his seat.

"What was that all about?" Molly asked. "Not that it is any of my business. You just didn't seem that happy about whatever you were talking about."

"That was Robert Fletcher," he said. Rick pushed his phone to the edge of the table, wishing it would fall to the ground and shatter. "He wants to buy my cabin."

"Buy your cabin? That's a good thing."

"Only if you are interested in selling."

"And you're not?"

Rick shook his head and grabbed his coffee, taking a long sip. "Nope. Robert owns Lemon Eagle Resort and wants to buy the cabin so he can tear it down and expand his property. He recently changed his offer to buy up most of my acreage while leaving me with the cabin and some yard space."

"And you don't want that, either?"

"Not at all. His guests tear up the forest with their off-road vehicles and make a bunch of noise. I'd get no sleep. And if he built more cabins back there, it wouldn't feel like the oasis it currently is."

"I'd love to live in a place where someone approached me to buy my house. Not that I own a house, but there are homes that sit on the market forever. If someone walked up to me with the right price, I'd sell."

"Even if it was your forever home?"

"A home is what you make of it. A house is a building, not a home. If you sell it for a profit, you could get something you'd like even more."

"You're sounding like Robert." Rick looked at Hudson, asleep at their feet. What would uprooting him from his home do to the old dog? This area is all Hudson has known. He wouldn't be able to wander in a new neighborhood. He'd become lost for sure. To confine him to a fenced yard would be no way for Hudson to spend his last months or years. "Sometimes a profit isn't worth the sacrifice."

Molly crossed her arms. "How much is a place in Lemon Grove worth?"

"Depends on the place."

"Okay. What has he offered you for your place?"

Rick took another sip of coffee. It was embarrassing for Rick to admit he was turning down Robert's offer of three million for a cabin he bought for four-hundred thousand. Any smart investor would jump at the offer, but he couldn't. He'd be giving up too much.

"I'm sorry," she whispered. "I shouldn't have asked."

"It's alright. I don't enjoy talking about money all that much, and it seems like that's all Robert Fletcher wants to talk about. My cabin is worth more to me than the money." Molly rotated her coffee mug on the table before lifting it to her lips. "The last offer he gave me was for three million."

Her mouthful of coffee landed back into her mug. "I'm sorry. What?"

"I know. It's a lot of money."

"Yeah. Are you serious? Three million?"

Rick picked up his phone and turned it screen down onto the table. "Yes, but I'm not interested in selling."

Molly laughed and lowered her mug. "Rick, I understand finding that special place you want to call home, but we're talking about three million dollars here. How many places in Lemon Grove sell for that amount?"

"None. I'm a fool for not selling. Hudson has lived his entire life here, and I can't imagine moving him away from the only place he's known. Even if I kept the house and sold the land, Hudson couldn't roam through the resort property. I know that Robert Fletcher would complain to me and demand I keep him off the land the minute I sold it, even though it hasn't mattered to Robert how many times his guests have been on my property over the years."

"You could find a place with an enormous yard for less than

three million dollars. Even half of that." Molly clasped her coffee mug in both hands and sighed. "I don't want to tell you want to do. It is your place, and it means a lot to you. I just think opportunities like this don't come along all that often. Do what is best for you and Hudson, and if you feel that means staying in Lemon Grove, then that's what you should do."

Rick raised his mug. "You're right." He took a sip as Patsy exited the café and rounded the corner holding a tray of biscuits.

"I thought I saw you two still out here."

"What have you got there?" Rick asked. Patsy never came outside with unordered treats. She was snooping for information to feed the rumor mill.

Patsy slid the tray onto the table and placed a plate of biscuits in front of them. "These are cranberry biscuits. I am considering putting them on the menu and wanted to get your opinion of them, first."

"Mmm." Molly was the first to take a bite and closed her eyes. "Oh, Patsy. These are delicious. I'd love to get the recipe."

"You can have it when you buy the café. Those kinds of secrets will go to the new owner. I can't be giving my secrets away for free."

Rick laughed and picked up his biscuit. "Molly and I were talking about your place. If she talks her business partner into it—"

"Shush." Molly took another bite and Rick winked.

Patsy's usual smile had grown twice as wide. "Lemon Grove is a special place. If you stay, I'm sure you will be very happy here. Keep talking to her, Rick. See if you can strike a deal for me."

"I'll do my best."

"Oh, stop." Molly pushed Rick's plate toward him. "Eat your biscuit."

Patsy scooped up their empty dishes and strolled back into the café, leaving Rick and Molly to continue their conversation alone. What Patsy had observed must have satisfied her and she was on her way to share her findings with her friends. Soon, everyone in Lemon Grove would know he was out at the café with Molly, and it didn't bother Rick one bit. In fact, he wanted them to know. If his town friends wanted him to be happy, they would help him convince her to stay.

"You were saying something earlier about opportunities," he said.

"Yeah. So?" Molly hid behind her coffee mug.

"The café is an opportunity."

"Not a three million dollar opportunity."

He rose from his chair and held out his hand. "Who said the opportunity had anything to do with money?"

CHAPTER SEVENTEEN

"So?" Carla sang into the phone. "How was your date with Rick?"

Molly giggled and glanced over her shoulder at the occupied campsites nearby, where new campers were focused on setting up their sites or preparing their meals. None appeared interested in her recounting the tale of her date with Rick earlier that day.

"He took me to the café for coffee and breakfast. It was nice."

"What else?"

"There is no what else."

"Oh, come on. Spill the details. Did he pick you up in his car?"

Molly adjusted her blanket over her legs and made herself comfortable in her camping chair. Carla would not let her get away with a shortened version of events.

"His dog, Hudson, arrived in the morning like he always does, and then Rick came in his truck. He had dressed up a bit."

"How dressed up? Are we talking about a suit? Did he look handsome?"

Molly laughed and pulled her knees to her chest. "Not a suit. Just a nice button-down shirt and jeans. He looked handsome. And he smelled nice."

"I love when a man smells good. Keep going," Carla crooned.

She reflected on Rick exiting his truck to greet Hudson. Carla wanted not only to know what he looked like, but Molly could tell she was fishing to learn how much interest Molly had in him. They were like high school students giggling in the corner over the cute boy in the hallway. Carla always had some guy that caught her eye, and Molly would listen to her friend gush over his positive attributes. Now it was her turn.

"Rick got Hudson ready, and he held my hand while we walked to the—"

"Wait." Molly heard a door close near Carla. "He held your hand?" she whispered. "Again?"

"What do you mean, again?"

"After the way you talked about the first time he held your hand, you made it sound as if he was only trying to keep you from tripping and landing on your face. If he held your hand again, he clearly likes you."

Molly smiled and tucked a strand of hair behind her ear, sliding her fingers down to the tip before letting go. Carla was probably right. Rick had made enough flirty comments on their date to communicate his interest, but Molly still needed assurance that his gesture was genuine. After Brad, she tended to be cautious and not become excited when some guy showed a slight interest. Holding her hand was a friendly gesture and not a public declaration. For all Molly knew, Rick might have a string of women he has been flirting with.

"Who knows what he's thinking?" Molly said.

"You always downplay everything. Why don't you ever just enjoy the moment?"

"I enjoyed the moment. It's you who is trying to make this a bigger deal."

Carla sighed, and Molly heard Carla wrestle with the phone. Most likely she was rolling her eyes as she moved the phone to her other ear.

"I only want you to be happy, Molly."

"I know."

"Then roll with it. Flirt back for once."

For once. Carla made it sound as though Molly never flirted, but she was only selective when she did. If Carla had her way, Molly would flirt with every man she encountered. "What do you call holding his hand?"

"A step in the right direction."

Molly closed her eyes and exhaled. This relationship was already moving faster than she was used to. They had only met and Carla viewed holding hands as a step in the right direction? Holding hands was enough for now. To roll with it, as Carla wanted, Molly needed to not resist as much as she had been. Jumping into something with someone as unknown as Rick seemed risky, and Molly wasn't sure how much risk she was willing to accept. Not when she planned to leave in a week.

"I've been thinking..." Molly said as she tapped her foot against the gravel pad.

"Don't do that, Molly. You always talk yourself out of good things when you overthink them."

"That's not true." The silence on the other end communicated Carla's disagreement with her statement. "Am I being ridiculous?"

"What do you mean?"

"To think this might work. He's here in Lemon Grove while my life is in the city. Rick isn't interested in moving back, so what would we do if things got serious? One of us would have to move and we have the coffee shop to run. I can't leave you to run everything."

"Don't worry, Molly. If this is meant to be, we'll figure something out." No hurdle was ever insurmountable to Carla. She would see that Molly was free to pursue whatever Carla deemed good for her.

"It's bad enough I've taken off for a couple of weeks and left you to cover for me. I mean, Lemon Grove is pretty far. I'd be looking at regularly taking a day or two off to visit him. If he came out to the city, I'd hate for him to have to sit in the coffee shop all day while I worked a shift."

"Again, don't worry." Carla chuckled. "I'm doing just fine with my cousin here. You need to stop worrying about me and enjoy what is going on with you. You've found someone, Molly. How long has that taken?"

"A long time." She hated admitting the truth. After Brad, she took some time away from dating while she licked her wounds. It took time to reach this point, and she had allowed the past to hold her back long enough.

"And you are going to ruin everything with doubt. Rick sounds like a great guy."

That's because he was a great guy. Had Molly not given him another chance at having their coffee date, she would have missed his best qualities. While the idea of a relationship made her heart beat fast and forced her to fight the urge to run in the opposite direction, a part of her insisted she stick around and see where this went. It was a quiet voice, almost drowned out by fear from her fragile heart, afraid of being led toward another heartbreak.

After giving him a chance, he had already proven he would follow through. He didn't run off when the first coffee date didn't work out, and he asked again. Rick had a kindness about him in how he treated others and his dog. Her quiet voice increased in volume, telling her not to miss an opportunity for him to prove he was worth the investment.

The idea of leaving Carla to manage everything on her own didn't feel right, but if Molly could arrange things so the business wouldn't suffer when she spent time with Rick, it might work. She only needed to find a solution where if Rick were a dead end, there would be nothing to lose besides her own time.

Buying Patsy's café seemed strange on paper. It didn't fit an urban business plan, but it did make sense in light of her budding romance. Owning the coffee shop in Lemon Grove would give her the ability to visit Rick and contribute to the business. Carla could be responsible for the day-to-day operations of the city shop, while Molly focused on Lemon Grove. If Carla meant it when she said they could make something work, then she might consider continuing their partnership with a Lemon Grove location.

Molly felt the excitement build within her as she imagined working on the other side of Patsy's counter, making coffees and treats for the tourists as they visited the town. She could share tips on the trails they should hike and the shops they should visit. And then she thought of Rick standing in the doorway, watching her as the sun shone behind him. She could spend time with him every day, and it would not limit them to weekend visits. It would take a move to Lemon Grove, but the little town was growing on her. It could work.

"I wasn't going to bring this up," she said. Molly paused, trying to think of the words to describe Patsy's café to Carla. Cute? Quaint? Busy? Successful?

"Okay…?"

"You remember how we've talked about expanding the business?"

"Oh!" Carla shouted. "That reminds me. I have news for you. Do you recall Peter, my realtor friend?" She paused long enough for Molly to open her mouth. "I told him a few weeks ago how we had considered expanding. So, get this." Carla was already out of breath. "He walked into the shop yesterday and told me about a storefront space coming available near 8th Avenue. It's perfect!"

It was always Carla's dream to find a place on 8th. To her, it was their destiny to find a shop on that street, and it seemed the opportunity had arrived. A location near 8th Avenue would be perfect. The street and foot traffic made it a prime location for a coffee shop, which was why it had been their first choice when they prepared to open their current store. When they made the decision to go into business together, they had to search for another location when nothing was available on 8th at their price point. Until now.

"Wait until you see it," Carla said.

"Are you saying you've already been there?"

"Yes. I'm sorry, Molly. I should have waited for you to come back, but when he told me about it, I had to check it out. These places go fast. If we want to do it, we'd have to move on it before someone else does." Her voice rushed with excitement.

There would be no space to talk about Lemon Grove now. Not with 8th Avenue being an option. "How much do they want for it?"

Carla went quiet, and Molly understood why. Molly would not like the price. Maybe Lemon Grove wasn't off the table.

"Think about how much we'd make once we opened."

"Carla, we can't be—"

"Don't say anything. Not until you see the numbers. I'm working on a business plan and once you read it, you'll see how we can afford it."

"I appreciate how much you want to find a place on 8th, Carla, but I don't see how we can afford it. Why not look for a place somewhere cheap for our next store?"

A cupboard door slammed in the background. There would be no negotiating today, at least not while Molly was hours away. "You're always looking for the easy route, Molly. We need to take risks in business if we're going to get anywhere."

There was Carla with her advice again. "Did Peter tell you this?" Molly asked.

"Peter didn't have to tell me. We need to make a move at some point, Molly, and I think this is our chance. Don't worry, I don't want you to decide on it until you get back. I can send you some pictures of the interior to look at on your phone. I already have ideas about how we can fix up the place."

More expense. The cost for the real estate was one thing, but the renovations would add more strain to their non-existent budget, and it was a challenge to keep Carla from blowing the budget on their first store.

"I'm sorry, Molly." Carla changed her tone. She was calm and soft. "You were trying to tell me something about your trip and I took over the conversation."

"Don't worry about it," Molly said. There was no point in bringing it up now. "We can talk about it later." It would be impossible to persuade Carla to consider Lemon Grove. Not since she had her heart set on the location on 8th. Besides the price tag, how could Molly compete with that? A café in Lemon Grove would cost far less than a store on 8th, and the cozy interior Patsy had created wouldn't need much changing. Molly could be content to keep it as is. Carla would disagree. She was all about modern design and chic atmosphere, even if it wasn't Molly's aesthetic. Who was Molly to disagree?

"Are you sure?" Carla asked. "I didn't mean to interrupt. I'd like to hear about what you have to say."

"It was nothing. We can talk about it when I get back."

"Alright. I'm excited for you to see this place. You're going to like it."

"I'm sure I will. I just want to make sure it is the right place. Please don't get too settled on it."

"You know me. I don't get stuck on anything."

That wasn't true, and Molly knew it. Carla was famous for latching on to an idea and never letting it go. If Molly were to turn down the new location, who knows what Carla would say. It could cause the end of their partnership. There had to be a good reason for the place on 8th not to work, since Carla had already convinced herself the budget would not be the issue. Molly would need to accept that Carla was ready to sign on the dotted line. Molly would either need to sign along with her or risk their friendship, and that wasn't a choice she wanted to make. She already had one relationship she was struggling with. She didn't need to worry about a second.

CHAPTER EIGHTEEN

*R*ick's fingers trembled with excitement as he pressed the phone to his ear. He was thankful for his old dog and his matchmaking skills. Even if he thought it was too early in the morning to bother Molly, he could always use Hudson as an excuse to hear her voice.

"Good morning," she said as she answered.

"Hey, you." What a stupid way to address her. "Has Hudson arrived yet?"

"He arrived about twenty minutes ago. When will I see you?" She cleared her throat. "You know. To pick him up."

Rick smiled and picked up his keys from the counter. "I am on my way out the door now. It would seem I have an empty calendar today. Not one work meeting. Would you like to visit that waterfall you tried to hike to with Hudson the other day?"

"He won't be too tired?"

"Not Hudson. In fact, he'll have a ton of extra energy when we get there."

Rick held his breath, waiting for Molly to break the silence on the other end. "Hudson seemed concerned about something on the trail the last time. Don't you think we should stay away if there are bears in the area?"

"If we stayed away from every place with bears, we'd never go into the forest. We just have to respect that this is their home and be cautious. As long as we keep talking on the trail, we'll be fine. I'll even bring a can of bear spray along as an extra precaution. How does that sound?"

He listened as Molly talked to Hudson, asking him if he wanted to go for a hike on the trail. Rick loved the way she included Hudson, talking with him and giving him extra love and care. None of the other women he dated ever gave Hudson this amount of attention. They treated him as a nuisance when he tagged along with Rick on dates. There was something special about this one. She cared, sometimes a little too much, but her caring caught his attention and held it.

"Okay," Molly said with an energy to her voice, as if the idea excited her. "What time will you be here?"

"About ten minutes. I'm going to stop and get some gas first."

"We'll be ready."

It relieved Rick that no one was around to spot him skipping to his truck. He had scored another date with the most beautiful woman at the campground. If he convinced her to stay, she would be the most beautiful woman in all of Lemon Grove.

He hummed to himself as he drove down the road toward the town, not remembering the last time he was this happy. His change in mood was because of her. Molly changed his life for the better by breaking his routine. Before her, he spent his days puttering around his cabin, making repairs that he should have paid someone else to do. Sure, it saved him money, but it filled the lonely hours. He didn't want to admit that the cabin was too large for a single guy and his dog. Yes, he had bought it believing he would one day have a family of his own, but sadly, it takes time to find that special someone. Longer than even he had imagined.

Had his schedule played out as planned, he would have married over a year ago. It seemed he was on pace when he started dating Valerie, and when he proposed it was right on schedule, but his questioning of that decision brought it to an end before it truly began. Now, in light of this new chapter with Molly, it could turn out that the wait was worth it. He could see a happier future with Molly. One where they would spend their evenings sitting around a campfire by the cabin with Hudson at their feet. The pair would explore the trails in their spare time and Molly would become a familiar face around town with his friends waving as they passed by.

He envisioned children in their future, filling the bench in the backseat of his pickup truck. Sliding his hand along the steering wheel, he laughed to himself. Not many guys he knew fantasized about having kids, and the pickup truck might end up being traded in for a minivan, but even that idea he found himself strangely without objection. He'd be proud to be the minivan-driving dad in Lemon Grove. While there were a few families with children, for those that were in Lemon Grove, the mothers drove the family vehicle. He had no problem being the one to change that.

If he had a therapist, they would surely tell him his desire for a family stemmed from his feelings toward his own parents. Too busy with company meetings, they were never around, and when his parents were home, they weren't interested in hearing about the interests of a child. He couldn't recall a single occasion when they attended one of his sports games. Time and time again, he would search the crowd to see the parents and guests of other players sitting in the stands and never once saw the faces of his own family. The only consistent attendee was his best friend's mom, whom his parents paid to drive him to games.

That wouldn't happen to his children. He would be present in their lives and celebrate the things important to them, no matter how insignificant they may seem.

Rick squeezed the steering wheel and exhaled to reduce the flipping sensation in his stomach. As he drove, he promised himself to do his best to make this work, not only in the present but also in the future. He wouldn't squander this opportunity. If Molly was as interested in him as he was in her, this had the potential to go somewhere. There was still much to learn about her, and from what he saw, she was definitely worth the effort.

Turning into the campground, the flip-flops returned, and he focused on slowing his breathing to regain control. The sound of the truck's engine and the gravel beneath the tires seemed amplified, along with the sound of his heart pounding in his ears. Through his windshield he watched the road bend with each occupied site entering his view, but there was only one site he wanted to find: site twenty-three.

He grinned as he spotted Molly standing at the end of her site with Hudson by her side. This was a sight he would remember for years to come. Molly was as beautiful as the day before and the day he met her. She had pulled her hair back into a ponytail that dangled behind her. She cinched her jacket at her waist and wore jeans that hugged her legs. It took all his strength not to jump out of the moving truck to wrap his arms around her.

Putting his truck into park, he opened the door. Hudson rushed past him and jumped inside, occupying the passenger seat while he wagged his tail. Rick fixed his eyes on Molly, who was laughing at Hudson's impatience. Rick reached his arms out and stepped toward her, expecting her to step into his embrace.

Molly grabbed his hands and held them in the space between them. Not quite the picture in his mind, but he'd take it. "He's been waiting for you."

"How about you?" he whispered.

"I've only been waiting for a little while. I had to clean up after breakfast."

It wasn't the answer he had been hoping for. Perhaps he hadn't made his intentions clear enough. He decided to go for it, giving her arms a pull toward him and breaking her hold on his hands. He wrapped his arms around her back and held her against his chest, resting his chin on the top of her head.

"I hope you slept well."

"I did," she said. Her arms drifted to his shoulder blades and Rick inhaled. For a moment, he considered canceling their walk to the waterfall. Standing here at the end of the campsite with her in his arms appealed to him more. "Are you ready to go?" Molly asked.

"If you are."

She leaned back and smiled. "Hudson may drive the truck himself if we don't get going." Molly's gaze shifted to the dog, now lying across the front seat, staring at them through the open door.

"I think you're right."

Rick held Molly's hand and led her to the passenger door and kept it open as she climbed inside. A gentleman never skipped the little things.

As they drove toward the parking lot at the trailhead to the waterfall, Rick snuck look after look at the woman beside him. The truck felt cozier with her in the passenger seat. It had been empty for far too long and when someone had sat there, they were the wrong person. She was the perfect fit for him, and he struggled to keep his eyes on the road. He wondered if she had noticed him looking at her. If she had, she never gave it away. Molly seemed content to look out the window at the view as it passed by or pet Hudson as he nudged her cheek for attention. It was a scene that warmed him and he wanted to see repeated as many times as possible.

Hudson whined as they turned the corner and his tail beat against the backseat. They were almost at the parking lot, and he was eager to get out to begin their walk.

"Are you ready for your walk?" Molly asked.

Hudson continued to whine and moved from one side window to the next.

Rick parked the truck and rushed to the passenger side, hoping to hold the door open for Molly. By the time he reached the other side, the door was already open, and she was climbing out. Not skipping a beat, Rick held the door steady as Molly stepped outside. If he couldn't open the door, he could at least be a gentleman and offer his hand, but her gaze was on the ground where her feet landed.

"It looks like no one else is here, again," she said, looking up and stopping on his extended hand.

Rick pulled his hand back and slapped his side, calling Hudson out of the truck. "It's usually quiet here. It's why I like it on the trail. There is hardly anyone to bother you."

"You won't find a place like this in the city."

"That's for sure. I've tried a few times to walk in the parks downtown and people were always crowding the path."

Hudson leaped to Rick's side and slapped his tail against the dirt. Rick grabbed Hudson's leash from his truck, just in case. They shouldn't need it on an empty trail like this, but he always carried one with him should he need to keep Hudson close. As loyal as Hudson was, he had a weakness for squirrels. Even though they surrounded him daily, he still gave the occasional chase. Should Hudson want to chase a furry rodent, he might need Rick to encourage him to leave it be while it protested from a branch above. It is a wonder Hudson ever makes it to his destination at the campground, given his love of nature.

"I know what you mean about people," Molly said, reaching for the leash. He let her have it. "They are always riding their bikes or crowding the path. There is no place for regular walkers to go for a stroll. Plus, I prefer not seeing high rises behind the trees."

"You're in luck." Rick watched as she clasped the leash to

Hudson's collar. He wouldn't get to run free today. "The only thing you'll see behind the trees today are mountains."

"Just what I was hoping to see."

Rick almost made another flirty crack about her wanting to see him on the trail but kept his comment to himself. He couldn't keep making remarks like that. He needed to take it slow and not scare her off. Things seemed to be going well, and it was easy for him to get carried away in his excitement. The only way to make sure he didn't say or do something stupid that would make her run in the opposite direction was for him to calm down. Already he wasn't sure what she was thinking. She might be still questioning her feelings, and he would not give her a reason to doubt what they have. Rick was determined to do all he could to convince Molly that this would work. That they should be together. Here, in Lemon Grove.

CHAPTER NINETEEN

*M*olly noticed a pit form in her stomach as they reached the point of the trail where Hudson blocked her path. She took some comfort in knowing Hudson never growled once on their walk with Rick and showed no signs of concern. He happily sniffed at the plants beside them and moved side to side with his nose to the ground. His ears stood upright, as did his tail. The warmth of Rick's hand against hers made her feel safe. Rick knew this area better than her, and if he wasn't concerned, she shouldn't be... or at least she would try not to be.

Her pace quickened as she heard the waterfall ahead. A small creek flowed beside them, carrying the water away from the falls. The sounds were familiar to her, recalling memories of camping trips with her family and friends. She didn't go often into the woods, but when she did, she enjoyed the sounds of nature. Her favorite photograph was of her family posing next to a viewpoint overlooking cascading waterfalls, which resembled more of a steep river than the towering ribbons of mist most would associate with the word. Her family had stood smiling as a friendly passerby volunteered to take their picture. She owned few photos with all four of them together on trips. One of the family most often took on the role of photographer, which meant they were not in the picture. The sound of the water brought back the warm memories, but from now on she would associate the sound of a waterfall with Rick.

He stood several inches taller than her, which made him appear strong, although probably no match for a bear. Rick promised the can of bear spray attached to his waist would be effective. He would surely protect her if they encountered danger on the trail and he smiled as she walked alongside him. Despite only meeting him a week ago, she found it easy to trust him.

"There it is," he said, pointing to a break in the trees ahead.

Molly saw the white pillows of water rolling over the edge of the cliff before dropping out of sight behind the trees.

"Is there a viewpoint?"

"Oh, yes. It will be worth the walk."

Eager to see the view, she walked ahead of Rick. Her hand, still holding his, lingered behind her. Rick picked up his pace and walked beside her. He gave her hand a squeeze and now walked faster than her. She matched his pace. Soon, they were moving at a light jog and laughed as they ran down the trail toward the falls. Hudson wagged his tail, running ahead of them as far as his leash would allow, stopping only to investigate a smell at the side of the trail.

"Wow!" Molly froze on the path as the viewpoint opened up before her. A large viewing platform at the rocky ledge jutted out into the open valley below.

Molly and Rick strolled toward the platform, damp from the mist and spray of the falls. The first drops hit the tip of Molly's nose, followed by her cheeks. The mist continued to gather on her skin, forming water droplets that rolled down to the point of her chin before dripping onto the front of her shirt. She looked at Rick, who rubbed the side of his face with his palm and ran the water through his hair, making it stand upright. He looked good no matter how he styled his hair. She watched a water drop roll down beside his ear and follow the line of his jaw, and she wrestled with thoughts of reaching across to wipe the drop away. It would be a sweet gesture, and one that would definitely communicate her romantic interest. Was she ready for what would come next if she did?

She still needed to talk to Carla about the coffee shop, but with Carla's heart so set on the location on 8th, there would be no discussing Lemon Grove. That would mean she would have to think about remaining in the city, and would that work for Rick? It would be ridiculous to date someone who she wouldn't be able to marry because neither wanted to move.

The view of the waterfall spoke to her and created an ache deep within her. She would hate leaving this behind... and her feelings for Rick. Their relationship could force Rick to trade away nature, with its rich dirt paths and tall trees, for concrete sidewalks and metal light posts. Or, if she moved to Lemon Grove, it would take Molly away from her friend and their business. The more she pondered it, the more she dreaded them needing to make the choice.

This was why people bought vacation homes and time-share properties. They hated leaving their new favorite place and dreamed of returning. Within days, Lemon Grove already became Molly's second home. How did a small town off the highway with so little to offer capture her heart? There really wasn't much to the place. If she wanted the best in life, she must remain in the city. But she never needed all the best.

Rick leaned on the railing that protected him from tumbling down into the ravine. She could tell he didn't care that the mist enveloped him and drenched his clothing in moisture. Molly turned away as heat rushed to her cheeks. How did she end up meeting a kindhearted and attractive guy like Rick? Carla would fight her for him. In fact, if Molly took a picture of Rick and sent it to her, Carla would probably suggest that Rick model for their shop advertising.

"What's on your mind?" Rick asked, now leaning on one arm to face her.

"Oh, I'm just trying not to think about work." She dared not tell him she pictured him posing for a photo, dressed in a suit while holding a silver tray balancing two steaming mugs of coffee with their coffee shop logo splashed along the bottom. He would be perfect to lure potential customers to their store.

Rick smiled and pulled her close. "I hoped this would take your mind off of it."

Molly wanted to wiggle free from his hold, but she let herself linger in his arms, carelessly allowing him to get close. What would he say when he learned Carla planned to expand the shop in the city? There would be no room for a future with him, no matter how much she wanted it. But his arm slipped around her waist as he held her close, and she didn't resist. Carla had promised she would help to make this work. If that was the truth, Molly must give Rick a chance. In the meantime, she would just need to be cautious.

Her phone chimed repeatedly in her coat pocket, and she pulled it out. Carla had sent twelve images.

"What's that?" Rick asked.

"My friend Carla. She's sent me some pictures. I can see them later." Molly stuffed the phone in her pocket and Rick nudged her.

"Look at them now. What pictures is your friend sending you?" The sparkle in his eyes showed his genuine interest. "Is this the friend you run the coffee shop with?"

Molly sighed and held the phone in front of them. "It is." He would find out eventually and they both needed the reality check. This won't work, and Rick might as well understand that now. "Carla found a property she's interested in."

"A place to live?"

"A place to expand the coffee shop. On 8th Street. If it had been affordable before, she would have had us open on 8th from day one."

"I see." His voice grew quiet, and Molly wondered for a moment if his grip had loosened before he tightened his grasp once again. "I can see why you're trying to keep your mind off of work."

"I'm not doing a very good job of it."

"Perhaps I can help." He pulled her toward him and cupped his hand to her cheek. Leaning in, he pressed his lips to hers.

Her mind swirled with every reason this wouldn't work. The list seemed endless from the coffee shop to her apartment, but her thoughts were quieted as she sank deeper into the moment. Molly had fallen into the warm embrace of a man who, it would seem, was a very good kisser, judging by the electrifying sensation of his lips against hers. Her mind rushed with imaginative thoughts of them spending day after day in each other's arms, running through the forest, laughing and giggling. The vision grew stronger and brighter the longer he kissed her. Reality hit. Soon, they must spend more days apart than they would together, and they would quickly discover their relationship would unravel the longer they were separated. With her at a distance counted in miles, they'd find they had less in common and what developed between them in Lemon Grove would disintegrate, along with her fanciful dreams.

Finally, he leaned back and their lips parted. Rick smiled and Molly exhaled. There was too much to think about. So much worry that shouldn't be in one's mind during a kiss. If she had allowed it, the kiss would have completely consumed her and made her completely forget the obstacles in their way. Rick made her want to be reckless. She couldn't be, no matter how much she wanted this.

"Did it work?" he whispered.

"Mmm hmm." There was a grin on her face. Even if her mind

had her thinking a million different thoughts, she wasn't about to hide that was an amazing kiss. She would, however, hide that she had thought about other things than his lips on hers.

Rick smiled and rested his chin on the top of her head. It was impulsive to kiss her like he had, but it was an opportunity he couldn't pass up. When else would he have the chance to kiss her by a waterfall? By romance standards, they couldn't be in a more perfect setting. The waterfall was a postcard, and the surrounding mist created a veil of reflected light. Surely Molly could appreciate the moment for what it was. He thought she had. At first, he felt her embrace the kiss. It was when he suddenly sensed her body tense that he realized the kiss needed to end. Perhaps he had overdone it and should have released her before she had second thoughts. Something made her tense up, and he doubted it was him... or at least he hoped it wasn't.

He had to compete with her friend, Carla, and their business. It wouldn't be an easy battle, but one he was determined to win. Her friend may want to open a second business in the city, and there was nothing wrong with that, but Molly shouldn't suffer because of it. Why should one sacrifice for the dream of the other? All he needed was a few more days with Molly to prove that this was worth whatever the struggle she was going through.

The kiss, as brief as it was, made him hopeful for more. Her lips were as soft as he imagined, and he felt relieved to have shown her how much he had fallen for her. He wanted to communicate his desire for her, his affection, his dream of a future. It was a lot to expect from a kiss, and perhaps his passion came across a little too strong, leaving her to misinterpret his intentions. While he came from a rich family background, he was never a playboy. He wasn't the type to flirt with a girl and ditch them after a few days. He was better than that. When she tensed up, he knew he had to let her go. She clearly needed some breathing room or a change of pace. That was fine. He would let her lead the way on that, but he wouldn't stop sharing memorable moments with her, such as standing by the waterfall while the mist continued to rain down on them, coating their skin in a thin layer of water.

"I like being here with you," he whispered.

She nodded her head against his chest and sniffled.

"Are you alright?"

Molly nodded again and gripped the back of his jacket.

He guessed the sniffle was a sign of something else. There was something bothering her… as much as he wanted to pull it out of her, he thought it best to wait for her to share when she was comfortable. In the meantime, he needed to make some decisions of his own. This woman would either stay in Lemon Grove or would go to the city to build her coffee shop empire. If he really wanted to be with her, he might need to rethink his own plans. Was she enough to entice him back to the city?

Rick tried not to think about the day that would inevitably come when she would need to return home. He had known the risk when he met her, yet he still took the chance. He had to. Rick would have beaten himself up if he had let her go without a try. Already, she had found a solid place in his heart, and he still had so much to learn about her. They might have a lifetime ahead of them to get to know each other. They merely needed time to give their relationship a chance to grow. With the number of meetings he had on his work calendar in the days ahead, time would be hard to find.

"I have an idea," he said.

"What's that?" She slowly slipped her head out from beneath his chin. Molly wiped her eyes with her sleeve and stared up at him with a smile.

Maybe she was thinking the same thing he was. Saying

goodbye was going to be hard. They couldn't waste their last days together being sad about their future separation. They had to make the most of them and he would lead the way. "I have work to do this week, but there is a Farmers' Market in town that I'd like to take you to."

"What's at the Farmers' Market?"

"The local shops and home businesses set up stands with their merchandise. There are fresh foods to try, and best of all, live music."

"Really?"

"We have a local band that has been a staple at the Farmers' Market for thirty years, they tell me."

She laughed and nodded. "That sounds like a wonderful idea."

"It's not for a couple of days, but I thought maybe we needed something to look forward to. I'd like to come by and see you in the evening, if that's alright with you."

"I'd like that."

Rick breathed a sigh of relief. Part of him had worried she would turn him down. Whatever was on her mind made her sad, and if his mother taught him anything, a crying woman meant bad news.

"I think you're really going to like it. You're into plastic beads and tie-dyed shirts, right?"

CHAPTER TWENTY

*M*olly stared at her steaming mug of instant ground coffee and shivered. For several minutes, she stood in place, revisiting the day before. Her thoughts had kept her awake that night as she replayed the kiss by the waterfall. It was a magical kiss and one she wished never ended. Wrapped in her sleeping bag, she still felt the warmth of his lips against hers and the gentleness of his arms wrapped around her waist. No one ever held her like Rick had. Any interactions with previous boyfriends had been, by comparison, lifeless and cold. Rick showed that he wanted her. She wanted him, too, but the timing... oh, that terrible timing.

If only Carla had never told her about the shop on 8th. With the knowledge of expanding the business looming in the back of her mind, it put a damper on the date with Rick, and no matter how hard she tried to put the thoughts out of her head, she kept thinking about the day it would all come crashing down.

Her hands shook, and a chill of cool morning air blew up the back of her jacket, sending a shiver through her body. The thoughts about Rick and needing to return to the coffee shop in the city and her apartment were as cold as the mountains. The reality of what was coming brought a melancholy air to her vacation. Molly left the city sad, and now the sadness crept back in and weighed her heart down. She should be happy and enjoying the excitement a new relationship brings. Instead, she was wallowing in self-pity and worry. As Carla said, if it was supposed to happen, everything would work out. Molly and Rick could be together, even if she had to be in the city with the business. Still, the nagging thought lingered: maybe she didn't belong in the city at all and this entire trip had given her a fresh look at her life. It wasn't only the relationship that she wanted, but this, the quiet lifestyle, all of it. As much as she wanted to support Carla, leaving all this behind would be a mistake. Rick was only one of many reasons to stay in Lemon Grove, and there was a perfect opportunity with Patsy's café to have employment. It was as if she was being handed everything she was asking for, and she was rejecting it out of fear.

"Shoo! Go away," a woman shouted from the campsite across from her. "Go on. Get!"

Molly stepped to the side to look around their parked pickup truck at the front of the woman's campsite. A large fifth wheel camper touched the tree branches and took over much of the space. A unit that large and new would cost Molly a couple of years' worth of income and probably even more debt.

"Hudson!" Molly called. He hadn't come by her site yet, but if she had to guess...

The dog came galloping across the road toward her with his tail wagging in the air.

"There you are. I was wondering where you were. Did you have a good walk?"

"Is that your dog?" the woman called from across the street. She planted her fists against her hips, which she tilted at an angle to one side.

"Oh, he is—"

"You shouldn't allow your dog to wander into people's campsites like that. If you're going to bring a dog to a campground, the least you can do is tie him."

Was that what she sounded like when she first met Rick? If so, she's lucky he talked to her after such a rude introduction.

"Hudson is an old dog and enjoys visiting with the guests here."

"Well, the guests don't want to visit with him. Every campground we've visited, the guests have followed the rules. They should expect you to follow them, too."

Molly sensed the heat rising within her. She wanted nothing more than to unleash her frustration on this woman who knew nothing about Hudson and was assuming Molly was the owner. If she gave Molly a chance to explain, she'd understand.

"I am going to be letting the office know about this."

"Go ahead." Molly laughed. The woman wouldn't be happy to learn Hudson has free rein of the property.

The woman's mouth hung open as she waved her hands in the air in frustration. "Do you think the owners of this campground want some person allowing their dog to roam free and disturb the other guests?"

"Since I've been here, you're the only person who has complained to me and I have been here for a week. Hudson doesn't bother anyone. Isn't that right, Hudson?"

Upon hearing his name, the dog sat on the ground facing the woman and nuzzled Molly's hand.

"Well, if you will not correct that dog's behavior, you leave me with no choice. Henry!"

A tired-looking man peered out from beside their truck. "Yes?"

"We're going down to the office. We will not enjoy ourselves as long as this woman assumes she can allow her dog to wander into our site."

"It's just a dog—"

She raised her hand to silence him and marched to the back of the truck where they had an animated conversation out of earshot.

Molly glanced down at Hudson and whispered, "You sure picked the wrong site to visit this morning. Didn't you?"

Hudson beat his tail against the ground and licked her fingers.

"I know. But not everyone likes to have a dog visit them when they're camping. Don't worry. You can visit me anytime."

The man and woman hopped into their truck and pulled onto the road. The man kept his eyes straight ahead while the woman glared at Molly, who wore a wide smile on her face.

"She's about to get a big surprise. Come on." Molly slapped her side and walked to her chair to drape her blanket over her legs and sip on her coffee. Hudson flopped down at her feet and let out a loud sigh.

Molly had come a long way since she first arrived at the campsite. While it was hard to watch the behavior play out in front of her, she was much like the woman when she arrived. After being in Lemon Grove for a week, she now found she appreciated the small town and its quirks. Having a dog wander into a campsite wasn't a burden or inconvenience, but was a privilege. Hudson had brought joy and comfort to her during her stay. In fact, Hudson had brought much more than that. While he didn't have a direct hand in it, his presence led her to Rick. It was an unexpected surprise, but it never would have happened without Hudson.

Hudson continued to rest at her feet as she pulled out her phone and smiled. No doubt, Glenda would get an earful about the dog wandering around and the rude guest they encountered. It wouldn't be difficult for Glenda to figure out who the couple was talking about, if they gave Molly's site number. If only Molly could be there when they learned Hudson wasn't her dog. Would they apologize or act like it was all Molly's fault? Probably the latter. Glenda would call Rick, but Molly assumed calling him herself wouldn't hurt. Besides, she hadn't talked to him since yesterday, and it had been long enough since she heard his voice.

Molly held her breath as the phone rang. Her heart raced as she waited for Rick's voice on the other end. The nervous energy was exciting, and she hoped the feeling wouldn't go away. Sure, with time she would calm, but she hoped she would always want to hear his voice on the other end of the line. This was what she should have experienced in the past, and now that she had found it, she wouldn't settle for anything less.

The phone line clicked.

"This is Rick. Sorry, I can't take your call right now." He even sounded good in a voice message. "Please leave your name and number and I'll call you back. Thanks." The beep rang in her ear and she took a breath.

"Hi, Rick. It's Molly." Leaving a message wasn't in her plans, but he would call her back and that would have to do. "Hudson is at the campsite having his morning visit. The guests across from me aren't thrilled and are on their way to tell Glenda about him." She sighed. "Anyway, call me when you can and I'll see you when you pick him up." Or when he was planning to come by to see her. Hopefully, he still wanted to see her. She would be heartbroken if he was avoiding her call because their relationship had already run its course.

Molly stroked Hudson's fur as she tried to ease her disappointment. She would talk with Rick soon enough, but talking to him now would have been so much better than leaving a message. Knowing Rick, he would arrive soon to pick up Hudson, unless he needed to be in the city. He never mentioned plans to leave Lemon Grove today, and he hadn't called her to ask that she look after Hudson. She needed to wait, and when she saw him, they could make plans.

Within minutes, the couple's pickup returned to the campsite, and the woman stepped out of the truck, slamming the passenger door beside her.

"You could have said it wasn't your dog."

Molly rose from her chair. "I tried to tell you, but you wouldn't let me—"

"That woman in the office is just as rude as you. We're leaving."

"Sorry to hear that."

The man climbed out of the truck, looking even more exhausted than before. In silence, he gathered his tools from the compartment in the side of his trailer and got to work preparing his unit.

The woman moved to the front of the truck and stepped onto the road. "People like you ruin campgrounds for the rest of us," she shouted.

"Like me?" Molly laughed. There had been no problems in the campground until this woman arrived. In fact, Molly had enjoyed the quiet of the place and the nondisruptive coming and going of campers. Most people kept to themselves and were pleasant whenever they passed by. But this woman...

"Had you at least been upfront about this dog and not had such an attitude about it—"

Molly gestured to Hudson and turned away. "Come on, Hudson. We don't need to listen to this anymore."

"See?" she continued to shout. "You're encouraging it to stay here. If the guests here would be consistent and send the dog away whenever it comes around, then no one would have to deal with it wandering through their site."

Molly took a breath and patted at the blanket on the ground. Hudson curled up and kept a watchful eye on the woman.

"I used to think the same as you when I first arrived," Molly said. The woman's face remained unchanged. "When Hudson first came to my site, I shooed him away, and he left, but he came back. He is very sweet and is loved by the whole town. Everyone knows Hudson."

"It shouldn't be the expectation that everyone has to visit with a dog. I don't like dogs and I don't want one walking in my campsite."

No surprise there that the woman didn't like dogs. "Well, I appreciate his visits. He comes and sees me every day and sleeps at my feet until his owner comes to pick him up."

"That owner should have his dog taken away." She took another step forward, pointing at Hudson. "Its owner should lock that dog in a yard and not allow it to come onto private property like this. When the owner comes here to get his dog, I am going to tell him as much."

Oh, boy. Molly noticed the gut twisting sensation of embarrassment. Rick didn't need to see Molly's old behaviors on display from another camper. Now that she could see how poorly she had behaved when they first met, she didn't want to relive it. She much preferred her fresh approach to handling Hudson. Giving him his freedom as an old dog seemed more humane than what the woman was demanding. Molly had felt the same at one time and didn't want to go back there or act similarly.

"He's a nice guy," Molly said, hoping to give Rick a chance at surviving the encounter.

"I don't care if he's a nice guy. He is a terrible dog owner, and he ruined our stay here by letting his dog do whatever it wants. We were hoping to stay here for a few days and rest, but we have to leave."

"I'm sure if you could see the positives of this place, you'd find a reason to stay."

"What is that supposed to mean?"

"I think you were looking for a reason to not like the place and you found it. I am sorry for your husband, who has to pack up your site."

The woman's mouth dropped open and snapped shut. Her hands opened and closed as she stomped her foot on the ground. "How dare you!"

Molly shrugged and turned away. There was no point in

talking to a woman who was determined to be miserable and attempted to make everyone around her share her misery.

She smirked when she spotted Rick's truck driving up the road, no doubt summoned by Glenda's phone call or he listened to Molly's voice message. He had no idea what he was about to drive into... or maybe he did.

The woman stepped toward her truck and crossed her arms over her chest. Molly spotted a smile on Rick's face as he pulled into Molly's campsite. He knew what was about to happen.

Rick barely set a foot outside of his truck when the woman shouted from her site. "Is that your dog?"

"Yes, ma'am." He flashed a warm smile in her direction. It had little effect on its target.

"What makes you think you should let your dog loose like that? What if it bit someone?"

He reached into his truck and pulled out two cups of coffee from the café. "I can assure you, Hudson has never bitten anyone."

"We could have been the first."

Rick didn't reply and handed Molly the cup with her name written in Patsy's handwriting. "I figured you might like one, since I was already in town when Glenda called."

"You're so sweet." Molly held the cup to her nose and took in the coffee's smell. Café-brewed coffee was far superior to the instant coffee she had made this morning. She had almost walked to Patsy's herself, but decided not to when heavy clouds gathered overhead. "Thank you."

"Oh, so you two are together," the woman shouted. "Now I understand why you were defending him."

Rick looked down at Molly and smiled. "You were defending me?"

Molly shrugged and pressed the coffee cup lid to her chin. It was still too hot to sip. "Maybe," she said. Yes, she had been defending him, even if she hadn't realized that was what she was doing. She felt as defensive over Rick's pet ownership as she did over Hudson's love of walking. To see the smile on Rick's face was worth the hassle of dealing with the woman.

Rick wrapped his arm around Molly to lead her deeper into her campsite, away from the critical eye of the guest. Even though it had been only a few hours, she had missed his touch and wished they were alone.

"I hope you're taking that dog home," she shouted. "It is people like you who ruin things for others." She turned and stomped back into her site, slamming the door to her trailer with a bang that echoed across the campsite.

"Did you hear something?" Rick whispered.

Molly shook her head. "Nothing but the chirping of birds."

Rick smiled and placed his hand to her cheek. Molly closed her eyes as he leaned forward and kissed her lips. It didn't matter what that woman thought. If Hudson's wandering brought Rick into Molly's life, she would never complain about a wandering dog again.

CHAPTER TWENTY-ONE

*R*ick whistled to himself as he pulled into his driveway with Hudson panting in the passenger seat. Seeing Molly this morning was just the pick-me-up he needed to get through the rest of his workday. He always found picking up Hudson to be a pleasant distraction from the onslaught of phone calls and emails, but to add in the chance to see her and hold her was the answer to beating the nine-to-five blues. Phone meetings exhausted him during a long workday. Knowing he would rush out the door and see Molly again would be the bright spot to his day and would be all he thought about as the minutes dragged on.

Rounding the corner to the front of his cabin, he discovered Robert Fletcher standing on his front steps with another man. Robert waved as Rick pulled up and groaned. One toothy grin ruined a perfectly good morning.

"Rick." Robert approached his truck and held out his hand. "I wondered where you had gone off to. Picking up your dog, I see."

"That's right." It was all he could say without blurting out his wish for Robert to leave. "You brought a friend with you."

"This is my realtor."

Rick didn't need any further information about the man. Holding a tape measure in one hand and a tablet in the other, he was here to size up the property.

"It is a pleasure to meet you." The man had a firm handshake and stared Rick in the eyes. "When Mr. Fletcher told me you might be interested in selling the property to him, I wanted to come here and check it out. He already went over the terms with me, such as you wanting to keep possession of the cabin and the surrounding yard space."

"The terms." Rick laughed and shook his head. "We haven't agreed to any terms yet."

Robert stepped forward and slapped the realtor on the shoulder. "What Rick is saying is that we are in the middle of discussions, and he is quite interested in the recent written offer I presented to you in our office this morning. Rick, here, hasn't signed on the dotted line, yet. In the meantime, I figured we might as well get the ball rolling. A property of this size needs measuring, which we will want the surveyors to do, of course. What I thought we'd do is make sure all appropriate paperwork is in order. When we're ready, I'd like the transaction to be as smooth as possible."

Rick imagined what it would feel like to strike Robert across his chiseled jaw. While Rick may not have tossed the recent offer in the trash bin, he wasn't ready to allow the men to stroll onto his property and "start the ball rolling".

Another vehicle pulled into the driveway and parked next to Rick's. It was an SUV with the resort's logo splashed along the side. Something about seeing the resort's vehicle on his property made Rick's stomach turn.

"Ah, they're here." Two men jumped out from the truck and greeted Robert with a handshake. "These are my developers. They wanted to discuss our plans for the property and the best use of the space. I figured we should involve you in the conversation, Rick, since you expressed concerns in the past."

"I appreciate that, however, I am too busy to—"

"Don't worry, Rick." Robert rested his hand on Rick's shoulder, giving him an uneasy feeling. "I already spoke with your father about our meeting today. In fact, he had his assistant adjust your calendar to allow us as much time as we need to go over things."

Of course, his father was meddling in the deal. It made Rick want to end the discussion sooner than later. What kind of deal had his father already worked out with Robert? Whatever they worked out wouldn't be to Rick's benefit.

The sound of a click caught Rick's attention. The realtor was snapping photographs of the cabin exterior.

"Hey." Rick raised his hand and stepped in front of the realtor's phone. "Why are you taking pictures of my cabin? I'm not selling it."

The realtor wrote a note on his tablet and stepped to the side, positioning his phone for another picture. "I am aware you might not be interested in selling the cabin. However, Mr. Fletcher noted you both needed to complete the deal, and there was the possibility you might revisit previous conversations." He lowered his phone. "Was I mistaken?"

Rick turned to Robert, and his disgust for the man grew. Robert was used to getting what he wanted and with the help of Rick's father, he was ready to get his hands on Rick's property no matter what. "I never wanted to—"

"Walk with me, Rick." Robert gestured to follow him behind the cabin, leaving the realtor and property developers to examine his property alone. Rick didn't enjoy leaving the men to wander and snoop around, but needed to speak his mind to Robert in private. Besides, Hudson would monitor them, even if he was a terrible guard dog. He glanced over his shoulder at Hudson, who lay at the feet of one developer, eager to get a few minutes of sleep.

Rick and Robert walked along the side of the cabin to the

backyard, where everything was as Rick had left it. The day before, he trimmed the grass and weeded the gardens. Anyone could see he put time and effort into making his space attractive. It was not something that happened overnight. He had to dig up overgrown roots, clear away piles of debris from leaves and twigs to waste from the previous owners. He transformed the space into something livable and beautiful. It was a private oasis for him to enjoy nature in silence.

Robert stopped by a pruned rosebush and plucked a leaf from its branch. Rick bit his tongue. He wouldn't dare to damage a plant on the resort. "Rick, I thought a great deal about my last offer. It wasn't enough to convince you on the spot, however, I believe it is as far as I can go. In fact, I considered taking it back. It is going to cost me a lot to expand, and if I am going to spend that kind of money, I need to make sure I get a good return on my investment."

"It sounds as though you have a problem."

Robert tossed the leaf to the side. "I don't. You do. I am revising my offer to include the cabin. If I am going to pay you three million for the place, I might as well have all of it. Besides, you already complain about my guests. Do I want to deal with you calling me every few months because someone came too close to your fence?"

Rick scratched his head and laughed. "Are you trying to talk me into the deal or out of it?"

"I want you to look at the bigger picture. You might enjoy this place now, but I have heard you've got your eye on something else... or should I say, someone else?"

The color drained from Rick's face. Had word spread around town already?

"Do you think she is going to want to live in a cabin like this? A woman like that needs the best you and the city can offer, not some run-down cabin in the middle of Lemon Grove. You had your fun and now it is time to settle down."

"I'm not sure what you heard, Robert. Molly and I have only just started to—"

"Molly?" Robert took a step back and laughed. "I was talking about Valerie. Your father told me all about your reunion in the city, and he's convinced the two of you are getting back together. Who is Molly?"

Rick didn't want to tell Robert anything that might get back to his father. He didn't need the drama. Molly was the woman he cared about, and not Valerie, who his parents would rather see him with. His father would have much to say when he found out.

"Does your father know?" Robert pressed. That man would not let it go, and now Rick's lack of response was only feeding his curiosity.

"As I was trying to tell you, we've only just met each other and there are no plans. And my father was wrong." He might as well say that much.

Robert smiled and soon let out a loud cackle. "I suspect it will upset your father when he hears this news. And this Molly of yours, has she seen the cabin? Is she prepared to live here? I assume she isn't from Lemon Grove since I don't recall anyone with that name around here." Rick said nothing, leaving Robert to laugh again. "My boy. If you are going to impress a woman, you need to have something to offer. This place is doing nothing for you, not to mention the fact that you make your living from your parents' business. If you call this setting out on your own, you haven't shown you have what it takes to cut the apron strings and be independent."

"You are crossing a line, Robert," Rick said through his teeth.

"I am trying to be honest with you. Women want men who make their own way. Sell your cabin and you set yourself up with a nice little fortune. Buy your young lady a nice apartment somewhere in the city. You'll both be happier there."

Rick tried to wear a fake smile to hide his hatred for the man. Despite his dislike for Robert, he was right. Rick had little to offer Molly besides a cabin and a dog. Would she have as much respect for him knowing his father employed him? It wasn't as if Rick had to fight for the job and go through the same interview process so many others have needed to do. His family handed him the job. Same with the paycheck that came with the job. It is why his father continued to hold the job over his head whenever Rick didn't do what they wanted. If Rick were to be in a serious relationship with Molly, who knew what other tricks his family would pull along the way. Even if his father didn't interfere with the relationship now, he might get involved later when he wanted to manipulate Rick into another decision.

He only hoped that Molly wasn't interested in being wooed by expensive gifts or a man who had to come up from the ground floor. Rick wanted her to like him for the man he was today. His family history shouldn't matter in her decision to be with him. Rick could walk away from all of it if doing so would make her happy. He'd even walk away from the cabin if it meant they would be together. But from what he could tell, she liked it in Lemon Grove. Like him, she was escaping the city to get away into nature. It was a bonus that they had found each other, and now she was assessing her next move. He could see it on her face whenever they were together. Her forehead scrunched when they discussed the café and the possibility of proposing the expansion to her friend. She wore the cutest expression and one that didn't match her confident opinions. When she knew what she wanted, Molly was firm in her beliefs. Her shoulders rolled back, and she stood straight. There was a fire behind her eyes and a tone that warned him not to argue, but when talking about the café and Lemon Grove, she grew quiet. A decision as big as uprooting one's life was not one to make lightly and wasn't one that Rick felt she could make right away. He couldn't decide to move to the city that quickly, although the thought was growing on him. The way he felt right now, if she would not move, he would.

"Well?" Robert said. "Do you agree with me?"

"I'm not agreeing or disagreeing with you. Molly likes Lemon Grove. I would like time to see what happens between us before deciding on something like selling."

"You're going to let a girl decide for you?"

"That's not what I'm saying. We'll decide together once we know what this could look like long-term."

Robert's smile turned downward, and he walked to the edge of the yard. "I don't have time to wait. My investors need me to be breaking ground in the next few months. I've offered you three million for this property, Rick, when it is hardly even worth one million."

Rick laughed and shook his head. "I'd argue with you about that one."

"You're wrong. It is worth a lot more to someone like me when it's sold to a development company and not to a private family. Who else is going to develop here, Rick? Lemon Grove has nothing to offer a smaller business. Lemon Eagle Resort is in the best position to invest in Lemon Grove. By turning us down, you will never get the same price for this property. As the cabin ages, the value will only go down. If we move on, we won't come back and offer this kind of money again. You are going to regret it when your relationship ends and you made a bad financial decision for nothing." Robert reached into his pocket and pulled out a business card. He pressed it against Rick's chest and held it with one pointed finger. "You are either stupid or even more stubborn than your father. I can't figure out which. I hope, for your sake, I'm wrong on both accounts."

Rick took the card and watched Robert stomp back to the front of the cabin as Hudson came bounding toward them. Robert stepped to the side, narrowly missing a collision with Hudson, who stopped at Rick's feet.

"Are you ready to go inside?" Rick asked.

Hudson wiggled in place and nudged Rick's hand with his snout.

"Alright. Let's go."

As they rounded the front of the house, Robert huddled with the men at the back of the developers' truck. They were quiet as they spoke animatedly, pausing only to scowl at Rick as if he had wasted their time. It wasn't his fault Robert brought them to Rick's property without a proper invite. If they were that upset by the situation, they should take it up with their boss. This property was Rick's for as long as his name was on the title. If he wanted to sell he would, and might if that was what it took to be with Molly. She hadn't asked him to sell. At least, not yet. All he needed was to know she wanted him forever and he would leave this place behind. It would hurt, but she was worth it.

CHAPTER TWENTY-TWO

*V*endors had their goods on display in the transformed park. The sun shone down on the green space where they erected stands of various sizes with table displays under tents for shade. Eager sellers smiled from behind their tables, each eying potential customers. Molly had already watched the nearby parking lot for Rick and after receiving a message from him saying he was running late, she wandered through the park while she waited for him to arrive.

She had never been to a Farmers' Market before, but already she was in love with the atmosphere. Baked goods from the vendors and the nearby food trucks filled the air with the smell of their delicious wares. Her stomach rumbled, knowing soon she could sample the pulled pork from the barbeque truck or the taco van. Hopefully, the trucks wouldn't leave before she and Rick were ready to eat. Long lines were already forming, making her worry there would be nothing left.

Molly strolled up to the first table where a woman sat knitting, paying little attention to Molly's attendance. The knitted towels were bright in stripes of neon and not a pattern Molly would want in her own kitchen, but they had character and were interesting to look at. She ran her hand over a towel. Rough wool made little sense, unless the creator designed them for decoration or to loosen dried on food.

"Are you going to buy anything?" the woman snapped.

"I'm just looking for now," Molly replied.

"Then don't touch."

Molly pulled her hand back and slinked away. That wasn't what she had expected from a local in Lemon Grove. Perhaps the reaction was because she was from out of town? Molly had only wanted to examine the material and decide if she was interested in purchasing something. She hadn't expected the woman to snap at her, and for that, the woman would not have Molly's business.

She moved on to the next vendor, hoping for a little more civil treatment. Baked goods lined this vendor's table. They had placed a few pieces of fudge on a plate with toothpicks sticking from the top, keeping the plastic wrap from touching the gooey surface.

"Are these samples?" Molly asked the woman behind the table.

The vendor picked up the plate and moved it away. "I only provide samples to people who live in town."

"Oh." Molly lowered her head and looked around the market. Did everyone feel this way? She hadn't expected people to be so rude at the market. Most store clerks in the city would want to make a sale, but these women seemed intent on not having her business. Did she give off an out-of-town vibe that made them want to avoid her?

"Are you doing a little shopping?" Rick asked behind her. She turned and saw his handsome, wide smile. "I see you found Amanda's fudge. Have you sampled her chocolate almond fudge? It's delicious."

Molly forced a smile on her face to acknowledge his compliments on the fudge she had been denied. She wanted to tell him how rude the vendor had been, but let it pass for now, especially given that she didn't want to cause a scene in the middle of the park. "I'm afraid not. I'm just browsing, for now."

"Then you must try it later. Amanda usually sells out, so don't wait too long." He gave the vendor a wink, and the sour woman perked up, holding her hand to her cheek. "Where are we off to next?"

Molly glanced over her shoulder and spotted a group of women huddled together whispering to each other. Now she understood what the rudeness had been about. Patsy had mentioned how the other women in town often asked about Rick, and this was their reaction to Molly getting his attention. Would she receive the same icy reception from the other vendors? Molly shrugged. "I was just wandering while I waited for you to get here. I'm not sure what all there is to see."

"There is going to be music down at the far end in a few minutes. Why don't we head in that direction?"

"That sounds like a plan."

Rick took her hand in his as they walked past the next few tables, causing the women to gawk at the sight of Molly and Rick strolling hand in hand. Molly enjoyed herself, if not because of the company, but from seeing the reactions. The women could think what they wanted of her. They were the ones being rude. If a vendor wanted to treat her kindly, Molly would purchase something from their table. Now, with Rick present, the vendors seemed to be warming in their interactions. Molly knew it was only for Rick's benefit, and not because the vendors further down the row liked her any better.

Despite the rudeness, Molly cultivated a pleasant smile toward each vendor they visited and allowed Rick to guide her from table to table. He seemed oblivious to the snarky comments and the grimaces from each of the women. Instead, Rick introduced her to each of his friends and unintentionally offended every woman in town by parading Molly around in front of them. Molly marveled: he was clueless... yet kind.

"You have an awful lot of friends in this town. I wish the city were like this. People walk by me all the time and don't care at all."

He laughed as he pressed his hand against her back to guide her around a group of people. "I may have introduced them as friends, but they are more like acquaintances. You don't want to get too close to people in town or they will share your personal business with everyone else. Besides, just so you know," he whispered, "I am well aware most of these women aren't interested in being my friend."

Molly smiled. "I think I figured that out already... about the gossip, I mean."

"Oh?" He looked down at her. "Tell me. What's the gossip?"

"Not you, too. You didn't strike me as the type to want to know all the news."

"I only meant I wanted to know what the gossip was about me these days. Not what they are saying about others. They all like to talk and I've heard some stories about you already."

Molly froze. "Really?" She felt herself grow pale. Knowing people had been sharing gossip about her reminded Molly of the high school days she was happy to leave behind. While she tried to convince herself that the stories they started didn't matter, deep down, they did.

"Yes. You are a mysterious woman who ran away from the city and is looking for a fresh start someplace new. They are all guessing what sort of trouble you were into that made you hide out in Lemon Grove."

"That's not true."

"Is any part of it true?"

Molly shook her head... then paused and smiled. "Maybe. I came to Lemon Grove on vacation, and the town has since grown on me... a lot."

"It has?" Rick's smile grew. "Enough to make you want to live here?"

To move to a town like Lemon Grove, she would need to be prepared to live with the quirks, such as the gossip. Most of the women here already showed that they hate her, but would it stay that way forever? At some point, they would have to forgive her for stealing their bachelor. Still, there was always the chance she and Rick wouldn't last, and then what? Would she move back to the city? Imagine the gossip then?

"I've thought about moving to a place like this, but that wasn't why I vacationed here. It was to get a break from work."

There was an expression on Rick's face. It was a look of mischievousness and concern. There was something he wasn't telling her.

"There's more, isn't there?" she asked.

He gave her hand a squeeze. "Glenda said the women are concerned you're toying with me."

"Pardon?" Molly turned and faced the women who continued to observe them in the park. She wanted to shout at them and give them an angry, death stare, but somehow plastered on a warm smile instead. She wouldn't feed the rumor mill. "Why would they say that?"

"Because they are afraid you'll forget about me when you go back home where the business executives in suits would woo you."

Molly turned her face toward the ground. There were no men in suits to woo her, and she was not interested in any men in the city. In fact, it seemed she had finally forgotten about the one she came to Lemon Grove to forget, finding a surprise in the small town instead.

"Well, I am not interested in any business executives in suits, so they can forget about that."

"You're not?"

"Nope. I like the more rugged types I find in the forest. Men with dogs."

"Ah." Rick smiled and gave her hand a squeeze. "Those are hard to find."

"You're right. Hopefully, I can find one at the Farmers' Market. Do you think any of the vendors might have one?"

Rick shook his head. "Afraid not. But I think I know where you could find one."

"Where?" Molly faked searching past Rick, leaning side to side to look into the crowd behind him.

"Here," he said. Rick pulled her close to kiss her lips and wrapped his arm around her waist.

Molly sensed the watchful eyes of the women glaring at them. She didn't want the kiss to be about silencing her critics and wanted it to only be about her and Rick. Molly would kiss him in a crowd, or anywhere. Still, she enjoyed the thought of the women being surprised by Rick's public display of affection. It wasn't a long kiss, but it was enough that no one would doubt they were an item.

"Come with me." Rick offered the crook of his elbow and Molly draped her hand over his arm. He guided her past the stalls to an open area where volunteers positioned chairs in front of a temporary stage.

"They're about to start," he said, pointing to a row of chairs. "Where do you want to sit?"

"Not too close to the speakers. I find the volume pretty loud at festivals." She hadn't been to a festival since high school and hated the way the volume had made her ears tickle.

"You won't find that problem here. There's no one that understands how to work the sound system." A loud squeal emanating from the speakers blasted through the park. Both Molly and Rick covered their ears. "See what I mean?"

"Another reason not to sit too close."

They sat near the middle of the rows and waited as the musicians took the stage. It was a band composed of two men on acoustic guitars, a fiddler, and a man on a trumpet.

"Is this a local band?"

"They are. The trumpet player is a retired sheriff. The fiddler was the mayor here for ten years, and the other two are teachers. They aren't too bad."

"What does that mean?"

"Well, they won't be going on tour, if you get what I'm saying. We are lucky to have a couple of guys who can play and make a little noise now and then. Have a listen. You'll see what I mean."

Molly chuckled and settled into her seat, leaning close to Rick as he draped his arm over the back of the chair. It was getting easier to forget about the reasons to resist him and cuddle against his shoulder. This was how a relationship should be. It felt natural and comfortable, even when preparing to listen to a market band.

"Thank you, ladies and gentlemen, for coming out today," the fiddler said. "I hope you all have visited our vendors. There are plenty of lovely items for sale. Amanda, do you still have some fudge left?"

Amanda waved from her booth and gave thumbs up to the band. It would seem the only person she didn't like was Molly.

"Save some for us, would you?" He stomped his foot and counted down. In unison, the band played and the joyful upbeat music rang through the speakers.

Molly's eyebrows rose. They weren't terrible. The music stayed on beat and they played in the same key. One teacher sang with more gusto than skill. She covered her lips to hide her smile.

Rick leaned over. "I said they could play. I never said they could sing."

That was true, and for good reason. At the end of the song, the audience applauded to show their appreciation for their local band.

Molly stretched out her legs and watched as the men set up for their next song. The audience smiled and cheered. This was a supportive crowd... at least toward the people from their community. Looking around, Molly wondered how many people had been born in Lemon Grove and how many moved here from elsewhere. How long did it take for the residents to accept them? How long might it take for them to accept her?

Molly brushed her hair out of her face and relaxed against Rick's arm. It was interesting to take in local culture. While these men weren't as skilled as the professional musicians she had seen at concerts in the city, it didn't matter. They made people happy, including Molly, who had tapped along to their music. It was more satisfying to support people with her enthusiastic applause than through the purchase of an expensive concert ticket.

"Rick?" she heard a woman say. They both turned. A tall, thin blonde stood at the end of their row. She wore an out of place tight, pencil skirt and a blue silk blouse. Her hair and makeup were perfect and her jewelry caught every speckle of light. She held her arms out wide to Rick and smiled. "I thought that was you." Her voice was high-pitched and irritating.

Rick rose, and he held out his hand to shake her hand. She ignored his gesture and wrapped her arms around him. Molly stood beside him, waiting for an introduction.

"Who is this?" the newcomer asked.

"This is Molly," he said. "She's a friend from out of town."

Molly felt her heart break. He had relegated her to being a friend. Just a friend. Whoever this was, Rick didn't want her to know that, moments earlier, they had just shared a kiss, unless it meant nothing to him.

"Just visiting?" the woman asked.

"Would you all take your conversation elsewhere?" a woman behind them shouted. "We're trying to watch the show."

"I'm sorry," he said to the woman behind them.

"I was hoping I might find your here." The blonde woman smiled and took a seat beside Rick. "I have missed these local shows."

Rick sat on the edge of his chair. His arm was no longer

draped over the back of Molly's seat as he folded his arms across his chest.

Nearby, women huddled together, whispering excitedly to each other. Their surprised expressions showed that the woman sitting beside Rick was giving them plenty to talk about.

"It has been too long since I've been here. The city was pleasant, but this... I've missed this place." She rested her hand on Rick's knee. "How have you been? I haven't seen you since the meeting."

"Fine," he said, brushing her hand away. "Perhaps we could talk later so others can enjoy the performance."

"That's why I'm whispering."

Molly smirked. If this were what this woman called whispering, she would hate to hear what she would consider a normal volume.

"I stopped by your cabin to see if you were there. It took me a while to find you here."

"The town isn't that big."

"Yes, well, you don't always make yourself available." This woman must be used to being the focus of his attention, not caring about others who are nearby, especially Molly. "Did you want to go get something to drink? It would be quieter away from all the music."

"Please, do," groaned the woman behind them.

"I think I'm fine," Rick said.

"Take that woman away from here." The woman leaned forward and waved a pamphlet in the air. "I am trying to watch my husband play."

Rick turned to Molly and shrugged. "I'm sorry. I guess the show is going to get cut short. They will play again later."

They inched their way out of the row with the blonde leading them toward the drink stand. Molly thought she saw the woman reach back for Rick's hand, but he pulled his hand away.

It was quieter by the drink stand, just as this interrupter had suggested, but the three of them were not alone. The nosey women had somehow followed them, finding their drama to be more interesting than the musical act, and stood to one side to observe them.

"What have you been up to, Rick?" she asked.

"Not much. Same old."

The woman inched her way closer to Rick and stroked his arm. "You are quieter than when I saw you the other day. What's wrong?"

Molly's eyes fixated on Rick's arm, which only minutes ago, Molly had draped her own hand over. Now, this woman was running her fingers up and down his sleeve to coax him to talk. Whoever she was, it was clear they had a history. A history that apparently wasn't over.

"I'm sorry," Molly said, taking a step back. "I should probably go."

Rick pulled his arm away and turned. "No, Molly. You should stay. Valerie was just leaving."

Valerie laughed and grabbed Rick by the elbow. "Don't be silly, Rick. I just got here. I told your father I was coming out to visit you and he told me to let you know you can have the rest of the week off. Isn't that great?"

Rick's gaze never left Molly. His eyes pleaded with her to stay, but Molly's cheeks burned as tears pooled in her eyes. There was something more to Valerie that Molly couldn't identify and didn't want to stick around long enough to figure out.

"I think I'm done here," Molly said. "You two appear to have some things you need to talk about."

"Molly." Rick took a step toward her, only for Valerie's grasp to hold him back.

"Let her go, Rick." Valerie hung on as Rick's arm straightened behind him. "I only need a few minutes for you to hear me out."

Molly didn't look back as she walked past a row of smiling female vendors who shook their heads and laughed. She had become one of the many caught up in Rick's ways. She never should have thought about moving here. Not because of some guy. She should have kept her mind on having a relaxing vacation and on returning to her job where she and Carla could expand their business in the city.

It was foolish to get caught up in imagining a life that wasn't hers and would never be. Hot tears pooled in her eyes. Her vision blurred as she walked up the road to the path leading to the campground. She had nothing to show for her trip to town. Instead, she returned empty-handed and with one less friendship. Molly couldn't be friends with Rick if he was hiding a woman like Valerie. She probably couldn't even remain in Lemon Grove, especially with everyone laughing and staring.

CHAPTER TWENTY-THREE

*M*olly wiped the tears from her hot cheeks. She didn't care if anyone at the campground saw her and the miserable state she was in. If her tears kept someone else from being hurt by Rick and his charming ways, so be it. She shouldn't have listened to Carla and her encouragement to not reject him. Molly should have trusted her gut and avoided Rick. He shattered her heart, and it took everything to keep herself from bawling in the middle of her campsite. Why would he choose her over a gorgeous blonde in her fancy outfit? Valerie in her dry clean-only fashion offered more than Molly in her plain shirts and jeans. It would be impossible for Molly to get her hair to lay that perfect with the limited products she brought with her. Besides, she shouldn't have to compete with anyone. Rick made her believe she was important and that he cared about her. If he did, he wouldn't allow Valerie to touch him like that. It bothered her even more that Rick kept it a secret that he spent time with the woman in the city. Something must be going on between them for Valerie to be that comfortable with Rick.

"Trust your instincts," she told herself as she pulled her belongings out of her tent. It didn't matter if it was mid-afternoon. Molly would not give him the opportunity to make a lame excuse for why Valerie was all over him. Instead, she would leave as quickly as possible and not stick around to hear his lies. If Rick thought about running after her, he would find her gone. Keeping secrets was not a way to begin a relationship. Molly was not about to become some long-term fling while he kept another woman on the line. "He can play that game with someone else," she said aloud as she gathered her things.

Molly shoved her sleeping bag into the trunk of her car and grabbed a nylon bag, returning to the tent to pull the pegs from the ground. She didn't bother to shake off the dirt, choosing instead to allow the clumps to fall into the bag along with the peg. Next, she collapsed the tent poles into a packable size before rolling the tent and its attachments together into a ball. If she was taking her time, she would have folded each corner of the tent, following every crease until it looked as tightly wrapped as it was when she pulled it out of the box. Instead, she crumpled the tent into a ball and threw it into the backseat of her car.

If she ever needed to evacuate a campsite, she now knew she could do so in under ten minutes. With her picnic table cleared, her laundry line tucked away and her chair packed, her campsite was empty. Now, to decide where to go? She would figure it out on the road. Molly pulled up to the office to tell Glenda she was leaving and was charged for the night. Glenda smiled as she refunded Molly for the remaining three nights. It was as if Glenda was happy to watch her go. No doubt the other women in town felt the same.

Her tires spun in the gravel as Molly hoped to not run into Rick during her last minutes in Lemon Grove. It was his fault she was leaving. Had he been trustworthy, then she would still be at the Farmers' Market, listening to local musicians and enjoying a meal from the food trucks. Instead, she was on the road with her tent in the backseat, wondering where she would choose to sleep tonight.

At the end of the road leading out of town, she considered both directions of the highway. Turning right would take her back to the city where Carla would lecture her about running away and wasting her precious vacation days. Returning home now would mean she would sit alone in her apartment feeling as miserable about her life as she felt the day she left on the trip. Turning left would take her past Lakewood to some unknown destination. She would be alone with her thoughts and no one telling her what she should do.

Turning left onto the highway, she sped down the road, leaving any thoughts of Rick behind her.

Rick grew impatient with Valerie and the flock of too-observant women huddled nearby. He felt like an object that everyone wanted and the only one he wanted had walked away. With her fingers still lingering on his arm, Valerie wasn't about to let him go.

"Come on, Rick. I came all this way to talk to you." The way she stared into his eyes, he recognized she wanted more than to talk. She wanted him to say things he no longer felt. He didn't love her. Not anymore. And he was not about to let her back into his life, even if it was what his father wanted.

He broke free and increased the space between them. "Valerie, I appreciate that you came all this way to talk, but I can't give you what you want."

Valerie laughed. "And what is it I want?"

"Us. We both know this would never work. We don't want the same things."

"Of course we do. You want to be successful and have a family. Maybe own a nice vacation home in Lemon Grove or nearby to visit now and then."

Rick observed the women sidling closer, hoping to eavesdrop

on their conversation. There would be no privacy in the middle of a Farmers' Market. He motioned for her to follow him as he walked past the vendors toward the road where he had parked his truck.

"Lemon Grove isn't where I want a vacation home."

"It isn't?" Valerie's voice rang with excitement. "That's fine, I can think of a million places to buy a vacation home."

He paused and turned. "I don't want a vacation home in Lemon Grove because I want to live here. Full-time."

Valerie worked to catch her breath as she considered Rick's words. She held her hand to her chest and her face wore a look of confusion.

"What about what you said at your father's meeting? That you were selling your cabin and moving to the city?"

"Someone was putting words in my mouth. Rather than fight it, I got through the day."

Her confused expression changed to anger as she pulled out her phone. "Your father assured me you decided to sell."

"And that is why this would never work. We both want different things."

She nodded and continued to touch the keyboard on the screen of her phone.

"Who are you writing to?" Rick asked.

"My father." Valerie slipped the phone into her purse and crossed her arms in front of her. "He told me it was a stupid idea to come here."

"He did?"

Valerie sighed and wrapped a strand of hair around her finger. She wasn't about to give up yet. "My father says you don't belong in the city. That you need your freedom. He likes you a lot, Rick. Your father, on the other hand…"

Her words took him by surprise. The number of years their families had done business together, it seemed their parents had a friendship that extended beyond the occasional business deal.

"Why do I have a hard time believing that?"

"Because my father tried to get along with your father for our sake. When he found out I liked you, he wanted to make it easy on us with your parents. Then we got engaged, and after that… I ruined everything."

"What do you mean?"

"He said we made a terrible mistake when we broke up and it wasn't until later, when I dated this guy, Michael, that I realized he was right." Valerie took a breath, and for the first time, Rick witnessed emotion in her eyes. "I had thought I wanted to do something exciting and travel the world. I never got the sense that traveling interested you. You had this little cabin, and this was as much of the world as you wanted to experience. It was stupid of me to think a relationship would be my answer to the adventure I wanted. Had I just told you I wanted to do some traveling, I am sure you would have given me the freedom to do that."

"I would have." Rick tried not to look at her eyes. He had stared into them many times in the past and had lost himself in those deep pools of blue. It wouldn't happen again. Now that he had Molly's eyes to lose himself in. "We're past that now and you have all the freedom you want to see the world."

Valerie raised her arms in the air and dropped them against her side. "I don't want that anymore, Rick. These past few months, I realized I've grown up. While living in a cabin in some small town isn't my dream, it's yours, and if I sacrifice for you now, one day you might try to live in the city to make me happy. We never know what the future might hold."

Rick shoved his hands in his pockets and kicked at the grass. Sure, he might consider moving back to the city one day, but it wouldn't be for Valerie.

"I appreciate you coming all this way to tell me this. It wasn't easy for you, and as much as you have tried to imagine living here, we both know you would be miserable. I can't ask that of you. Perhaps Michael wasn't the guy for you, but there will be someone who won't ask you to live in a small town and will want to see the world with you. Don't give up on that dream. You're a special girl, Val."

She wiped a tear from her cheek and rubbed the side of his arm. "You were always so sweet." Valerie looked past him at the women whispering in the distance. "That woman you were with... where did she go?"

Rick looked over his shoulder and gestured toward the trees. "Probably back to the campsite where she's staying."

"Is she someone special?"

"She is," he said, trying not to sound too enthusiastic over his new relationship. He didn't want to crush Valerie after her failed attempt to win him back. "I should go. After our reunion, I expect we need to talk."

Valerie wrapped her arms around him for a friendly hug. "I'm going to miss you, Rick. I apologize if I messed things up for you and...?"

"Molly," he said.

"That's a cute name. She seems nice."

"Hudson likes her, so that's a bonus."

Valerie smiled. "You still have that dog? I can't believe he's still alive."

She never did like Hudson and was now most likely relieved not to be saddled with the responsibilities of being a dog owner. It is another reason Rick was happy about not reuniting. Hudson didn't like Valerie and would have a sour look on his funny face if he saw Valerie walk through the front door of the cabin.

Rick continued toward his truck with Valerie following close behind, and followed soon after by the town gossips. Valerie stood by the driver's side door as Rick climbed into his truck and rolled down the window to share a few last words.

"Stay in touch," she said before he pulled away.

He took two long, cleansing breaths. Finally, he had rid himself of Valerie and said all he needed to say. Rejecting her was the easiest decision he had to make. Without a doubt, Valerie was not who he should be with, and he couldn't wait to scoop Molly into his arms and kiss her again. His heart pounded harder against his chest as he pulled into the campground. From now on, he wanted to experience the twisting in his stomach every time he drew close to her, knowing he would only find relief when he held her. He wanted to tell her, without a doubt, they were meant to be together, and he didn't want Molly living in the city to be a barrier. They would make it work. They had to.

His truck came to an abrupt stop. He had slammed the brakes when he saw her empty campsite. Rick looked over his shoulder at the sites he passed by. Surely he hadn't taken a wrong turn. The campground wasn't that big, and the showers were across the street from her site. Bile rose into his throat. Where had she gone?

The truck moved faster than the posted speed limit as he drove past site after site, not seeing her tent or any sign of her car. Molly was gone.

He stopped at the office and rushed inside, where Glenda was on the phone with her back to the door.

"That would have upset me, too. I never expected that from him. You don't flirt with another woman in front of someone," she said to an unknown caller. He cleared his throat and Glenda spun around in her chair. Her face turned pale. "I've gotta go." She curved her lips into a smile and placed her phone on the desk. "Hi, Rick," she said with a shake to her voice. "What can I do for you?"

"Molly." His voice tightened when he said her name. "Where is she?"

Glenda looked at the map on her desk, acting as if she was trying to remember the name. "Molly... oh, yes. She checked out about fifteen minutes ago."

The room spun, and Rick leaned against the office wall for support. "Fifteen minutes ago? Did she say where she was going?"

"I'm afraid not. I refunded her for the days she didn't stay, and then she left. Seemed to be in a bit of a hurry."

Now he knew what people meant when they said they couldn't breathe at the thought of someone disappearing from their life. Something was crushing him on the inside and, ashamed that he had already worn his emotions on his face, he had to rush out of the office. It should embarrass him to think of others seeing him rush out of the building with tears pooling in his eyes. He didn't care. Molly had left, and he understood what he had done. To her, he made a choice when he allowed her to leave so he could continue his conversation with Valerie. He shouldn't have allowed that to happen, and this was the consequence.

Rick fumbled through his phone contacts and listened as the phone rang. If he waited long enough, Molly might pick up the phone. As soon as she answered, he would tell her how sorry he was for the visit to the Farmers' Market being such a terrible date, and that Valerie had gone home. All he wanted was to hear her voice and for her to forgive him for messing everything up.

The phone rang with no sound on the other end besides the default voice message from the phone company. She didn't take his call. He only had one other option. He could go to Patsy's and see if she had gone to the café. After that, the only other place he would think to look was the city. Maybe her friend, Carla, at the coffee shop, could tell him where to find her. He feared that the longer Molly didn't hear what he had to say, the closer he came to losing her forever, and Rick couldn't imagine his life without her.

CHAPTER TWENTY-FOUR

*M*olly drove a tent peg into the ground, narrowly missing her finger. This was Rick's fault… No, it was her fault she moved to a new campsite so late in the day. Now, at dusk, she struggled to get her tent up before the last bit of light disappeared. Had she stayed away from Rick like she originally planned, she would still be at her campsite in Lemon Grove with a clear head and comfortable campsite. Leaving meant driving for longer than expected in search of an empty spot, and she ended up at a more rustic campground to pitch a tent for the night. She considered getting a hotel, but every hotel she saw was along the noisy highway and none had vacancies. When she saw the advertisement for the Bent Crane Campground, she took her chances. She would commit to one night and tomorrow she would decide if the campground was worth staying another day or two.

At least it wasn't raining. That was the only thing that kept this from being some sort of nightmare. After driving through tears, she didn't need tears and raindrops. Still, the weather was cool and her teeth chattered as she worked to assemble her tent. It took time to untangle the mess Molly made when she crumpled the tent and stuffed it into the back of her car. If she hadn't been in a rush, laying out the tent at the new site and locating the door would have been easier. The rope ties had become a tangled mess, and she needed them to stake down the fly.

She fought back more tears. Not only was her tent a mess, so was her life. Nothing ever turned out the way she hoped. By her age, she should be in a serious relationship and planning a wedding. What was this pattern with her and men? Why couldn't she find a guy worth her time and her heart? She seemed destined to be alone. Perhaps she needed to accept her situation and would be happier if she stopped trying to find happiness with someone else. But she was happier when she was with someone. She enjoyed sharing her dreams with another person and having him share his with her.

Molly always imagined coming home to someone and not to an empty house. She needed someone to be happy to see her when she returned from a long day at the coffee shop. Some friends adopted pets for this very purpose. To be their furry greeter. Had it come to that? Would she get a pet so she didn't have to be alone?

Wiping a lone tear from her cheek, she felt a smudge of dirt brush against her skin. Now she would have a streak of mud on her face, and since her campsite was nowhere near the facilities by the campground office, she would remain covered in dirt until she readied herself for bed. At least the lack of daylight would keep the other campers from seeing her looking like a disaster.

Now she recognized her mistake in booking all two weeks in Lemon Grove instead of breaking up her vacation into two locations. She could have used her schedule as an excuse not to get caught up with Rick. Knowing he had two weeks to show her who he was, she gave him a chance. Limiting her stay to one week would have made it easier to turn him down. She could have moved on and avoided the heartache.

Molly took another swing at the peg and caught the side of

her thumb. She gasped and whimpered. No one would care if she howled out loud, and it was best to not draw attention to herself. For the rest of her trip, she would remain under the radar with no one knowing who she was or, most of all, ask her out on a date.

She tossed her belongings in the tent and prepared her bed. The cool air surrounded her, sending a chill to her bones. She would need the extra blanket here. What a difference a little elevation could make. While it was cooler here, she still questioned why smoke hung in the air. The fire ban extended to the entire region, and the campground wasn't exempt. The attendant gave her a gentle reminder about the fire ban when she registered. No campfires were visible, so the smoke came from elsewhere. While she missed roasting hot dogs and marshmallows over the fire like she had enjoyed as a child, maybe the fire ban was a good thing. She didn't want her experience in Lemon Grove to taint her childhood camping activities. Marshmallows would always be associated with good thoughts. Now, she would make fresh memories here at a cold, private campground where smoke lingered in the air.

With the cool dampness of the morning dew sending a small shiver up her spine, Molly stood outside her tent. The attendant promised views of the nearby lake from her campsite, but a thick layer of smoke had settled in and a bright orange glow emanated on the other side of the hill. A strong wind beat at the side of her tent, pushing more and more smoke down into the valley bottom, which forced Molly to wrap her blanket around her. She choked down her breakfast cereal as her eyes stung and her throat burned. After yesterday, she had been looking forward to waking up to the sparkling shimmer of the water. Of course, the location would disappoint her. The entire vacation was a disappointment.

She sighed and then gagged and coughed. There would be no swimming today, or hiking. Any physical activity in the smoke would irritate her lungs, so her best option was to sit and wait it out, hoping the wind would blow the smoke away. Once the weather pattern changed, the smoke would surely subside. Still, there was something unsettling about a wildfire being so close. It would have to jump the lake, or circle around it for her to be in any danger. Molly didn't know how far embers might travel, but if they blew across and lit the surrounding trees, the thought of needing to outrun a blaze terrified her.

Once again, the tears pooled. This was supposed to be a nice vacation, not one filled with frustrating and frightening experiences. She pulled her chair to the edge of the campsite and imagined she was looking down at the water. Even the sun was obscured. A small glowing circle attempting to push through the hazy morning light.

A camper emerged from their trailer and coughed, as did another traveler across the road. It was a miserable place. Music played in the distance. Someone was trying to mask their disappointment with loud music. If only this campground shared the same rules for noise as Lemon Grove.

Molly couldn't tell if her sore throat resulted from the smoke or her growing emotions. She never would have left Lemon Grove had she known this was what awaited her. She should have moved to Lemon Eagle Resort or to a different site and asked Glenda not to tell Rick where she was. At least there she had privacy with the trees and underbrush. Here there was only grass and a small hill to minimize the view of her neighbor. If there was no smoke, the site would be hot in the summer, and no trees meant no place to string a tarp for additional shade or for her laundry line. To get out of the sun, she would need to hide in her tent where the temperatures would surely climb. Molly wasn't sure if she wanted the smoke to clear or not.

She sat in her chair, grinding her foot into the gravel pad. People had come with their trailers and boats expecting to play on the water, but judging by the miserable looks on their faces, they lacked energy in the smoky conditions. The wildfire was ruining everyone's plans.

Molly checked her watch. There was a visitors' center up the road and she decided that checking it out would be better than sitting around in the cold, feeling sorry for herself. Getting moving would be better with her irritated eyes and a burning throat.

Jumping into her car, she navigated around kids riding slowly on their bicycles and drove toward the visitors' center. They must know of something she could do when the weather or fires weren't accommodating outdoor activities. If she was lucky, they might even have coffee. She would take anything besides the instant garbage she had back at camp.

Compact cars and travel trailers filled the parking lot at the visitors' center. Everyone appeared to have the same plan as Molly. Inside, she stared at the many pamphlets for the area and, once again, she was disappointed. The town only offered outdoor experiences, and the rest of the pamphlets were for restaurants and museums. While she wanted a slower pace, a museum would push it a little too far.

"We have several shops," she heard a representative say to a weary-looking couple. "Our parks are also beautiful."

The clang of metal got her attention. A man in his sixties walked inside with a chihuahua trotting on a leash alongside him. It sniffed at the air and sneezed as it crossed the room.

Molly thought of Hudson and how there was no dog at the campground to warm her feet in the morning. She missed Hudson and his morning visit during breakfast. Molly walked over to the man standing at a wall-sized map. She leaned down and stretched her hand out to the little chihuahua. It sniffed at her fingers and growled.

"He's not friendly," the man said. "He doesn't like many people."

"I guess so," she said, rising to her feet. "Sorry to bother him."

The man walked away, leading his growling dog toward the next display. Hudson never rejected her and always sought her out for attention. She missed the way he would crane his neck around to get more attention, demanding more scratches and hugs.

Soon, a rush of excitement came over her, and the accompanying thought made perfect sense. She should get a dog. There must be a local humane society nearby to visit, and with dogs in need of a home.

She smiled to herself, thinking of picking out a dog and bringing it back to her apartment... with no access to a yard. Molly sighed. When she returned to the city, the coffee shop would keep her away from home all day. She would not be home to let a dog outside and it would be miserable spending its days by the window staring at the outdoors from three floors above. Adopting a dog wouldn't be possible as long as she lived in a place without access to a yard, and definitely not with her lifestyle.

Molly sighed and gave her head a shake. It was a pleasant dream while it lasted, as brief as it was. The thought of owning a pet had brought excitement that she would not forget. One day she would live somewhere that would be dog friendly. The dream might be what would drive her to continue to build their business. They would become successful enough to allow Molly to afford to live someplace where she could own a dog and make sure it was happy.

With none of the pamphlets interesting her, Molly returned to her car, disappointed, and drove back to her campsite. At least she had done something besides sit around in her camping chair.

As she drove back, her eyes watered more than before. Was it possible the smoke had become thicker? Her throat tickled, and she coughed as she entered the campground. Only a few feet onto the property, the campground attendant waved her over.

"Good afternoon," the attendant said. "We are letting campers know there is an air quality advisory for the area and are giving guests the option to cancel their reservation. We will charge you for the night, but we will reimburse you for the rest of your reservation with no penalty."

"Thank you," Molly said. "Is the fire a threat to the campground?"

"Not to the campground, but the air quality has led to a public health advisory for folks to remain inside. Weather reports predict the smoke will continue to blow in for the next couple of days, which will make it even worse. It wouldn't surprise me if they upgrade the alert and ask visitors to return home."

Molly thanked the attendant and continued to her site, where the smoke had lowered to the treetops. Her lungs burned as she coughed. There was no way she could stay. She checked her watch. If she left now, she would make it home before nightfall, or she could reach Lemon Grove and set up her tent in the daylight.

She rubbed her eyes. Why Lemon Grove? She could go anywhere. It didn't have to be Lemon Grove, where she might run into Rick. But if she returned to the campground, she could visit with Hudson again. That was appealing. But where Hudson was, Rick would stop by to pick up his dog. That was not.

Rick would need to understand that the only reason she would interact with him would be to hand over Hudson after his morning visit. It would not be to talk to Rick or to encourage a relationship. Molly would set up boundaries, even if he would be disappointed. Rick wasn't worth her time. Molly would return to Lemon Grove to get away from the smoke, and that's all.

There was no reason to overthink it. She needed to leave. It would have been nice to stay and enjoy the lake, but that would be impossible with a wildfire burning nearby. Molly tossed her sleeping bag into the trunk again and began disassembling her tent, this time folding it properly. She would not deal with a mess in Lemon Grove. The rattling around the campground signaled she was not alone in the decision to leave. The smoke had become too much for the vacationers. She now hoped to get packed up and leave before the others blocked the exit as they waited in line to have their fees reimbursed.

With her site packed, she jumped into her car and headed out toward the gate where a line of five cars were already waiting to check out. Molly tapped her steering wheel and stopped. She wasn't in a rush and needed time to think about what she would say if she saw him again. She knew it would only be a matter of time before he'd come by. It would be hard to see him. He had hurt her after she had promised herself she wouldn't let anyone else hurt her again. As risky as it would be to go back to Lemon Grove, she'd return for Hudson, clean air, and coffee. There was nothing else for her there.

CHAPTER TWENTY-FIVE

*A*ll Rick could think about was Molly. He was thankful for friends like Patsy, who agreed to keep Hudson for the day while he left Lemon Grove to find her. It seemed like the right move at the time, to chase after Molly, but now he wasn't so sure. What would she think when she saw him standing on her doorstep? Or at least on the doorstep of her coffee shop? He checked the waiver she signed when he took her on the hike to Lakewood, and she had only provided her phone number. It would have been better if he had her home address, especially since what he wanted to tell her would be best said in private. He wanted to make his feelings perfectly clear to her and leave no room for doubt in her mind.

He felt the stickiness of sweat against the palm of his hand on the steering wheel. No doubt the rest of him was just as sweaty and he would look like a mess by the time he reached her coffee shop. There would be no time to change, and he never brought another set of clothes with him. Rick hoped she needed a couple of hours alone after she left the Farmers' Market, and after calling her phone multiple times, and leaving several messages to ask her to talk about what happened or if she was coming back, he made the quick decision to rush out the door to search for her. He never should have talked with Valerie for so long. He had no interest in her, and yet, Molly's countenance changed after Valerie's arrival, and he did nothing about it. It was Valerie who was intent on talking with him and it took time to break free from her, but before he distanced himself, Molly had already left.

All night, he sat on his couch with his phone balanced on his knee. It was only after the phone slid to the hardwood floor that he was startled awake. The first thing he did was check his messages, and found nothing. For hours, he paced around his kitchen, trying to convince himself to eat breakfast to pass the time. He didn't want to do anything other than talk to Molly. Calling her number again, while his default response, would definitely not win her over, and he convinced himself doing so would scare her off even further. If she needed space, he needed to give her some. It tormented him to think, with each passing minute, Molly drove further and further away.

His panic spurred him to jump into his truck and earned him a speeding ticket an hour outside of Lemon Grove. The officer took little time to review his information. Something about hearing Rick's confession of love must have affected the man behind the badge. It also didn't hurt that he knew the three officers who patrolled this stretch of highway. A little further away, and Rick doubted his story would have any impact, even though it had done nothing to get him out of receiving the ticket he deserved. The officer did share some encouraging words of wishing him luck in winning Molly back, as though the officer hoped for a fairy tale ending.

Rick pulled into an empty stall down the road from the coffee shop and walked up to the store window. He saw the line of customers waiting in the queue to make their order while others sat at tables and benches positioned around the walls of the store. Behind the counter, two workers, neither of which looked like

Molly, rushed to fill customer orders. Rick took a breath and stepped inside.

Soft jazz music played on the speakers above, and the smell of fresh coffee greeted him. Customers were engaged in conversation, creating a layer of mumbled words and cheerful laughter. It was a modern coffee shop with modern art lining the walls and the artist's information noted on cards below. They displayed mugs and small bags of coffee beans on shelves for customers to purchase. The space was decorated in dark colors of deep blue and the floor was a slate gray tile. It was a stark difference from the rustic decor of Patsy's café.

He stood in line and rubbed his sweat-covered hands against the side of his jeans. Customers came dressed in business attire, from men in suits and ties to women in blouses with coordinated skirts or pants. This was a city crowd. He had left this kind of attire behind for the casual life of jeans and plaid, but if he needed to dress like this again for Molly, he would. She was worth it. He would adapt and live wherever she was, if it meant living in the city, in Lemon Grove, or wherever else their lives took them. He needed to see her and tell her. She just needed to hear him say it.

A woman from behind the counter watched Rick for a moment before turning back to a coffee machine. She might not have meant for him to see her staring, but he had. He stood out in his small town attire, but he couldn't be the only man to walk into the coffee shop looking like he just stepped off a worksite. If the staff here were used to serving the office, white-collar folks, it now puzzled him why Molly even gave him the time of day.

His foot tapped against the ground. Beside him, a man looked down at the floor and back up to Rick with a scowl. Rick glanced down to find a pile of dried mud laying on the floor beside his boots. He turned away. He would not let some stranger at the table beside him, who probably had never worked outside a day in his life, shame him over a little pile of mud.

The line continued forward, and he inched his way closer to the front. The menu listed names of fancy coffee drinks, many of which he had never heard of, or appealed to him. He knew his favorite drink, and that was all he would order, unless Molly one day convinced him to try something new. The workers behind the counter remained the same, and Molly was nowhere to be seen. His legs shook as he considered turning around. It was a bad idea to drive all this way. Molly would hate him for sure for making a scene in the coffee shop and for following her home.

"Can I help you?" asked a young girl behind the counter. She looked old enough to still be in high school.

"Yes. Um…" He should have used his time in the line to make a choice. "Coffee."

"What kind?"

Rick scratched the back of his head. "Black." The girl looked at him with a puzzled expression. "Large?" he added. "I'm sorry. I am not from around here. I just want a regular coffee. Whatever you recommend is fine."

She giggled and pushed a few buttons on the register. "That will be two dollars."

If Rick had coffee in his mouth, he would have spit it out from the shock. Two dollars for a coffee? Still, it was for Molly and he would do his part to keep her business going. "Is Molly working here today?"

"Molly?" She glanced over her shoulder to the other woman behind the counter, who now appeared to have another reason to stare at him. "No. She's on vacation this week. If you're looking to speak with an owner—"

"No, thank you." Rick paid for his coffee on the debit machine and stepped to the side. "That's fine. I was just hoping she might be…" He smiled. "Thank you."

The second woman approached the counter and grabbed a paper cup from the rack. "Where are you from?" she asked with a smile. A pleasant way of saying she knew he wasn't from the city.

"I'm from Lemon Grove," he said. Not that she would care.

"You must be—" Her cheeks turned a rosy shade of pink as the coffee cup she had been filling overflowed, spilling coffee onto the counter. "Oh dear. Sorry. Please give me a minute to clean this up."

"Would you be Carla?"

She looked up at him as she wiped the counter clean. "Yes. I am. I overheard you asking about Molly."

He cleared away a lump in his throat. If anyone would know where Molly was, Carla would. He could be one step closer to knowing where Molly went.

"My name is Rick." After saying his name, Carla's mouth dropped open. "I was hoping to talk to her about something, but I can't get ahold of her. I figured she might have come here."

"She's not here," Carla said, gesturing for him to follow her to the far end of the counter, free from customers' listening ears. "Molly mentioned the two of you had met. I wasn't expecting to see you come by the coffee shop, though."

"I wasn't expecting to come here, either. She left the campground the other night, and I haven't been able to reach her since. I was hoping you have talked to her and can at least tell me if she's okay."

Her friend smiled and slid the coffee on the counter toward him. "She's fine and a little embarrassed."

"Embarrassed. Why? She did nothing wrong. I mean, she left without giving me a chance to explain—"

"What was there to explain? She had fallen for you and then you paraded this other woman in front of her to make her feel like she wasn't even there." Carla wiped the cloth over a clean section of the counter. "If she doesn't want to talk to you, then I think you need to do the right thing and leave her alone."

He lowered his gaze to his hands, now clasped around the paper cup. "Valerie is my ex-fiancée, and I was trying to be polite.

It isn't easy to explain. If I tell you everything, perhaps you could talk to Molly for me? Tell her what happened?"

Carla sighed and ran the cloth along the edge of the counter. "I don't know if I should get involved."

"Molly said you are her best friend, and you opened this place together. She had wanted to talk to you about purchasing the coffee shop in Lemon Grove, and didn't want to upset you when you told her about the shop on 8th that you want."

"Wait, what shop in Lemon Grove?"

"She never told you?"

"No." Carla looked over her shoulder at the line of customers. "Can you give me one second?"

Rick nodded and watched Carla whisper into the clerk's ear before disappearing into the back room, emerging with another employee who quickly got to work pouring coffee. Carla poured a coffee for herself and stepped around the counter, gesturing for Rick to follow her to an empty table at the far corner of the store.

"I think it is sweet that you came all this way to look for Molly, but I don't know if what I say will convince her of anything. She seemed really hurt when she called me."

"I had no intention of hurting her. Things have been complicated, and I can explain it all to her if she'd talk to me."

"What is so complicated?" Carla rotated her coffee cup on the table. "Your ex-fiancée is still in the picture—"

"She's not." He tried not to sound defensive, but the words flew out of his mouth and Carla leaned back in her chair. "Sorry. Valerie is the daughter of a man my father does business with. My father has a way of controlling my life and he never agreed with me breaking up with her in the first place."

"So, why is she back?" Carla kept her eyes fixed on him as she took a sip from her coffee.

Rick shrugged his shoulders and sighed. "She wanted to see if she could get back together with me, I guess. I told her no. Molly is who I want to be with. When I met her, she filled a hole in my life that Valerie never could. Valerie liked nothing about Lemon Grove. It is my home. It is a part of me and what I love. I enjoy being outdoors and being in nature. Valerie likes city living and her father's business. If I were to be with her, I'd have to give up everything to be with her and I never felt strongly enough that it was the right decision. With Molly, it's different. I'd give it all up for her, and yet, I don't think she'd ask it of me. I think we'd find a balance."

"Balance? You mean, driving back and forth from the city to Lemon Grove?"

"If that's what it took. Yes."

"We have a coffee shop here. Are you saying she'd give up the coffee shop for you?"

"She wanted to talk to you about expanding the business to Lemon Grove. The opportunity is there, and she loves the area."

"Molly has always been a nature lover, but I can't see her living in Lemon Grove, though."

"Why not?"

"Because that would take her away from me and everything we've built here. You've only known her for... a week? Maybe a few days more than a week. She can't throw her life away for someone she just met, even if I encouraged her to give you a shot."

"I'm glad you did."

"But you broke her heart."

Rick shook his head. "Not intentionally. She is who I want to be with. I am not running around with Valerie on the side. If we found that driving back and forth to see each other doesn't work, I promise I'll be the one to take the step to move closer. She deserves that much from me. As much as I'd hate to give up my cabin, Molly's happiness is the most important thing to me. I can be happy anywhere with her. It doesn't have to be in Lemon Grove. Please, help me fix this."

"So, that's why…" she said with a breathlessness to her voice.

"That's why what?"

"That's why Molly fell for you." Carla cleared her throat. "Alright, I'll do my best to help you, but you have to promise me you'll get your father to stop trying to match you up with ex-girl-friends or fiancées or whoever else he has lined up. You can't hurt Molly again."

"I will tell him. Will you tell her I was here?"

"Of course. I'm her best friend. We don't keep secrets from each other." She smiled. "Don't worry, I'll tell her I like you and I think she made a mistake leaving Lemon Grove."

"Is that the truth?"

Carla shrugged. "It might be." She laughed and raised her coffee cup in the air, toward Rick. "To Molly's happiness."

Rick raised his cup and tapped it against Carla's. "To Molly."

For the first time in what seemed like forever, his clammy, nervous hands were dry and comfortable. With Carla on his side, he felt like he finally had a chance to fix this. But what to do to get through to his father?

CHAPTER TWENTY-SIX

*A*fter pulling into Lemon Grove, there was only one thing Molly wanted. Sitting in the parking lot of Patsy's café, she couldn't wait to order a good cup of coffee. She smelled the sweet scent of coffee beans from outside, and was happy to be back in the land of convenient coffee. A day away had been long enough, and even though it was later in the afternoon, she would risk being kept awake by caffeine if it meant she could get the good cup of coffee she missed while she was away.

Molly stepped out of her car and walked along the sidewalk, when she heard the familiar clang of metal. By the picnic tables, Hudson rose to his feet at his water dish. Molly froze. If Hudson was at the café... she turned in place, looking for Rick's truck, which was nowhere in sight. Hudson was now at her feet and licking at her fingers dangling at her side.

"Hey, Hudson. How are you?"

He nuzzled against her palm, pushing her hand against his face, encouraging her to stroke his fur. She obliged, bending down to give his cheeks and the top of his head a good scratch.

"Where is he?" she asked. "Did he go for a drive somewhere and leave you behind?"

Hudson's tail beat against the ground, acknowledging her voice. She gave his head a final rub and gestured for Hudson to return to the water dish. Hudson groaned and wandered back to his shady patch of grass, where he flopped to the ground.

Molly checked the sidewalks and parking lot one final time and took a breath before stepping into the coffee shop. The regulars she had seen before, sat in their chairs, deep in conversation. They stopped and stared at her as she walked inside.

"Molly!" Patsy cried out from behind the counter. Her face beamed as she leaned onto the surface. "Rick has been looking everywhere for you."

"He has?" Molly tried to hide the emotions rising within her. As her heart raced at the thought of Rick searching for her, Molly's anger fought back, reminding her of his betrayal. He had ignored her at the Farmers' Market, choosing instead to turn his attention to another woman. She had reason to act surprised hearing he was looking for her, and only needed to convince Patsy she wasn't hiding from Rick.

Patsy straightened her back and nodded. "Oh yes. This was one of the first places he looked after he saw you left your campsite. He said he didn't know where you had gone off to and that you might be angry with him."

"Why would I be angry?" she asked. Molly stared at the menu. If she looked at Patsy, her eyes would give away the truth. Her actions embarrassed her. It occurred to her that it might have been better to confront him and say what was on her mind instead of rushing off in the height of her emotion, to a campsite at a smoky destination.

"Well," Patsy quieted her voice. Molly turned to see the customers watching their conversation, interested in what they had to say. "From what I heard, you left after Rick's old fiancée stopped by. There rumors that the two of them are back together."

Molly laughed and leaned against the pastry display. Not only was she gorgeous, he was going to marry her… or still might. She took a deep breath. "Whatever he wants to do with his life is good for him, I guess."

"True, but we all thought you and Rick had been hitting it off rather well."

"You and *who else?*"

"Just me and some friends who watched the two of you these past few days. I have never seen Rick so taken by someone."

Molly laughed louder this time and faked surprise. "Me and Rick? What gave you that idea?"

"I guess I thought when the two of you came here the other day, and they said at the Farmers' Market the two of you…" Patsy's smile lessened as she pulled out her notepad. "I should learn to mind my business."

A wave of guilt rushed through Molly. Patsy was right, and the last thing Molly wanted was to make her new friend feel bad for seeing the truth. There had been something between her and Rick, but she didn't appreciate the entire town talking about it, especially when it was over. Whatever had existed between them was no longer of any importance to her. If the town was going to make a big deal about it, she was going to regret having returned. Hopefully, her conversation with Patsy would end the gossip.

"Don't worry about it," Molly said, trying to be polite to someone who showed kindness to her during her stay in Lemon Grove. She still needed a friend around these parts. "Why is Hudson sitting at the front? Did Rick go somewhere?"

"Yes. To find you."

"Really?" Her guilt increased. Because of her, Hudson was now sitting outside the café alone.

"Rick asked me if I would watch Hudson for a few hours while he tried to find you and make things right. I figured he must have caught up with you. He left early this morning."

"I haven't seen him since the Farmers' Market. Hudson has been here all day?"

Patsy smiled and pulled out a jar of dog treats from the cupboard. "Hudson knows if he stays put, there are more treats coming his way. Since he has already been to the campground this morning, he won't go wandering off. He likes to stick close to where the food is. He's a smart one."

Molly chuckled and shuffled in place. She would miss Hudson when she left this town for good. She already missed Hudson, and wished there was some way she might spend time with him, even when she was no longer on good terms with Rick. Hudson had done nothing wrong, and it wasn't his fault the two of them no longer got along. It would confuse a dog to not be able to see someone who had given him love and attention. Then again, he has spent years wandering into a campsite where people only visit for a few days at a time. This felt different to her. She had made room in her heart for her furry friend, and how could a dog not sense that she cared? They had to be more intuitive than humans gave them credit for.

And there was that guilt again, building strength and consuming her thoughts. She dreaded the end of the week, when she would pack up again.

Patsy leaned toward the pass-through window into the kitchen. "Sarah, would you mind covering me for a bit?"

"Sure thing," a voice called back.

"One second, Molly." Patsy grabbed two coffee cups and prepared two steaming mochas before returning to the counter, passing one to Molly. "Come with me." Molly reached for her purse and Patsy shook her head. "It's on the house."

"Thank you." Molly was certain it wasn't often that Patsy gave away free coffee. She had to make money to stay in business. It wasn't as though Patsy would turn Molly into a regular customer when she had to return to the city in a few days. It would be an excellent strategy if Molly was staying, but she wasn't. Not when things were as they were with Rick.

Patsy led her outside to the picnic tables and sat at the same table Molly had shared with Rick. Hudson lifted his head when they approached and let out a loud sigh before rolling onto his back for a scratch on the belly from Patsy. "Good boy, Hudson." Patsy stretched out her legs and groaned a little herself. "I'm getting too old to be on my feet all day."

"You're not that old."

Patsy's laugh echoed around them. "My goodness. I should have retired years ago."

"How long has the café been for sale?"

"On and off, here and there, for two years. I have been waiting for the right buyer. One day, the economy will force me to sell it to someone who doesn't share my vision for this place. I've been told once or twice I need to give up control and let the next owners have their way with it. I'm just not ready to do that."

Molly nodded. The exterior walls of the café looked as loved as the interior. While time had aged the building, Patsy had taken care of it. A testament to hours of cleaning, painting, time and money. It was easy to understand why Patsy would be hesitant to sell to just any buyer.

"I didn't bring you out here to talk about the café, although I am confident you would be a great fit, if you were so inclined."

"Then why did you bring me out here?" Molly took a sip of coffee and exhaled. She would need to learn Patsy's secret recipe, although she doubted it would be easy to get it out of her when her secrets would be part of a purchase agreement.

"I wanted to talk to you about Rick and figured you'd be more comfortable away from prying eyes and listening ears."

Molly held a hand to her cheeks, fearful her color had changed. Talking about Rick was not something she wanted to do. She was here for coffee, not to discuss the man who had broken her heart and made her the talk of Lemon Grove. "Maybe that isn't such a good idea."

"I disagree. Besides, I gave you a free drink, so the least you can do is talk to me until you finish that coffee." Patsy's trap had closed and Molly had no choice. "Tell me, why did you run off?"

"Because I can't compete with a tall, leggy blonde, and she clearly wanted him back, if she didn't have him back already."

"What makes you suppose she has already got him back?"

Molly kept her focus on the coffee. If she looked up, she would stare straight into a pair of warm and caring eyes. Patsy was the mothering type, capable of pulling everything out of Molly with only a few simple questions. Even though she wanted to avoid the conversation, she wanted to share her story with someone other than Carla.

"Have you seen her?" Molly asked.

"I have."

"Then you are aware she's gorgeous... and she knows it. I stood there while she strutted in front of him like I wasn't even there."

"And what did Rick do?"

Hot tears flooded her eyes as she recalled the events. It had hurt to see Valerie stroking his arm and chatting with Rick like she owned him. After seeing a future with Rick, in an instant, she lost him.

"Rick talked to her."

"And?"

"He didn't tell her to go away."

Patsy picked up her coffee and took a sip. "What do you know about Valerie besides that she is gorgeous? For what it's worth, I don't think she's anything special. It's all clothes and makeup."

"I know she is his ex-fiancée. That's about all."

"Then you don't know that Valerie's father has close business ties with Rick's father, who makes his life very difficult if he does anything contrary to his father's plans."

"I didn't know that."

Patsy took another sip of coffee.

"You're going to say I would have found that out if I had asked him instead of running away." She glanced furtively over her cup.

"I wasn't going to say anything... but you're right. Knowing Rick, he would have told you. You have made a powerful impression on him and I have never seen him this way, not since he first moved here and he fell in love with that cabin. You should have seen him acting like every day was spring. The ladies loved his positive attitude and lined up for a chance to be looked at like he looked at his cabin. He only had eyes for that cabin, even when they brought him casseroles and desserts to win him over. Now, he only has eyes for you. I don't agree for one second that he has any interest in Valerie. After the way she treated him, and how I saw him look at you the other day when the two of you sat here, I'm convinced he's in love with you. Why else would he have asked me to watch Hudson so he could take off after you?"

Molly cradled the cup of coffee and felt a tear roll down her cheek. She wanted to agree with Patsy about Rick. How nice it would be if it were a big misunderstanding, and she was wrong about what happened at the Farmers' Market. Even if she were, she would leave in a few days. Would it be worth patching things up with Rick, only to leave again?

"So you think it was ridiculous for me to leave?"

"You did what you needed to do. It is good to be alone with your thoughts now and then."

"I didn't come back because of Rick."

"But you came back. Maybe try to think about what made you want to be here instead of going home?" Patsy smiled and rose from her seat. "I think I have said enough. It isn't my place to interfere with you and Rick. All I want is for that boy to be happy. He has done so much for me, and I don't want to see him miss out on a good thing because of outside meddling. Give him a chance to explain and I think you'll get all the answers you need. Besides, I still want you to buy my café and that won't happen as long as the two of you aren't getting along."

Molly laughed and stood beside her. "I wish I could buy it. It would thrill me to own a place like yours."

"Well, when you're ready, I hope you will make me an offer."

"Of course."

Molly watched Patsy give Hudson another scratch before reaching into her apron pocket to hand him a treat. Hudson rolled over and pulled the treat from her hand and munched the cookie into smaller pieces. Patsy waved and returned to the café, leaving Molly by Hudson's side.

"I hope you will come and visit me tomorrow. And I guess it will be okay if you brought Rick along with you. I'm still mad at him, though. Just because I'm willing to talk to him doesn't mean we're getting back together, okay?"

Hudson looked up as he munched on the remnants of the treat. Molly smiled and knelt beside him. She hadn't expected to come to the café and have a talk with Patsy about Rick. She had come for coffee and was leaving with a fresh perspective. Patsy knew Rick longer than Molly. Things were more complicated than a simple visit from an ex-fiancée. Perhaps what she had expected from Rick was unrealistic and possessive, or maybe even controlling. If the roles were reversed, she would be the one running from someone so emotional over the sight of an old flame. Yet, Rick was in his truck looking for her. He wasn't angry over her reaction and instead wanted a chance to explain and win her back.

She spent a few more minutes petting Hudson before she walked back to her car. Soon, she would need to have dinner and, in the meantime, she would need to set up her campsite, hopefully for the last time.

CHAPTER TWENTY-SEVEN

*H*e had stood at the front doors of the company building for too long, waffling over what he would say to his father. He wasn't sure whether ten minutes, fifteen minutes, or even an hour had passed. Rick recognized the stress had upset his stomach and tormented his mind as he second-guessed his plan. He knew he had no other option. If he wanted to be with Molly or anyone else, he would never be happy as long as he allowed his father to interfere. He needed to make clear he was his own man, capable of making his own decisions. Unfortunately, his father would not take the news kindly.

He lifted his chin and took the last step through the door, to the elevator, and rode up to where he found his father's office empty.

"He's in a meeting," his secretary said, holding a stack of papers. "Did you need me to make you an appointment?"

"I'd like to speak with my father without an appointment." It seemed impossible to have an unscheduled father and son talk anymore.

"I'll see what I can do."

"Could you please tell me where he is? It won't take long."

With directions from the secretary, Rick moved down the hall, refusing to look at any of the faces in the offices he passed by. Some of them he recognized from his days in the office, and were faces he doubted he would meet again after what he was about to do.

The doors to the meeting room at the end of the hall were closed. Through the glass wall, he spotted his father at one end of the table, and several business associates in seats around the table, with Valerie's father at the far end. Rick took a few deep breaths to calm his nerves and cracked open the door.

"...And that is why we need to move on this," his father said. "There is no time for us to be sitting around discussing this when we need to take action and—" A look of surprise replaced a scowl on his face. "Rick." His father rose from his chair and straightened his blazer. "I wasn't expecting to see you today."

Rick stepped into the room and to one side of the door. "Sorry to interrupt. Am I able to speak with you for a moment?"

"Of course." His father remained in place at the end of the table, waiting to learn what Rick had to say.

"It would probably be best if we spoke in the other room."

"I can't leave these people to chat, Rick. We're in the middle of a meeting. Say whatever you need to and do it quickly so we can get back to business."

Rick looked at each of the associates and Valerie's father. This was not the place for the conversation he had planned, but he needed to get back to Lemon Grove and find out from Carla if she had talked to Molly. He cleared his throat.

"I'm sorry for having this conversation in this room with all of you, but my father would like us to speak in here." His father lowered his chin and stared into Rick's eyes from across the room. It was a paralyzing stare, daring him not to say something his father disapproved of, and Rick resisted the urge to back through the door into the hallway. He took a deep breath to calm his nerves and spoke. "I have decided it is time for me to leave the company." The executives exchanged glances across the table. Valerie's father leaned back in his chair and crossed his arms as Rick's father stood stern-faced at the end of the table. "I have been with this company since I was old enough for employment, and while I am grateful for the opportunity you gave me to learn and grow, it is time for me to step out on my own and do something different."

His father laughed and approached him. "Come on now, Son. This is no way to negotiate a raise." He grabbed Rick by the bicep and attempted to push him toward the door. Rick stood firm.

"I'm not trying to negotiate anything." He shrugged off his father's grasp. "I've given this a lot of thought. It will be healthier for both of us if I'm not working for you. I want to be your son and not your employee. I realize this isn't easy for you to understand, but there are things I want to do and I don't want to worry about the stability of my employment because we disagree about the decisions I'm making in my personal life."

"Is this about the cabin? I swear, you have become increasingly stubborn since you moved away. Had you stayed in the city, you would see things differently."

"You mean, I would look at things your way." Rick gestured toward the door to continue the conversation outside of the room, and now it was his father's turn to stay put. He was going to save face.

"Who do you think will hire you when they learn you walked away from your own father?"

"I'm not walking away from you. Only the business. Every time I want to talk to you, I need to make an appointment with your secretary, when all I want is to stop by and talk to my dad. Even after work. The business is hurting our relationship and the best thing for us is for me to walk away."

"What do you know about relationships? I found out what

happened with you and Valerie." He leaned to the side. "She paid you a visit, and you turned her down. Isn't that right, Charles?"

Valerie's father glanced down at his arms.

"Valerie and I talked it out. We aren't getting back together and there are no bad feelings. Besides, I met someone, and I'd like for you to meet her sometime."

His father laughed and shook his head before strolling back to his position at the head of the table. "Talk with Jolene to make an appointment and we can talk about this further. For now, I need to get back to my meeting. In the meantime, if you want to quit, you can clear out your desk."

"I don't have a desk here, remember? I work from home."

His father said nothing and stood with a smile at the end of the table, attempting to regain the attention of his guests. "Again, I apologize for the interruption."

Rick backed through the door and eased it closed.

"Wait up, Rick," Charles Thomas called out.

Valerie's father moved into the hallway and closed the door behind him as Rick's father glared at them through the glass wall, still holding his place at the end of the table.

"That was a very brave thing you did back there, Rick."

"Thank you. He never really understood what I was getting at."

"I heard you loud and clear. It is what I've always appreciated about you, Rick. You're a man who follows his heart rather than chase the money. It is why I had always hoped you'd end up with my Valerie…" He grabbed Rick's shoulder and give it a squeeze. "She told me she went to see you the other day. I'm glad the two of you talked. I'm also happy you were brave enough to tell her the truth and didn't string her along like others have done. You're a good man and I will one day have to accept the fact that I won't have you for a son-in-law."

Rick glanced at his father, who was busy addressing the

associates in the room. He now paid no attention to the two of them in the hallway.

"Rick, I wanted to ask you something. You can refuse me, if you want." He reached into his pocket and pulled out a business card. "I want you on my team. What you did in there was outstanding and showed character. I want people who put their family above business. There are too many people in this city who would do anything to get ahead, but you have principles, and when I see someone like you, I don't want to see them get away. It would also appear you need a job."

"I do." Rick held the business card in his hands. "I'm just not sure if I can accept. You would want me to be in the city and I—"

"There's no rush. And I have many employees who work remotely across the country. Where you live is of no concern to me as long as you get the job done and do it well."

"How would Valerie feel about it? I don't want to make things awkward for her."

He smiled and gestured for Rick to follow him to the elevators. "Valerie will be fine with it. She is hoping the two of you can remain friends and it won't be awkward when you run into each other. Of course, you would only run across each other when you'd be in the city, and I doubt we'd see much of you around the building when you have that place of yours in Lemon Grove."

"Yeah, about that..." Rick sighed and watched a load of passengers get off the elevator. "I've considered selling the place."

"You're not selling to Robert Fletcher because your father wants you to, are you?"

Rick shrugged and shoved his hands in his pockets. "I might sell to Robert, but not because of my father. Did Valerie tell you I—"

"Met someone else? Yes, she did. She said she felt rather intimidated by her. The young lady was quite attractive from the sounds of it, and kindly left the two of you to talk. It takes trust to leave a man alone with another woman."

"I don't believe our relationship was quite ready for Valerie's arrival. I haven't been able to reach Molly since she left Lemon Grove."

"Hmm… I see." Charles' voice grew quiet.

"She owns a coffee shop with a friend in the city, so I came here hoping I could find her, but she wasn't there. I thought I would talk with my father while I was here and make it clear with him where I stood. He has held things over my head for too long and I need to be free to make choices without it affecting my relationship with my father or with Molly."

"Now that you've had your conversation with your father, what are you going to do?"

"Go home, I guess, and keep trying to talk to Molly."

Charles slapped Rick on the shoulder. "If she's worth the risk of standing up to your father, you shouldn't give up on her. She'll turn up eventually, and when she does, you will talk things through. And on another note, I like that cabin of yours. It would be a shame to sell it to Robert. If you are serious about wanting to sell, call me. I am looking for a vacation property."

"I will keep you in mind, for sure."

"Well, I'd better get back in that meeting room or your father will wonder if I don't want to deal with him anymore, either." Charles pressed the call bell for the elevator and squeezed Rick's shoulder. "You're a good kid, Rick. Do consider my offer. I think you would make an impressive addition to the team and you'd be very happy with us."

"I will consider it."

Charles stepped back into the meeting room and Rick watched his father barely acknowledge his return. As Rick stepped into the elevator, he exhaled and thought about the offer Charles had made. Working for him would be an excellent option if it weren't for the connection to Valerie. If talking to Valerie had made Molly bolt, how would she react to hearing Rick took a job with Valerie's father? But being out from under his father's thumb would be a good thing. Yes, it was a tough conversation to have with him, but it was the right thing to do. The only problem was it left Rick without a job. He had enough money to get by for now, but it would eventually dry up. There were people around town who would give him the odd job here and there, but it wouldn't be enough to keep him from going into debt.

Knowing he had a job offer made the bitterness of his split from his father more bearable, but he had no choice. His father's need to keep up appearances in front of his associates was more important than giving his son five minutes of his time. To appear in control, he told Rick he could clear out a desk he didn't have. The most he could do was return the company laptop he had in his office at home, but he hadn't worked from the city building in years. His father was putting on a show for the others in the room. The only hope Rick had came from the comment that they could continue the conversation later. Unfortunately, his secretary would need to book the meeting. It wouldn't be a father and son chat, but an employer to employee conversation. As the elevator reached the bottom floor, he realized that he was ready to leave behind the need for his father's approval. The only approval he needed was his own.

Today had become a fresh start. No matter what played out romantically, he would continue on a journey that would lead him to greater independence and freedom. His chin lifted and a smile spread across his lips. He was a free man. While he loved his parents, he had his own life and, with each step, he felt himself drawing closer and closer to Molly.

In the parking lot, he pulled his phone from his pocket and found a missed call from Carla. The phone shook in his hand when he saw she had left a voice message. What if Molly told Carla she didn't want to speak to him?

"Hey, Rick. It's Carla. I tried calling Molly, but she didn't pick up. She sent me a text message saying she had been driving when I called. She said she'd call me back later. I just wanted to let you know I tried. I'll call again when I have something to share. Take care."

At least he had Carla on his side. There was still hope he could talk to Molly, and hopefully soon. Rick longed to hear her voice and hold her in his arms again. He needed to tell her what he had done, and why: because there was nobody else for him but her.

CHAPTER TWENTY-EIGHT

*M*olly stood beside her tent and took a deep breath. Only a slight smell of smoke hung in the air, no doubt carried to Lemon Grove on the wind. It felt good to breathe in fresh air once again, and even better to stand next to her assembled campsite. Luckily for Molly, Glenda hadn't booked anyone into her original campsite and Molly quickly got to work putting things back together. She smiled to herself as she recalled the way Glenda sighed as she registered Molly back into trusty campsite number twenty-three. It would seem she wasn't pleased to discover Molly returned, but it was Glenda's interest in Rick that most likely played a factor in the reaction.

Dusting off her hands, Molly removed her camping chair from the trunk of her car and popped it open before flopping into the seat. It had been a long day, and she was ready to rest. It wasn't only the physical exhaustion from disassembling and assembling her equipment, but the emotional weight of leaving Lemon Grove and what she would face when she returned. Her body was reacting in its own way, and she would climb into her bag soon enough for some well-deserved sleep.

She pulled out her phone and checked the display. Three

missed calls. Two from Rick and one from Carla. And then there were the text messages, mostly all from Rick apologizing and another two from Carla asking her to call when she was available to talk. With nothing else to do, she might as well tell Carla she was, once again, in Lemon Grove because of wildfires. At least someone should know where she was in case of an emergency.

Her bed was warm, and she was glad she cleared away the largest stones before placing her tent. While her sleeping mat was thin, it was comfortable when not lying on a stone. She slept well, even if she initially struggled to fall asleep. It was Carla's fault that Molly lay wide awake for several hours while the rest of the visitors slept in their trailers. Had Carla only told her on the phone call about the coffee shop and how well her cousin was doing in Molly's place, she would have fallen asleep immediately. Instead, Carla's words echoed in her mind.

"He came into the shop… looking for you."

Rick was in the city?

"He said he can explain what happened. He doesn't love her."

Why would he choose her over the leggy blonde?

"I think you should believe him."

Molly lay on her back, staring up at the roof of her tent, thinking about the Farmers' Market. Now that she was calm, she could recall the signs she hadn't noticed before. Rick moved away from Valerie and leaned toward Molly. He gave curt responses to Valerie's comments. Maybe Patsy was right when she said Rick had moved on from Valerie and was interested in a relationship with Molly.

Her heart wrestled with swirling emotions. Perhaps he was worthy of another chance? Rick had made many attempts to talk to her and went out of his way to speak to Carla. Giving him the opportunity to talk about what happened might clear the air and allow them to at least be friends. But now she would be the one who would need to get him to talk to her after refusing to take his phone calls and avoiding him for so long. The rejection must have hurt. Surely he would probably react in a similar way and make her sweat over him not returning her calls. But was Rick really like that? The man she knew seemed to not hold a grudge. He had tried to talk to his ex-fiancée when she came to the Farmers' Market, when others might have ignored her instead of trying to find a balance between ending a conversation and keeping Molly comfortable. She finally understood his awkward predicament, and the understanding carried over into the morning. As soon as Hudson would arrive, she decided she would call Rick herself and tell him she was back in town… and invite him to talk when he came by for Hudson.

Noises echoed through the campground: the sound of visitors clearing out their sites. She checked her watch. Hudson should have come by already this morning to sniff around her tent and beg for attention. Maybe Hudson was mad at her for leaving and found another family to visit? Hopefully not. She had been looking forward to seeing him and had her chair and blanket ready. As soon as he came, she would sit in her chair and let him lay on the blanket at her feet.

Another thirty minutes passed and there was still no sign of Hudson. Now, Molly found herself standing at the end of her site, looking up and down the road for any sign of the dog. The occasional trailer drove by as campers left the campground, but Hudson still hadn't arrived. Molly locked up her car and walked down the road, following the loop around the campground. Hudson understood how to take care of himself and he didn't have to come visit her at her site if he didn't want to, but something nagged at her to search. She had to know if he was here. If she spotted him at another site, flopped on the ground to take in attention from other visitors, it would give her relief. If she didn't find him, she would need to call Rick. After completing the loop, she checked her site one last time before walking to the campground office. The door was closed and Glenda left a sign hanging from a hook indicating she would return in two hours. With Hudson not sitting at the office door and no sign of him at the campground, Molly couldn't wait any longer. Hudson was late, and if injured, it would be best to find him before something worse happened to him.

She pulled her phone from her coat pocket and dialed Rick's number.

"Molly." His relief was clear across the phone. "Thanks for calling me back."

This conversation had to wait. While Rick wanted to talk about what happened at the Farmers' Market, it was far from Molly's mind, at the moment. "I'm sorry. I had a lot on my mind. But, I'm back in Lemon Grove. Hudson hasn't arrived at the campground yet. Did you let him out today?"

"He should have been there a while ago. I was wondering why no one had called me."

"I've walked around the campground to see if he was visiting someone else, but I don't see him. Glenda's office is closed."

"He might have found something on the way there and got distracted." Now, Rick's rushed voice wobbled with concern. "I'm going to make some calls to ask if anyone has seen him. I'll call you back as soon as I know anything."

"Okay," Molly said. "I'll wait for your call."

She choked away a lump in her throat. Waiting for Rick to call her back seemed like hours, yet after the many checks on her watch, it had only been ten minutes. She hated to think Hudson might be waiting for them to find him while she was pacing around her campsite. At least she had Rick calling around to see if his neighbors in Lemon Grove had seen Hudson making his morning rounds, and she hoped someone had spotted him. His calls seemed to take more time than necessary. Surely Rick wouldn't waste time and leave her to worry.

Molly wanted him to call, not only with news that they had found Hudson, but to hear his voice again. She wanted to give him time to talk about what happened. After talking to Patsy and Carla, she needed to hear his side of the story. Only, it seemed impossible to hear it now when Hudson was missing. It would have to wait until they found him, hopefully in good shape.

The sound of gravel under tires alerted her to Rick's truck coming up the road. She strained to see into the cab of the truck, only to spot the empty seat beside him.

"Hop in," Rick said, bringing his truck to a stop at the end of her site. "We can check a few of his favorite spots."

Without hesitating, Molly tossed her blanket into her tent and jumped into the seat next to Rick. Clearly, no one had news of seeing Hudson.

"I called everyone," he said. His eyes shifted back and forth from one side of the road to the next, checking the woods lining the shoulder. "I have a suspicion I know where he might be."

"You do?"

Rick drove at a crawl as they both looked out the windows. "He has a few places he visits. It doesn't happen that often." He pulled out onto the highway and drove no faster than the posted speed limit, perhaps slower. While Molly wanted to rush, going faster could also mean missing a glimpse of him. Slower was better.

"Thanks for bringing me along to search for him. I figured you might not want to talk to me after—"

"I've been wanting to talk to you. You've been on my mind every day."

"Yes, but leaving and ignoring you was a little immature."

"You're here now." He smiled and adjusted his grip on the steering wheel.

Molly rubbed her hands against her knees. Rick was sitting only a few feet away, and she loathed the distance between them. It lingered there like a huge crevasse neither felt safe enough to cross. Some of the distance was his fault, but she couldn't put the blame solely on him. Her temper and desire to run away had contributed to the void. Her actions must have had some impact on him and their relationship.

"I appreciate you giving me space to think," she said, even though he hadn't given her space at all. If she had listened to his voicemails and read his text messages, he would have over-whelmed her with his pleading.

"I figured if you wanted to talk, you would have responded."

Molly fidgeted in her seat. She had wanted to respond to him, but her anger kept her from dialing his number. There was a part of her that wanted to understand why he hadn't turned Valerie away and another part that wanted to forgive him. "She seemed really into you, so I thought I was getting in the way."

"She was the one getting in the way," he said. "Valerie and I were over a long time ago."

"But she said she saw you in the city. When she said that, I thought—"

"It was my father. He called me back for a business meeting and tried to set us back up as part of some plan of his. He has these ideas about merging companies with Valerie's father and forcing him out as a competitor, so no better way to do that than have me marry the man's daughter. When she saw me in the city, Valerie remembered she enjoyed the time we spent together because neither of us are like our families, but we aren't meant for each other."

"If you were engaged, you must have loved her."

Rick turned off the highway onto a dirt road and followed it through the trees. "When you spend enough time with someone, eventually you become connected in some way. It never felt the same as... with you." He stole a glance and smiled. "Valerie likes you and thinks you are very sweet."

"I hardly said anything. And I left."

"She's used to women who are dominant and ready for a fight.

She saw how upset it made you and how upset it made me when you left."

"So now what?"

The truck came to a stop in front of a boarded up cabin with a chain-link fence surrounding the yard, and Rick laughed. "There he is."

Molly leaned forward to get a view of a dilapidated cabin and Hudson. In its prime, this would have been a cute cabin when there was paint on the exterior and someone made repairs to its roof. Leaves and small twigs now covered the wraparound deck, which could use a good sweeping and a few boards to replace the railing. Abandoned, a chain-link fence kept visitors out.

Hudson lay on the top of the steps. His head rested on his front paws, but he didn't look asleep. He appeared sad and barely acknowledged their arrival.

"He comes here sometimes," Rick said, exiting the truck.

She hopped out and stood beside him. Her hand brushed the side of his and she felt a rush through her arm. It had been too long since they last touched. "What is this place?"

"This cabin belonged to Hudson's previous owner before he passed. Hudson comes here now and then to visit, even though the old man is gone." They walked over to a gate in the fence where a padlock hung from a chain to prevent trespassers from entering the yard. "I worry about how he'll be when they demolish the house. Robert Fletcher bought the property to expand his resort a few months ago. Soon, there won't be a house for Hudson to visit." Rick slapped his legs. "Come on, Hudson. It's time to go."

Hudson lifted his head and looked at Rick with sad brown eyes. His ears hung low as he lowered his head back onto his paws.

"He's in one of those moods." Rick pulled off his jacket and handed it to Molly before he gripped the chain-link and climbed.

"What are you doing?"

"He will not get off the porch unless I get him."

Rick made quick work of the fence and was up and over before Molly could talk him out of it.

"How did he get in there?"

"He's a dog." Rick dusted off his hands. "He dug under it. This should only take a minute."

Molly watched Rick cross the yard to the front porch, where he sat beside Hudson, stroking his back and the top of his head. She couldn't hear him but could see Rick's lips move as he spoke to Hudson. Watching him consoling the dog brought tears to her eyes, and she covered her face with Rick's coat where she caught a whiff of his scent, bringing back memories of the day on the Lakewood Lake trail. She would rather have her arms wrapped around him than his coat. For now, his arm was around Hudson as he draped himself over the dog and nuzzled into his ear.

Hudson's tail beat against the front porch and he rolled onto his side for a scratch on his belly. Rick obliged as Hudson became more animated, eventually springing to his feet. Rick ran to the fence and climbed as Hudson ran behind the house, presumably to find his exit.

As Rick climbed down off the fence, Molly handed him his jacket and wiped a tear from her eye.

"Are you alright?" he asked.

"That was really sweet."

"He needed me to remind him he's not alone. He has us."

Molly nodded and stared up at his warm eyes as he smiled back at her. "Us," she whispered.

Rick wrapped his arm around her waist and pulled her close. Molly slid her arms over his shoulders as he leaned in, pressing his lips against hers. With Hudson at their feet, they held each other, enjoying kiss after kiss until Hudson flopped to the ground and sighed.

CHAPTER TWENTY-NINE

*R*ick submitted his official letter of resignation to his father. There were no doubts in his mind when he made a follow-up call to his father to confirm with him directly that he was leaving the company. While his father commented on his disappointment and expressed his anger, he never tried to convince Rick to stay. His minimized reactions gave Rick the hope he needed that the separation would benefit their relation-ship in the long run, even if it seemed bruised at present. Rick received a much warmer reception when he called Valerie's father and accepted his offer of employment, with one condition -- he wouldn't start until after Molly returned to the city, leaving him free to spend his time with her before she left.

He couldn't have asked for a better result. The time he invested in Molly was exactly what they needed as he picked her up from the campground to take her to Patsy's for breakfast, lunch, and dinner. She seemed to enjoy the adventures he took her on, showing her the many attractions and viewpoints around Lemon Grove. As these tours and adventures continued to be enjoyed in her smiles and relaxed body language, he was more and more certain that she was what he had been looking for. Someone to share these moments with, who would appreciate them as much as he did, and he would not let her get away. It would take time to fully accept he would be leaving his cabin for the city, but for Molly, he would do anything if she asked. But in her remaining hours in Lemon Grove, she never said anything about it.

Rick took her to the café, where they ordered breakfast. Patsy seemed quieter than usual as she took their order.

"This is your last day, isn't it?" she asked as she poured their coffee at the table.

"It is." Molly stared at Rick. There was sadness in her eyes, mixed with a twinkle of hope. While they wouldn't be able to spend time together as often as they enjoyed the past few days, there would be many days ahead and phone calls in their future. "Rick and I are going to pack up my site once we're done with breakfast."

Patsy placed the coffee urn back on the heater. "Well, that's too bad. I enjoyed seeing your lovely face around here. I'm going to miss you, although I have a feeling Rick will miss you even more."

Rick reached across the table, holding Molly's hand in his. The distance would be difficult and downright painful, but if things worked out, it would be worth the wait. Her hand fit perfectly in his and he loved to touch her soft skin. Thinking of holding her again would be what would get him through the week, until the weekend when one of them would travel to visit the other. Visiting on the weekends would have to be the temporary solution until one of them made a more permanent move. With no business ties to sever locally, he was the first to volunteer to close the gap between them. Molly told him he didn't need to commit to it. At least, not yet. She spent time at his cabin, enjoying the backyard with Hudson by her side. She encouraged him to keep it for now, and if they could afford two homes, she did not see a need to sell a property they both enjoyed together.

With neither Rick nor Molly interested in conversing with a third wheel, Patsy returned to her place behind the counter, leaving Rick and Molly to gaze into each other's eyes. There had been plenty of staring over the past several days, with Rick wanting to etch each of Molly's features into his mind. He refused to miss a single detail. He swore the closer her departure time approached, the more beautiful she became, and it was increasingly difficult for him to accept she was leaving.

Once their breakfasts arrived, neither was in a rush to eat, as each hurried moment moved them closer to the time she would leave Lemon Grove.

"You don't have to leave when you check out," he said, holding her hand a little tighter.

"My site will be packed—"

"You can spend the afternoon with me and then go home later."

Molly half smiled and placed her other hand on top of his. "I would like that, but I promised Carla I would look at the property on 8th this evening. The realtor is saying there might be another offer coming in this week, so she is concerned we will miss out on it if we don't decide soon."

She didn't sound excited whenever she spoke of opening a new branch of their coffee shop. For someone who wanted her business to grow, Rick interpreted her lack of enthusiasm as disappointment. As much as he wished there was nothing in the city that would keep her from him, he didn't want her to avoid being successful for his sake. He gave her hand a squeeze before lifting it to his lips.

"I hope it is as perfect as Carla says it is. You two deserve this."

Molly turned and faced the window. A tear rolled down her cheek.

"What's wrong?" he asked as he ran his thumb over her knuckles.

"I don't want to leave you."

"We already talked about this. I'll come visit you when I meet with Valerie's father to complete my orientation, and then I'll come again on the weekend."

"I hate that we will be apart for a week at a time."

"I know. At least we have technology to help tide us over. I will be happy to stare at your smiling face on my computer screen whenever I want." And he meant it. He already made her photo from their hike the new background on his computer, and photos from their sightseeing adventures had become a rotating screensaver. Whenever he found himself at his computer, he would see her.

Molly wiped away the tear and took a breath. "I need to check out if I am going to get unpacked and cleaned up before I meet with Carla."

Keeping her hand in his, Rick nodded and rose from his chair. The time had come for them to prepare for goodbyes.

The drive back to the campsite was quiet, and neither said a word, leaving their silence to say everything they couldn't. Packing up her tent was quiet besides the clicking of the poles. Their combined efforts made the clean up go faster than either wanted, until they stood in the empty site inches apart.

"Are you sure you have to leave right away?"

She buried her head against his chest and let out a sob. He rubbed her back and swayed as they stood on the empty gravel pad. A few agonizing minutes later, she gave him a final tender kiss goodbye and climbed into her car to drive out of the campground.

Rick stood in the campsite, where he kicked at stones and stared at a patch of ground that still bore the imprint from the soles of her hikers. They had looked cute on her feet. Her entire wardrobe had made him chuckle, at first, but he recognized how much that city girl had been longing to be in the wilderness. It wrenched at his heart to see her go, but he had to hope the pull of the mountains and their budding relationship would be enough to bring her back. Only time would tell, and he would give her all the time she needed.

Molly sensed her heart breaking as she drove out of the campground. She refused to glance in the rearview mirror as she pulled away, wanting her last memory of Rick to be the sparkle she saw in his eyes before she climbed into her car. She didn't want to replace it with the visual of him standing in the campground looking sad as she pulled away. Leaving was hard enough without replaying his saddened face in her mind.

If only she didn't have to go back to the city. She had finally found a relationship that seemed to go somewhere good, and now she had to leave just as things were gaining momentum. Wouldn't that squash what was only getting started? Running a coffee shop in the city was the life she had chosen and, for now, her relationships needed to fit within that reality. She knew Rick understood. It didn't change the fact that this separation wouldn't be easy. With enough time, it might be possible to sell off her share of the company and have Carla buy her out. When they had started their business, they were both young single women and both knew things would one day change.

With Rick starting a new job, they had a plan in place for now. It was better than him remaining in Lemon Grove and not being able to see each other at all. She never thought she would regret the life she had chosen, yet here she was wishing her life could be different. If only she had the freedom to not return to the city and remain in Lemon Grove with the man her heart knew was the one for her. He had shown her what it was like to have someone put her first and made her feel loved through his words and actions. His kindness melted away any judgmental thoughts she had toward him, and to her surprise, her heart had opened to the irresponsible and irresistible dog owner.

As she relived the happy moments she had shared with Rick, the heart-crushing emotions eased. She looked forward to more moments to come, and even though obstacles stood in their way, she was confident they would overcome them.

CHAPTER THIRTY

*M*olly breathed in the scent of freshly brewed coffee. Normally, it would excite her to try new beans and learn new recipes, but today her mind kept wandering to thoughts far outside of their busy coffee shop. The line of waiting customers extended from the counter to the door. Molly tried to recall the last time the shop was this busy. There were no promotions and no nearby events to draw the crowd, but the constant pace kept Molly and Carla running all day.

"It's been like this all week," Carla said, grabbing another carton of milk from the fridge. "I brought in extra help to keep up with the demand."

"This is unbelievable. I never imagined we would be so busy."

"Same, but I hoped we would be." She winked.

It was what they dreamed about in their early days of planning their business. They hoped for days of having a line extending down the block as coffee lovers spread word to one another about the quirky shop with the best tasting coffee and incredible service. The moment had finally arrived and so did the people.

Molly glimpsed the faces of the crowd, who somehow seemed

content to wait as their workers buzzed about fulfilling their orders. The team worked fast and kept the line moving. Their customers were cheerful as they received their coffee and the tips came rolling in. With each transaction, Carla and Molly exchanged looks and smiles. This was a big lift financially, but if this was the new normal for their store, it was positioning them well to expand their business. It was a simple decision. They had landed on something special. Regulars were coming back, and new customers believed the hype. All this with minimal advertising on their part.

The phone rang, and Carla excused herself from the rush to take the call. Molly stepped in to replace Carla, completing her drink orders and grabbing pastries from the display cupboard. She had assisted three customers by the time Carla returned, shaking her head with a frown on her face.

"What's wrong?" Molly asked.

"They sold the place on 8th this morning."

Molly paused, pouring coffee into a paper cup. "But we had an appointment to take a second look after our shift today."

"Someone swooped in and put an offer on it. The realtor says there is no point, and it is a done deal."

Carla's dream property was gone and there was no telling how long it would take before another property would become available. Molly reached out to comfort her friend. "I'm sorry, Carla."

Carla smiled and waved her off before washing her hands and returning to serving customers. It was rare for Molly to see her with tears in her eyes. If Carla was trying to hide them behind a smile, she had failed. There was little Molly could say to improve her mood, and with such a long line of customers, it would be impossible to sneak away to do more to comfort her. Instead, Molly focused on the task ahead of her and moved through the orders as quickly as possible. The rush would soon be over, and then she and Carla would be free to talk about their next steps.

It was an hour before the crowd had slowed to where the staff could catch their breath. Molly's back ached, and she had burned her fingers with hot coffee. Finally, she noticed Carla working at a slower pace and found an opportunity to pull her into the back room for a conversation.

"So, what do you want to do?"

"About what?" Carla asked.

"The place on 8th? Now that it isn't available, was there another place you wanted us to look at?"

Carla sighed and shook her head. She looked down at her feet before looking back up at Molly with a wistful smile. "No, but I'll bet you do."

"I don't—" Molly froze and her cheeks reddened.

"Rick told me about the shop in Lemon Grove. You've been home for two weeks, Molly, and you have been miserable. I know you've only been looking at the place on 8th for me." She wiped a tear from her eye. "Rick makes you happy, and I am willing to consider the coffee shop in Lemon Grove. If your relationship is going to be a long-term thing, then we need to invest in a place that won't make you commute to see the love of your life."

Molly giggled to herself. "Are you serious? You really wanted that place on 8th and I don't want to disappoint you because we went with the store in Lemon Grove."

"If I show you another place in the city, I think you will be the one missing out on an opportunity." Carla glanced out at the busy shop. Customers were entering the store, but none of them were waiting long. Their staff handled the flow on their own. "We're doing well here, and if the place has as steady an income as what Rick described, then we wouldn't be taking a loss on it. We'd continue to be in an excellent position. Then, when a new place comes up in the city, we'd be opening up a third location."

Molly flung her arms around her friend and squeezed her tight. "I can't believe you're considering this."

"Just keep me in mind when you spot another eligible bachelor in Lemon Grove that would be good for me. I could use a little Lemon Grove romance."

With Hudson in the seat beside him, Rick pulled up at Patsy's café. It had been a long week of meetings and orientations, getting familiar with the new working environment. It went much smoother than expected, but still, he was ready to unwind with some local Lemon Grove coffee and a pastry. Hudson followed him out of the truck and flopped down by the picnic table as Rick entered the café. The regulars were sitting at the table eating their lunch, but Patsy was not in her usual spot behind the counter or out by the tables waiting on customers. Knowing she would be out momentarily, Rick stood by the counter and waited.

He had hoped to spend his Saturday in the city with Molly, but she warned him she wouldn't have time for a visit and instead had encouraged him to stay home. Doubts crept into the back of his mind and he worried for a moment it might be the start of Molly growing tired of their relationship. Distance took its toll on many relationships, and while his feelings toward her hadn't changed, perhaps hers had. It deflated him to contemplate perhaps the relationship had already run its course. If it was the distance that ate at their future, he would do anything it took to restore things back to what they had been when she visited Lemon Grove.

As if he could read Rick's thoughts, Robert Fletcher walked through the door with his realtor beside him. A smile appeared on his face as he approached Rick with his hand extended outward.

"Rick. It is always a pleasure to see you."

"Hello, Robert."

"We haven't talked in a while. I heard you left your father's company. That was an unexpected surprise."

"I decided I needed to make a change."

Robert laughed and leaned against the pastry display. "Are you considering any other changes?"

"I have been thinking a lot about making additional changes," Rick said as Robert straightened and looked at his realtor with a broad smile. "In fact, I was considering calling you."

"What brought on this change of heart?"

The door to the café kitchen opened as Patsy stepped into the room, wearing a big smile and wiping her hands on a cloth. "Oh, I'm sorry," she said. "I didn't know I had anyone waiting. I was just in the back showing the place to the new owners."

"The new owners?" Rick asked. The kitchen door opened, and Rick gasped as Carla and Molly stepped out of the kitchen.

"Hey, Rick." Carla giggled and walked past him to an empty table, where she pulled out her phone.

Molly stepped forward and greeted Rick with a kiss on the cheek. "Surprise."

"Did you really buy this place?" he asked in disbelief as he attempted to swallow his heart in his throat.

"We still need to sign papers, but Carla is behind it and is going to make some phone calls to get things moving along."

Feeling his knees weaken, Rick placed a hand on the counter to steady himself. This was why she discouraged him from visiting the city? She was here. In Lemon Grove. "What does this mean?" he asked.

"What do you think it means? I think it's pretty clear." Molly smiled and held his hand. "I want to buy the café and live here, in Lemon Grove."

"You're moving here?"

"Unless you don't want me to."

"I want you to," he said with an eagerness that carried to any listening ears. He didn't even care. "That's all I ever wanted."

"This must be the young lady I've heard about." Robert's smile disappeared. Having overheard their exchange, Rick knew Robert could guess what he was about to say.

"Yes. This is Molly, and I think I won't be looking to make additional changes after all."

"Moments ago, you said you were considering making additional changes," Robert said, glancing at his realtor, who nodded his head. "That might as well be a verbal agreement."

"We didn't discuss anything," Rick said, with a smile. "Besides, I believe I have found myself a better deal."

Rick led Molly out of the café to their picnic table, where Hudson gradually rose to his feet to greet them with loud whines. The dog nudged Molly's hand and beat his tail against the ground as she scratched his back.

"It's good to see you, too, Hudson. Have you been a good boy?"

"I think he's missed you. I've found him at your empty site many times this week."

Molly knelt beside Hudson and rubbed behind his ears as Hudson licked her cheek. "I get kisses? I'm a lucky girl." She rose to her feet and wrapped her arms around Rick's waist. "I know I could have told you we were coming to look at the café, but I didn't want to get you excited about it if Carla didn't like it."

"But she does like it?"

"She loves it and she loves Patsy. Rick, I am so excited that I'm here, I can barely contain myself."

"Then that makes two of us. I was a little worried when you didn't want me to come see you today." He squeezed her tight. "Now I understand why, and I couldn't be happier."

She eyed him with a mischievous grin. "You mean, it wouldn't make you even happier if I moved here?"

"I am happy just imagining it. I can't wait for the day you call Lemon Grove your home."

Molly's smile broadened and she leaned closer. "I've felt like it was from the day I arrived."

Rick ran his hand against her cheek and held her close as he kissed her lips. He couldn't wait for their lives to begin in Lemon Grove. His heart had found the perfect house, the perfect canine companion, and now the perfect woman for him. At last, he was complete.

EPILOGUE

*M*olly loved her new home only a few steps from the café. It was much more spacious than her city apartment, and she preferred the view of the trees surrounding the town to her view of the city skyline. She had a backyard with a small vegetable garden, and she decorated the front yard with flower beds. The first few weeks she had spent injecting her personality into the space by painting room after room. Rick came by to do some minor repairs, showing off his skills.

Since Molly had moved to town, Hudson no longer hung out at the campground. Instead, he had found a new path, walking from Rick's cabin to Molly's home. If she wasn't there when he arrived, he would carry on to the café, where he would wait by the picnic table for Molly to check on him and give him a treat. Rick would arrive at lunch and they would visit together. Hudson had grown accustomed to the routine, and Molly relaxed, knowing Hudson slept nearby instead of wandering alone in the campground. Rick also appreciated the new routine, not having to drive to pick up Hudson every morning. Hudson seemed content, especially when presented with a daily treat at the café.

The businesses were doing well with steady customers in Lemon Grove and in the city. Thankfully, the local business had not lagged with the change of ownership, when they realized that Molly had no plans to change the menu or the atmosphere. The slower pace of the café and the company that Patsy provided thrilled Molly. Even though Patsy had passed on the ownership of the business, she continued to work there as an employee, sharing her knowledge and recipes while engaging with the customers she grew to love over the years. The two had become close in the months Molly had lived in Lemon Grove, with Molly spending many afternoons playing board games and piecing together puzzles with Patsy in her kitchen.

Carla walked through the door of the café, making Molly squeal at the sight of her friend.

"You didn't tell me you were coming," Molly said, giving her friend a hug.

"I don't have to tell you everything. Besides, I wanted to surprise you."

"I'm definitely surprised."

The moment was disrupted when Patsy called Molly to join her at a freshly wiped table in front of the window. She pointed outside and smiled. "I think there is a customer who wants to talk to you."

Molly followed Patsy's gaze and spotted Rick standing outside with Hudson. Molly waved and untied her apron, handing it to Patsy.

"I'll be right back," she said. Molly rushed outside to the handsome man waiting for her. She would never grow tired of his daily visits.

Rick exhaled and held out his hand to stop her before she threw herself into his arms, as usual. "There you are. I was wondering when you'd come out."

She looked at him quizzically. "Were you waiting long?"

"I've been waiting forever." Molly noticed Rick's hand shaking faintly and she gasped as he dropped to one knee. "Molly, since the day we first met, I realized you were the one. Even Hudson knew." The dog tilted his head and Molly held a hand to her lips. "Will you make me the happiest man in Lemon Grove? Will you marry me?"

Molly's thoughts swirled. Her mind flashed through the months before, having met Rick and how she had happily uprooted her life to be with him. Now, she was the owner of a café in a small town, and a growing business. Her life had only been better with Rick and Hudson in it. Molly looked at the window, where Carla and Patsy hugged each other and wiped tears from their eyes in anticipation of Molly's answer.

She stared deeply into Rick's eyes, and her heart soared. There was no doubt in her mind -- this was the man she would spend the rest of her life with. "Yes," she said. "I will."

Rick pulled a small box from his pocket and lifted the lid to reveal a three-stone diamonds set in a white gold band. He held her hand and gently slid the ring onto her finger. Rising, he pulled her against him, allowing her joy-filled tears to dampen his shoulder.

"I love you, Molly," he whispered. "I can't wait for you to become my wife."

He lifted her chin and wrapped his arms around her waist as he pressed his lips to hers. Molly's heart raced and thumped as Hudson's tail beat against the ground beside them. A little plume of dust rose behind him, and a gentle breeze caught it as the bright sky smiled down from above.

LEAVE A REVIEW

Reviews go a long way to help authors. They help other readers find books they may want to read.

Help spread the word about this book by leaving an online review and by telling your friends.

Thank you for reading. I look forward to bringing you more great stories in the near future.

ABOUT THE AUTHOR

HEATHER PINE grew up on the West Coast of Canada, surrounded by mountains, lakes, and forests. She enjoys reading books as much as she enjoys writing them. Her fondest childhood memory is reading the family tent during a thunderstorm.

www.heatherpine.com